UNTRACEABLE

JAKE CROSS

Copyright © 2020 Jake Cross
The right of Jake Cross to be identified as the Author of the Work has been
asserted by him in
accordance to the Copyright, Designs and Patents Act 1988.
First published in 2020 by Bloodhound Books
Apart from any use permitted under UK copyright law, this publication may
only be
reproduced, stored, or transmitted, in any form, or by any means, with prior
permission in
writing of the publisher or, in the case of reprographic production, in
accordance with the
terms of licences issued by the Copyright Licensing Agency.
All characters in this publication are fictitious and any resemblance to real
persons, living
or dead, is purely coincidental.
www.bloodhoundbooks.com

Print ISBN 978-1-913419-47-9

ALSO BY JAKE CROSS

Hide

This one goes to anyone seeing these words. Readers are the reason I do this. Hopefully this novel makes you come back for more.

THE START

Two years after Don Jones lost his home in a fire and moved to Sheffield, he was killed off by Ian Smith, who fled to Newcastle under the guise of a man who'd decided to relocate after his wife shacked up with his best friend. Three years after that, Ian Smith vanished and Peter Jackson, rising from his ashes, resettled in Glasgow with a claim that he'd lost his job and had chosen a new home by sticking a pin in a map.

Don Jones had waited tables. Ian Smith had worked a night-club door. Both guys had left their jobs with no notice, and Peter Jackson was going to do the same when he winked out of existence. But for now, he lugged potted plants and bags of stones out to customers' cars for minimum wage. He kept to himself, didn't talk about his past, never asked others about theirs. Sometimes someone at the garden centre offered a night out or asked to pop round to his bedsit, but Jackson always refused. He was considered strange by his colleagues, but was polite to customers so the boss never had a problem with him. Every day he worked hard and mostly in silence and then returned to his rented bedsit and spent the evening alone. He'd performed this unsociable routine for eighteen months and would continue it until he felt too rooted, too stale. Then he would get the map and the pin and a new name and a new bullshit story to explain why he was in a city where he had no friends and no family.

Today the man, whose real name was Matt Armstrong, woke early and alone, as always. He sat up in bed and reached to a square piece of duct tape stuck on his shoulder. He peeled it away, exposing a micro SIM card. His phone was on the bedside table, next to a slip of paper with his latest fake name on it. The slip was there in case the boss called: wouldn't do to have his sleepy head forget his alias. He slotted the SIM and the battery into the mobile.

He went into the bathroom to shower while the phone booted up. Only one man other than him had the number for that SIM card and in seven years Matt had never received a call or a text on it. Every day for seven years, he'd prayed he never would. If that was again the case when he checked after his shower, he'd tape the SIM on his shoulder, put the original SIM back in the phone, and head off to work to enjoy another day as Peter Jackson.

It was as he was stepping into the shower that he heard the unmistakable double-beep of a text message received. A cold snake of fear slipped down his spine.

It had taken seven years, but finally it had happened.

I HEARD YOUR SISTER JUST GOT KILLED, the text message said.

1

Emotions he'd kept in check for years bubbled up in an instant, but they subsided quickly. Just like that. Like a spike on an electrocardiogram. And then it was all over. He'd survived news of the most despicable and wrenching kind, and now his mind would be stronger for it. Like an instantly healing broken bone.

Karen, his sister, was gone, but nothing could happen to her now. There could be no more bad news. Now, selfish as it might sound, he could set her aside. It was the rest of his family he needed to think about. Their pain. That was the right thing to do. So he would do that.

He composed a reply text message: THANK YOU. That was it. The recipient was an old army buddy whose life he had once saved. His reward: the guy would keep tabs on Matt's family and let him know if anything happened to them. Anything bad. Only the bad. And only by text message, to a number Matt kept only for that reason. And the guy had done his job.

Matt put his phone in his pocket and thought. He had to be practical here. He had to go back. He had to contact the rest of the family, even though they wouldn't want him there. He had to go to the funeral, all that stuff. But he also had to find out what had happened. There might be something in the news, but he didn't want to hear a story that might be embellished or erroneous. He would wait until his mother or the police explained, even though the wait, the knowing nothing, was making his head spin with wild theories. *Killed.* That word could be so vague, but undeniably it meant something bad and quick. Victims of disease weren't considered to have been *killed*.

He just prayed that her death hadn't been someone else's fault.

Matt had also decided that four months in Glasgow was going to be it. He felt he couldn't return here after the funeral, even if he found out nothing foul had happened to his sister. He would have the memory of learning about her death right there in his bedsit. He wouldn't be able to enter the place again without thinking about her, and thinking about dead loved ones too much was akin to ripping at healing wounds. So he would have to get a new flat, and if he had to look for somewhere new to live, why restrict himself to the same city? Why not move on, start afresh? Again.

Home?

His biggest fear over the last seven years, and something he worried about every day, every hour, had been something bad happening to someone he loved. And now it had, but the aftermath had proved to be bearable. So what else could hurt him after this? No stubbed toe had ever been felt by a man who just had his eyes torn out. So maybe he could go back, wriggle his way back into his old life, rekindle things with old friends. With his family.

Home?

He packed a few things. He called his boss at the garden centre, said he wouldn't be in today, duty calls. The guy said no problem, see you tomorrow. Matt said okay, even though he knew he'd seen his last of the garden centre. He turned off the bedsit's mains electricity and wrote a note for the landlord and left him a month's rent in cash. He also left the TV he'd bought, and the few ornaments he'd acquired, and his expensive multi-gym. The last thing he did before locking up and leaving was take a fistful of sand from a bucket in his backyard and dump it into his left pocket.

In the car, with his bag in the boot, he fired up the satnav. And sat staring at the screen. He had taken the device when he left London, but he had never used it, preferring a pin and a map. So for the first time he was seeing a list of destinations in its memory, places input by his mother, and it was one of those that drew his surprise.

Go home.

He clicked it and watched a little arrow whiz across a map and alight on a spot in London. It made his skin prickle.

Go home? It might never be home again.

As he passed through London, Matt started to notice places he remembered, mostly unchanged, and that felt good. He needed that. Seven years now away, and in all that time he'd lived in cities he hadn't really known. The routes from whatever crap job he had to whatever crap bedsit he occupied were imprinted deeply, but the cities themselves were never given a good shot. Work, home, work home. But even his familiarity with London was hazy and eroded, and it put sorrow in his heart. There was no place on Earth he really knew well, that he felt was home. It was as if he were an alien visitor to the planet. But he would change that. Because he was back, and his plan was to stay.

His mother's house was in Muswell Hill. When he turned onto her street, the nerves hit him. Seven years away, no contact. She hadn't known where to find him to tell him his sister had died. How many other times had something in the family necessitated her trying to find him? Maybe there was a nephew somewhere, seven years old and wondering where this elusive Uncle Matt was.

The house was as he remembered it, except the front garden was different. The grass was gone, replaced by crazy paving. And blinds had replaced net curtains in the big kitchen window, which was out front, living room round the back. Last he'd known, Mum had been driving a Vauxhall Corsa, but there was no car in the driveway. He had an awful thought that his mother had moved. Some strangers were going to answer the door, tell him the previous owners had sold up and moved to Zimbabwe.

It was mid-afternoon, though: she could be at work. She was a seamstress working in a shop in the Strand. His brother, Danny, had moved into the City of London while Matt was in his final year in the army. Again, seven years ago. A lot could happen in seven years.

He chose to go around the back. The back garden was the same as always. Plain grass, an old shed, nothing else. French doors led into the living room. They were closed, but the full-length vertical blinds were open. He got right up to the window and looked in.

The living room was little different to the one in his memory. The TV was newer, and the ancient coffee table had gone, but that was it. Everything else was how he remembered, which helped dampen his nerves. Then he noted a new picture on the wall, amongst the seven *Dogs Playing Poker* reproductions that had been hung for as long as Matt could remember. A baby, lying on a blanket, facing the camera. In front of him, lettered blocks reading JOSEPH.

Shit. Someone had had a baby after all. He might be an uncle. Danny's baby?

Or the child of a dead woman?

His mother walked in from the kitchen, a cup of tea in hand. She saw the figure at the window and stopped abruptly. Tea spilled onto the carpet. He tried the sliding door but it was locked. She approached, dragged the door open, and drew him into a silent hug. She began to shiver and he knew she was fighting emotion. Then the tears came.

He instantly felt terrible, certain that his return must have nailed home the fact that it had taken the death of one child to bring home another. His arms encircled her, but the closeness felt awkward, as if the years apart had made them strangers.

Mum finally let him go, dabbed at her eyes and turned away. She took a slot on the sofa amid scattered embroidery materials, a place that accepted her neatly, as if she'd carved a niche there over time. Unwilling to mention Karen until his mother brought up the subject, and unable to think of anything else, he said, 'How's the shop?'

'Oh, it closed,' she said. 'Come in. Don't be a stranger.'

He realised he was still outside. He put his feet on the carpet and shut the door. But he remained within two feet of it.

'The shop closed,' his mother repeated. 'I still do curtains, but I work from home now. I've only lost the social side, but I go to bingo a lot. I like having free time.'

It was impossible to read her during this emotional period, but he wondered if she was being defensive. Mum had always hated sympathy.

He nodded. 'Where's John?'

She picked up a length of material and a measuring tape, and fiddled with them. He realised he'd broached a tender subject. 'We parted. It was amicable. He's working overseas a lot now. But let's not talk about that. I checked for you on Facebook.'

He was glad to get off the subject of her boyfriend, but this new topic crushed him under a wave of guilt. 'I don't use it.' He felt the need to explain his absence, but she smiled at him, and he felt that urge no more. *You're back, that's all that matters,* the smile said. Besides, what could he say? Explain his bizarre reason for skipping out? That would go down a treat.

Matt and his mother chatted for half an hour. It was awkward at first, like small talk between strangers confined together, but soon both of them lightened up as old comfort returned. By the time his brother arrived, it almost – almost – felt as if Matt had never been away. But he noticed that she didn't once ask where he'd been for the last seven years, as if concerned about the answers. And she didn't mention Karen, her dead daughter, his murdered sister. His theory was that she was seeking the correct time.

Then he heard the front door open. Danny came in fast and froze, staring at Matt. He had a briefcase, a suit, long hair in a ponytail. Changes, changes. Last Matt remembered, Danny spent all day in rock gear, playing with his band.

The family together, minus one, of course. Matt had expected them to sit at the dinner table and catch up, but Danny had flicked his head, a follow me gesture, and left the house without even a word to their mum. And Matt had followed. He was thoughtful enough to tell his mother that he was going to chat to his brother and would be back soon, just in case she thought he was eloping again. She nodded, fully understanding.

Now they were in Danny's car, a flash BMW M5, car of

choice for the yuppie crowd. South on Archway Road, fast as the traffic would allow. Matt scrutinised his brother. Danny was two years older but looked ten years younger. Matt had noticed the bike rack on the back of the car and guessed Danny rode around London to keep fit. The suit was tight around Danny's shoulders. The guy was building muscle, too. Changes, changes, but not for Matt. He had been treading water for seven years, nothing changing but his name and his age.

'I won't ask where you've been,' Danny said. First time he'd spoken since the house. 'It's your business. Mum won't ask, either.'

'She didn't,' Matt said. He was thinking about how nobody had mentioned Karen. It was puzzling him. 'It was weird.'

'You expected a party?'

He couldn't tell if that was sarcasm. 'I expected to be told off, actually.'

Danny swung a turn. 'She didn't mind you running off. Grown men go get their own lives. Expected it, maybe, especially after you ran off to the army. Although a call would have been nice. She was over the moon when I finally got my own flat.'

And Karen, when she left?

'Mum split from her boyfriend, I hear,' Matt said.

Their father had left the family when Matt was two and he knew nothing about him. Mum had stayed single until just a couple of months before Matt had left for the army. John, who she'd met through her shop, had been a decent guy, fairly well-off because he ran a business in China. Very kind and loving to Mum, always treating her, praising her, and she had finally been able to share the burden of running a house and having children. His arrival into her life had been a convenient excuse for Matt, he remembered.

'Yeah, they started to grow apart,' Danny answered. 'He was working away a lot. But don't worry that you'll have to move back in. She's happy now. She goes out more and she's got new friends at the bingo. It's good.'

He'd told his mum, and Danny, that he felt like an intruder now that he was grown up but still living at home, and now that Mum had someone to help around the house. But it seemed his 'convenient excuse' for leaving home all those years ago hadn't fooled Danny. Eager to shift the subject, he said, 'Nice suit. Didn't make the rock star, then?'

'We still play the odd gig.'

At least something was the same. 'Still doing The Doors covers?'

It was a pathetic silence-filler, so Matt didn't mind when Danny gave no answer. He drove fast, with a clear intent. Matt realised this wasn't just a drive so they could talk in peace: his brother was taking him somewhere specific.

'Family will be down,' Danny said after at least a minute's silence. 'They'll be asking questions. We've avoided them so far. Questions, that is. We're hoping for next week for the funeral. You're going to come, of course?'

'Of course.' Now they were taking baby steps in the right direction. No outright mention of Karen, but a nod towards her. But there was a knot in Matt's throat. No date for the funeral might mean the coroner hadn't released the body yet. Which meant an inquest. And an inquest hinted at foul play.

Silence again. At least five minutes this time. Matt looked around the car and the man. The BMW was a top-end model, so Danny was doing well for himself. He wore a wedding band, so a wife had entered the picture at some point. There hadn't been any kind of steady girlfriend in Danny's life when Matt left, just a string of casual ones, all part of the wannabe rock star lifestyle. He looked over his shoulder. Directly behind him, the rear seat had food crumbs in the seams, while the half behind the driver was clean and pristine. An accumulation of crumbs over time, from someone who only ever sat behind the passenger seat, where the driver could easily see him. Changes, changes.

'How's Joseph?' he said, relief having hit him like a wave. He had feared the baby in the photo back at the house might be Karen's. Barely into the world and already his mother dead.

Danny looked at him. 'Brilliant. He's three now. I just dropped him at his mother's and they're off to the cinema.'

Dropped at his mother's? Matt didn't want to hear a sorry story, so changed the subject. 'How's work?' More small talk.

'Not now,' Danny said, and pulled the car quickly to the kerb.

Wherever Danny had chosen to take him, they had arrived. Matt saw a residential street with small shops scattered. Take-aways, a dry-cleaners, some others. On the surface nothing appeared off about the street, but he felt a grim aura pulsing from it. He had registered the road name, on a sign on a wall back at the corner. Barker Street.

'Red-light area, in case you're wondering,' Danny said. Matt wasn't wondering. He'd worked that out already, but not why they were here. Danny took an item out of his glovebox. It was something laminated, A5 size. He held it to his chest.

'Caz sometimes said she thought the next time we hear about you, it'd be two cops at the door, telling us the bad news.'

There it was, finally. Karen had been mentioned. He hadn't dreamed her his whole life after all. He waited for Danny's story. Cops at the door, bearers of bad news.

'That's how it's supposed to happen,' Danny continued. 'Someone dead in your family. Cops coming to the door.' He smacked the steering wheel with his forearm. 'Not when the guy who finds the body is a goddamned pal of some reporter and tells the press all about it first.'

Danny held the laminated thing out for him. He was

supposed to take it. He didn't take it. He didn't see it. He saw nothing as his world sank inside him.

The nightmare was real, then. All the facts were there, proving it: body found outside, inquest ordered, and a text message with the word *killed*. No heart attack, car crash or hidden disease had killed his Karen. The truth was forcing upon a mind that was losing the battle to keep itself locked shut, and the truth was going to be that his sister had been murdered.

Matt looked out of the windows again. He knew what Danny was trying to show him, but he didn't need to see it. Danny was trying to show him a laminated article from a newspaper. A morning edition to which some eager reporter had brought a stunning, late story, possibly having called his editor before he alerted the police. The story is in print and in the shops before the cops can identify the dead woman. And a city boy in a suit buys the local paper on his way to the office and learns of the explosion to his world long before a sympathetic officer can knock his door to tell him. Matt knew all this and as he looked at the street beyond the window, he realised he knew something else, too. Why Danny had brought him here.

'She was a prostitute?' His head spun. 'Did you bring me to show me where she worked?'

'That's what this bastard who wrote the article says. I say he goddamn assumed she was a prostitute because of where she was found. Or just because she was out alone on a Saturday night.'

The laminate was still under Matt's nose. He didn't want to see it. He'd seen all he needed. He didn't want it to exist. His gut was twisting at the brand-new knowledge that his sister had been found murdered on Sunday morning and it was now Tuesday. For two days she had been dead and he hadn't known. Two days in which his family had been suffering, while he was just a few hours away and lugging bags of ornamental stones and compost in a world of oblivion. While his family had cried, he'd had a bath, enjoyed a meal, laughed at comedy on TV, and slept like a log, unaware of the vicious blast crater in his universe. That part stung as badly as anything he'd ever experienced.

'And she was killed around here?'

'Not just killed, Matt. Murdered, and dumped in a patch of waste ground like trash.'

The last sentence put a painful throb in Matt's stomach. He forced his fist into it. He looked for this waste ground. Wasn't there. Danny saw his roving eyes.

'It's a few streets or so over. But this is where she worked, the police said. They think the body might have been moved after death. She was found on her back, but there was blood that ran out of her ear and to her lips, so she must have been face down at some point.' He held out the laminate again. Matt didn't take it, but he could see part of it. Six lines of smaller print beside a photo that he avoided looking at, both under a headline: LOCAL PROSTITUTE FOUND STRANGLED.

Strangled. Now he knew everything. Knew too much. Knew too where this knowledge was going to lead him. Someone out there had done this to her, to her family, to Matt. He felt the affront as a pressure behind his eyes. He rubbed his nose where it parted his eyes. He was grinding his teeth, and that part was anger. He knew he was at the start of a journey he couldn't avoid. It was in his DNA, but he was scared at the prospect.

He immediately thought of his mother, learning of her daughter's death and shady job all in one go. Matt asked how she felt about it.

'The prostitution? She already knew. Karen was arrested for it a couple of times, and the only address they had for her was Mum's house. And there was a funny thing that happened about nine months ago. But she doesn't mention it. She doesn't like to even think about it. Maybe she thinks it'll all be a dream if she ignores it. It tips the 10-4.'

An old saying of Danny's: tipping the 10-4 meant upsetting the normal balance of things. That went part way to explaining why Mum hadn't yet talked about Karen. Not Danny's stupid theory, because no matter how vile Karen's lifestyle, it wouldn't make a loving mother try to forget about her daughter. So this had to be about Matt: he'd been away so long that he had no idea Karen sold her body, and Mum didn't want to immediately heap awful facts upon the terrible. Maybe she'd asked Danny to take Matt aside and impart the news.

His mind turned to something else Danny had said. 'A funny thing nine months ago? What are you talking about? Is it connected to this?'

'Mum thinks some evil punter of Karen's killed her. Maybe she charged too much, or bit him by accident, or–'

'Don't talk like that, Danny.'

Danny took a long time before answering. 'I just meant that Mum doesn't seem to care. You see these murder investigations on TV, with families in court to see the killer get convicted, so they can get justice. Well it's not like that for Mum. "Won't bring her back," that's what she said to me. Karen's gone and that's the end of it, and she doesn't want to dwell on the crime. She didn't care about knowing the autopsy results, she keeps sending the family liaison officer away because she doesn't want to talk about the crime. And she's happy to accept some evil punter theory and move on.'

'Mum thinks a client might have killed Karen? What do the police say? And you sound like you don't believe this evil punter theory, as you call it.'

Danny gave him a condescending look. 'You're on that band-wagon, too?'

'I'm not sure of the official statistics, Danny, but as a profession amongst murdered women, I'd say prostitution is right up there at the top of the list. Prostitutes hang about in the dark and they go off with strangers. I hate to say it, but it makes total sense to me that some sick bastard killed Karen for pleasure. What do the police say?'

'There was no clear evidence of forced sex, Matt, and a sick bastard out for kicks would probably have raped her. So I think there's more to it than that. But that's exactly the line the police are giving us.'

'What do they know? What have they said?' Matt snapped, impatient now for an answer to a question he'd asked three times.

His anger was a shade of Danny's. He spat, 'They've said enough to let me know that they don't know anything. They've spoken to some of the street women here, but no one knows a bloody thing. Of course they don't. They reckoned she was homeless. Mum wanted to know if there was a flat somewhere, so we could get her stuff back. There's no stuff, apparently. Unless the girls are lying. There could be some clues there, if she had a flat. And they spoke to some mingebag they thought might have been her pimp, but he wasn't arrested and he was let go soon afterwards. Didn't know anything, had no idea who Karen was. But he would say that, wouldn't he? With his bloody solicitor holding his hand, knowing the police can't put scissors on his balls to get the truth.'

Matt stared out the window, took in his surroundings, and right there it dawned on him. Mum might have tasked Danny with taking Matt away in order to tell the story, but Danny had his own reason for bringing Matt to a red-light area.

'Take me back,' Matt said with a croaky voice. When Danny paused, Matt added: 'I know why you brought me here. You want me to talk to the women out here.'

'I need to know the truth, Matt, even if Mum is happy

enough to move on without it. I need it. Christ, I thought you'd love the idea of a hunt.'

'Take me back, Danny. This isn't a good idea. The police have questioned these girls, and they don't know anything. Which I'd expect if Karen's killer was some random lunatic who chanced upon her.'

'No, no, they wouldn't want to tell–'

'Besides, it's too early,' he cut in. 'Even if these women were willing to talk to someone who's not a policeman, it's too early, as you can see. There's no women out. We'd have to wait till after ten. If we were doing this, which we're not. Now take me back.'

Danny looked angry. His mouth moved a couple of times, but he seemed to bite back whatever wanted to come out. He threw the car in gear and squealed the tyres as he jumped away from the kerb.

They drove home in silence. When Danny pulled up outside their mother's house, he gave a weak excuse about errands to run and drove away. Matt took a very slow stroll down the garden path, while pretending to look at something on his phone. It was a show for Danny's eyes in the rear-view. As soon as the car was round the corner, lost from sight, Matt back-tracked and hopped in his own vehicle. His mother would likely be annoyed that he'd vanished again, but he would be back tomorrow. One more day after so many years wouldn't hurt her.

Matt knew his brother well. Danny had expected his brother to return to the family fold upon hearing about Karen's murder, and from the start he'd planned to use Matt for some detective work. Matt, the tough army boy, would go chat to the girls. Matt would go get the truth and danger be damned.

Danny knew his brother well, too.

2

As if Karen was surfing social media up there in heaven, many people had written miss you messages on her Facebook profile. Dozens. Young people, mostly, so probably colleagues from her university days – her profile still said she was studying nursing. Matt wondered about what had turned her to prostitution. Had university been an attempt to get off the game, get herself a life, or had selling sex started as nothing more than a means of paying her way while studying?

He would talk to Mum about getting the profile deleted. But for now it was beneficial. Without asking questions of his family, he could scroll and click and learn about the sister he had become estranged from. But soon delving into the life she'd lived since he'd abandoned her became too hard on his emotions.

Back to the job at hand. It was closing on 10pm and the darkness here on Barker Street, in the red-light area Danny had showed him, had livened the place up. A host of unsavoury characters passed by his car. Matt didn't doubt that he would be accosted within moments if he stepped out of the vehicle. Women wanting to suck him for a price. Men wanting to sell him jewellery or just take his shoes. House prices were probably bottom of the barrel in such a place.

Matt exited the car. Locked it. Started walking. A hundred metres up, the road hit a T-junction. A sign said the new street was called Albert Road. Left, he could see larger commercial establishments, still open. A Tesco Express, a taxi rank, others. More life up that way. To the right, the lighting grew worse. Down that way the street was purely residential and dim, almost eerie, as if the local authority had set such an area aside for the strange of society to lurk in. Big houses, old, three storeys, looking like mini haunted mansions in the moonlight. More people, mostly standing around. A dotting of girls, plying their trade.

He crossed to the other side of Barker Street, where there was a streetlight virtually right on the corner. He stood on the corner of the junction, hidden in a shadowy recessed shop doorway, waiting. Watching both streets. Didn't care if he looked suspicious. It would keep people away from him. It took forty more minutes. In that time, six different girls passed him, but none approached. They were only interested in the guys in cars. Like the one that pulled to the kerb sixty metres down the haunted mansion part of Albert Road. Other side of the road, facing his way. Matt moved that way. A guy stuck his arm out the driver's window when a prostitute in a jogging outfit came close. He held something in his hand, some piece of paper. The woman gave him the finger and walked away. By this time Matt was level with the car, on the other side of the road. The driver hadn't seen him. He sprinted across the road just as the car started to pull away, yanked the passenger door and slipped inside.

'Jesus goddamn Christ!' Danny yelled. He hit the brakes.

'I could have been a guy with a knife, you idiot,' Matt

snapped. 'And right now you'd be in the road, watching me drive your flash BMW away into the night.'

'Yeah? Well I had no choice, did I? You wouldn't help.'

Matt snatched the paper Danny held. It was a Polaroid photo of Karen, from some Christmas party Matt had missed. One of many. 'You'll get nothing this way, Danny. You might look like a drug dealer in this car, but you go asking questions like that in the dead of night, wearing a bloody suit, and you come across like a police officer. I saw the success you had just then with that girl.'

'What are you doing here, anyway? I thought you weren't bothered about the truth. You could have stayed home and believed your evil punter theory.'

'I came because I knew you'd come, soon as I told you I wouldn't go asking questions. And I told you ten o'clock onward would be best so I wouldn't have to wait around all evening. Now go home.' He snatched a pen that protruded from Danny's breast pocket. 'Give me money. I need money.'

Danny gave him a shocked look. 'I hope you don't mean to–'

'No, it's not for buying sex. And you'll get it back.'

Danny didn't know what was going on, but he complied. He had eighty pounds in his wallet, six tens and a twenty. Matt took it. He rapidly drew a smiley face on each note, then pocketed pen and money. Danny just watched, puzzled.

'So now what?' he asked.

'Now you tell me about this so-called funny thing that happened nine months ago. Whatever it was, it's the reason you spit on the evil punter idea.'

Danny gave a pause. 'You could ask Mum.'

'Or I could leave Mum to wallow in her ignorance, if that's her way to cope. How can you expect me to look beyond an evil punter if you don't tell me what you know?'

Another pause from his brother. Matt sensed doubt and

realised that he wasn't going to be the first person to hear Danny's murder theory. And whoever else had been party to it had scoffed at it.

The story came out in short sentences and throughout Danny stared ahead, out the window. Nine months ago Karen had been arrested after an off-duty policeman had solicited her for sex. Karen had recognised him from somewhere, and afterwards had told him so. Then she'd tried to threaten him, according to the officer: he had to give her more money, or she would report him to his bosses and tell his wife. The officer had not only refused, he'd arrested her for blackmail, taken her to his station and come clean about the whole thing, including telling his wife.

Here Danny looked at Matt, awaiting a response. Matt had been expecting more. At first he didn't understand, but something sparked a moment later. 'You think she did it again? She tried to blackmail a client, but this time she picked someone who couldn't afford to just come clean. So she was killed to keep a secret. That's your theory?'

'I don't have any proof, but yes. She did it before, and maybe she's done it lots of times and gotten away with it. So, do you think I'm full of shit, like the police do?'

'I have no evidence either way.'

'So what are you going to do now? There could be evidence out there, maybe in the heads of her fellow sex workers.'

Matt opened the door and got out. 'And now we're back to that, are we? Look, Danny, I'll go have a word with one of them. But not with you around. Go home.'

'I want to know what you find out, Matt. You come straight to tell me, okay?'

Matt repeated his order for Danny to go home. He made a point of standing and watching until his brother, realising he'd get no answer to his question, left.

When the car was gone, Matt took out a photo of Karen that he'd printed off her Facebook profile, and then walked back to the corner and took up his spot again. Not quite right on the corner, where the safe shadows were, but six feet from it on the Barker Road side. Right on the kerb, which was a spot that gave him maximum exposure under the streetlight.

It took another twelve minutes. Foot traffic was heavier now. Lots of girls, plying their trade. When they passed him by, he made crude remarks. Did they do group discounts, could he get a loyalty card, could he film the sex for his website? He was told to fuck off. When cars passed by, he stepped into the road and stared at the drivers and wrote blatantly on the blank side of his folded photo of Karen and made sure they saw him do it. The girls started to notice that potential punters were driving away. The 10-4 was well and truly tipped. Because of the guy down at the corner.

Twelve minutes of this game, then they came. A black three-door Volkswagen Golf turned off Albert Road and onto Barker Street and drew up at the kerb by his feet. He'd seen it go past him before, he realised, while he was hidden in the doorway. Down came the passenger window. A rugged white face above a tight plain T-shirt stared at him. Bright blonde hair, stringy, like some rag mop head turned upside down.

Other side of the car, the driver stepped out. Black guy, jeans and another T-shirt, this time blue, also plain, too tight, or just tight enough to show his muscled physique the way he wanted. A handsome Adonis who could make women swoon. He came around the front of the car. The backseat passenger, big and fat and white, oozed slowly out of the same door, and waddled the other way around the vehicle. With a big belly and facial tattoos and far too much hair on his meaty arms, here was a man who would prefer men to quake rather than women to swoon. Both mean-looking bastards took a spot that boxed Matt in using the car. The white guy in the Golf stayed right there, glaring.

Big Belly said, 'I run this area. These are my girls. I watch out for them and they pay for the privilege–'

'Just say you're a pimp,' Matt cut in. 'Or a procurer, if that sounds more business-like.'

The black guy sniggered, but not at Matt's joke. It was the sort of snigger you might do if you saw a guy about to walk into a lamp post because he wasn't watching where he was going. Like he thought Matt was unwittingly running into major trouble with his mouth.

Big Belly said, 'You're scaring my clients off. That costs me money.' He snatched the folded photo off Matt. 'And what the fuck is this? You writing number plates down, dickhead? You a cop?' He looked at what Matt had written, but he didn't see registration numbers. He saw senseless doodling. Puzzled, Big Belly crumpled the sheet up and dropped it. Thankfully, he hadn't opened the paper to see the photo of Karen. 'I think you've cost me 200. So you owe me 200. Now.' His chubby palm came out.

Matt held out the cash Danny had given him. 'I got eighty.' He was prepared for something to happen here. It didn't, really. The black guy snatched the money and pushed him towards Big Belly, who stepped aside, booted Matt in the ass as he went past, and said, 'Get lost.'

Ten seconds later they were back in the car and gone.

Matt drove and worked out the area. A quarter-circle area some 600 metres down the straight sides – Barker Street and Albert

Road – and a long, curving main road called Edison Avenue. Those streets and everything within: the pimp's zone, he figured.

The zone, however, didn't encompass the waste ground where Karen's body had been found. That was a hundred metres from Edison Avenue, beyond a green area and a row of shops on its far side. Matt didn't know if the waste ground's location was significant or not. He would find out, but not yet. He refused to cast his eyes to the right each time he passed the waste ground. If he saw it, he would picture Karen's body, and he did not want to do that. Yet.

The black Golf made circuit after circuit of the zone. A nice, plodding fifteen minutes for each trip. Sometimes the Golf dipped down a side street, but it always came out again and continued that anti-clockwise rotation. Roads Albert, Barker, Edison. The circuit was about 2.5 kilometres because while the straight roads were short, the main road curved out far and wide. Edison Avenue was a bustling thoroughfare, and a jolly social place for prostitutes. Fifteen or more he saw. They lurked in doorways and side streets. Driving through, you'd hardly notice them. Eyes had to know what they were looking for.

The Golf also made regular stops and girls would hand money over. Sometimes passenger side, sometimes driver's side. He couldn't work anything out from this. No one ever got out. Matt kept his distance. He lurked just around corners or pulled in behind larger parked vehicles. There were a few places where he could duck left down a side street, make a turn right onto a second side street, and drive to the end and get ahead of the Golf, just in case the guys in front noticed the Mondeo behind them. Deep down the second side street he would wait, and watch the Golf cruise past, before pulling out to follow again. Easier to see the occupants from the side. Same three guys, same seating arrangement.

Two hours he followed the car. Circuit after circuit, and

always dead on fifteen minutes each time, even with the money stops and the side street detours. It was obvious to Matt that the plan was to have the car present at each of the vital spots in the zone every quarter of an hour, probably to discourage unwelcome activity from the girls or from rival pimps.

He was beginning to think he should peel away, because soon someone on the pimps' payroll might report a dodgy car cruising around, or a law-abider might tell the police. Either would ruin his plan. Deciding to get ahead of the Golf, he took a left off Albert Road. A couple more turns put him on a road that connected to Barker Street. He parked ten metres from the junction. Ahead, Barker Street running past. Thirty seconds until the Golf sauntered by, he figured.

It didn't. He gave it thirty more.

Nothing.

Panicking, he drove too fast to the junction, screeched to a halt, looked right. Twenty metres up was the corner, the spot where Albert Road and Barker Street met. Where the pimps had accosted him. The Golf was supposed to turn left, onto Barker, but it hadn't. Which meant it must have continued straight across, continuing down Albert towards the brightly lit part with the shops. Matt swung right and raced to the junction. He looked left, and there was the Golf, parked at the kerb right outside the Tesco Express. Hello again, mingebags.

He waited. Risky sitting right in the road, at the junction, but he waited, nose sticking out just far enough so he could see the Golf beyond the corner wall. Two vehicles came up behind him. He put his hazards on and stuck an arm out the window and waved them past. Six minutes he waited, worried that the police might pull him for kerb-crawling, that some local was calling Big Belly, then the black guy, the driver, came out of the Tesco carrying a plastic bag of goodies. He got in the Golf and it pulled off. Matt swung left and followed.

A kilometre later, after two turns, he was deep in a housing estate. And this one looked okay. Semis, no terraced houses. Driveways with cars. Garden ornaments. The odd water feature. No prostitutes. A mildly affluent estate within throwing distance of a run-down shithole.

There was a house with an overgrown lawn and a four-year-old hatchback sitting in the grass. One of the three guys got dropped off there. White front passenger, mop hair. He had the food that the other guy had bought. He went in the house, no wave, no look back. Big Belly struggled his bulk out of the car with all the finesse of a whale being born and got in the vacated front seat.

Matt followed the car a mile to a commercial street. The shops were all shut but there were people around. Guys and gals in classy clothing, all walking, passing through, as if heading home from a club or theatre. Nobody lurking. No prostitutes. The Golf stopped outside an Indian takeaway, but the place was closed. Big Belly got out and scuttled down a thin alley beside the shop. Matt looked up at two windows on the first floor. Both were dark. He waited. The Golf drove away. He didn't follow. He needed confirmation of which of the pimps was the boss. Two minutes later, one of the lights upstairs went on. Anaemic light washed the pavement. He saw Big Belly approach the glass and draw thick, old curtains.

He had his answer.

Carl had once woken up in a police cell, five officers hovering over him, shouting, waving their sticks. That was scary. He'd woken a few months back right here in his bedroom, looking at the barrel of a gun held by some cocaine freak he'd sold shit stuff to. That was scary. But this one topped both. His eyes fluttered open and saw a guy kneeling on his bed, between his spread legs. The quilt had been cast aside, so Carl was naked, utterly exposed. The guy, just a silhouette in the dim light, waved hello. The other hand held a pair of scissors between Carl's legs. Big scissors, Carl's own pair from the kitchen. He recognised the purple rubber-handle covers, even in the gloom. Open blades, cupping his balls. There was enough cold pressure there to make him realise he really shouldn't move. He shouldn't try anything smart.

There was enough light for him to recognise his assailant. The guy from earlier, on the street corner. Just a normal-looking guy back then. But he seemed like the devil now, despite the smile.

'So you're the procurer,' the man said. 'The man who watches out for the girls and who they pay for the privilege–'

Carl's voice was broken. 'What you talking about?'

'I'm talking about the brain-dead, slimy, pimp mingebag who runs prostitutes out of that zone.'

Carl shook his head. 'No, man, that's Dean, the fat guy, the one who booted you. He even said he was the boss. You heard that.'

'I don't think so. You live in this nice house, nice new car in the garden. Your bulldog Dean lives in a bedsit above a shop. And Dean's supposedly the top dog, yet he spent all evening in the back seat, cramped, struggling to get his fat ass out. He got real bored of that back seat when they dropped you off.'

Carl thought quickly. 'Okay, man, it was the other guy, the black guy. You got me. Black guy, he's the boss. I ain't supposed to snitch on him, but you got me. That black guy. It ain't me.'

The man squeezed a bit more with the scissors. Their cold touch became hot with pain. 'The boss drives his cronies around all night, does he? And runs into shops for them? Proper little errand boys, these crime barons. The food from Tesco. It's down in your kitchen.'

Carl said nothing. Only a weak table lamp lit the room, but he could see clearly the glint off the scissors. And his own sweaty chest and legs. And the slow rise and fall of the chest of the man threatening to cut his balls off. Slow and steady, like he did this threatening people shit all the time.

The man held up money. A twenty-pound note. His finger tapped a place. In the gloom Carl saw a smiley face drawn in pen, about the size of a ten-pence piece. 'This is mine. I marked it. Your so-called boss took it from me, yet I found it in your trousers.'

Carl deflated. *Come what may,* he thought. 'Okay, you win. It's me. I control that area. Tell me what you want.' He relaxed a sliver. He thought this guy sought something other than blood.

The guy put the note away, came back with a photo. 'Did you run this girl?'

The fear was back. Carl recognised the picture. She'd been one of his girls. Found dead the other day. 'Aw, Christ, are you family? Jesus, pal, the cops talked to me about that, about her. Cleared me. I was away, man, far away. I had nothing to do with that. The cops talked to me, man. I didn't kill her.'

'I believe that. That's why your balls aren't where your eyes are. But she was one of your girls, even though she was found outside your zone. I want to know what you neglected to tell the police. And yes, I'm family. She was my sister.'

A memory flashed into Carl's head: he recalled some comment ages ago from that girl, something about a brother who'd served in the army. Somehow, his fear hit a higher gear. He knew a couple of army guys, and what they'd experienced in Iraq had thrown their heads out of whack. 'Nothing, I don't know anything, man. The cops cleared me. I told them every-thing. Go ask 'em. I was well upset about that.'

'I'm sure they considered you a very helpful member of the community. With your solicitor holding your hand, knowing the cops don't use the old scissors-on-balls tactic. I just had to use that trick when I heard it.'

The blades closed a notch and the pain level went up. Carl panicked. He lived alone and his neighbours knew to keep their distance, so he was aware that he could be left to bleed to death right in his own bed and not be found for days. And the cops wouldn't hit the blues and twos in their rush to solve his murder.

'Yeah, okay, I knew her, but look, like you said, she was outside my zone. I don't let the girls go outside my zone. That's not safe. I don't know how she got there or what happened. I can't see everything. I just cruise the same few streets, man. I swear. If girls go off the reservation, I ain't got no control, I ain't got no eyes. I wish she hadn't, man. I was well upset about that.'

'"Well upset", were you? Do you know her name?'

Carl thought hard. Girls who came to work for him gave a name, of course, but he knew most were probably bogus. He didn't care because he and his boys referred to the bitches by nicknames. He wondered if he'd anger this guy more by giving a wrong name, as opposed to no name at all. He played it both ways.

'I don't know. She only told me a nickname, Red, because of her hair colour. She never told me her real one. She liked Red.'

The guy considered this, then nodded. 'Now listen very carefully. When I leave here, I'm going to follow any leads I get. What you need to do is hope that when I get to my next destination, there's enough information there to move me forward. Always forward, you understand. Because you know where a guy goes when he can't go forward?'

Carl knew exactly what the guy was saying. 'Back. He comes back.'

'Right. He comes back. Right back here, with the scissors. So you need to push me forward, keep me going. But you don't know what information will push me onwards, however insignificant, however bad it might make you appear, so it's vital that you answer my questions in as much detail as possible. Understand?'

Carl understood. He understood fully. He nodded vigorously, so vigorously that the mattress shivered and the scissors brought another wave of pain.

'Okay. So, you know your girls. I'm sure if one of them had a regular client, or a weirdo who liked her to dress as his mother, you'd know. And if one of them had a sideline in blackmail, you'd know that, too. She'd probably need your help with that, for collecting money or showing some muscle.'

Carl shook his head. 'I don't know anything about blackmail. Jesus, what do you think I am? If one of them blackmailed some punter, it's nothing to do with me. And they wouldn't tell me something like that. All I do is protect the girls.' He was careful to add: 'As long as they stay in my zone.'

'One night with a woman, nice and anonymous. But a regular guy, coming back to a girl he likes, will start to open his mouth. He'll maybe talk about his job, his boring wife, whatever. Tell me about any of her regular clients. Especially high-profile or rich ones.'

'I swear to God, I don't know. These people don't make appointments, man, and I'm sorry if that sounds sarcastic. I don't want to know about clients. If the girls have a regular, I don't know about it unless the guy steps over the line.'

The man looked like he was thinking. Like some new revelation had hit him. Then he seemed to snap back to the moment, and Carl realised he'd dodged another bullet. 'That night she was murdered. Cast your mind back. When did you last see her? What did she say to you? How many clients did she have? Tell me everything. Just talk, now, fast.'

Carl talked, now, fast. He explained that on the night before she turned up dead, she had approached his car on Barker Street around seven that evening and claimed she was sick, could she go home? He had said yeah, sure, go rest, take care. Actually, he had threatened her with a kicking and told her that he'd be getting a lot more than his fifty per cent of her takings tomorrow, for his inconvenience. But he wasn't about to tell this guy that part. Then they'd driven off and she'd walked away, and that was that. Earlier in the evening she had been missing on two of their cruises round the zone, so obviously she had gone away with punters, but he hadn't seen who. None of the girls knew who, either, because he made sure there was no sisterhood. 'And that was it, man. I never saw her again. I heard about her death the next morning, in the papers. Honest. That's it, that's all I know.'

The guy stared at him for a long moment and Carl knew he was assessing what he'd been told. Working out if it was bullshit or not. Carl tensed, figuring he'd know the outcome of that assessment if things got a lot more painful.

The guy nodded again. Carl relaxed a little.

'Did she have a residence somewhere?'

Carl shook his head. 'No, but look, man, this'll prove I want to help. The girls told the police she was homeless, but I know she used to crash at some of their places now and then. I told them not to tell the cops that in case the cops searched their flats and found stuff about me. But she never used those places for sex.'

'So where did she take her clients? Is there a place outside the area that girls go to?'

Carl shook his head. 'No, man, they stay in the zone so I can keep an eye on them. I mean, to watch, you know, make sure everything's fine.'

'They must have regular spots where they go. Did she have a

favourite spot?' The words seemed to taste bad on his tongue, Carl saw. Something the guy didn't want to think about: his sister having a comfortable dirty doorway or alcove where she did her sex stuff.

'I can tell you that. There's a place where a lot of the girls go. Too much cop activity around, so they don't use the streets. I don't like them to trust cars, either.'

The man snorted. 'Don't pretend you're worried about their well-being. Where's this place? Is it safe and secure?'

'It's hidden. No one else goes there. Just the girls. You know the street we saw you on?'

'Don't tell me,' the guy said. He reached behind him, plucked something from the bed and threw it on Carl's chest. A pair of Carl's blue jeans. Taken from his wardrobe. It unnerved Carl to know that the guy had been snooping around before he pulled the scissors. 'Show me.'

The guy moved the scissors away. Carl took a deep breath of relief and grabbed his balls, but there was no blood. The guy shuffled back and got off the bed. He still held the scissors, but the weapon was a much less lethal item now. Carl considered rushing him, even naked. Then he remembered that the guy had broken in, found the scissors, crept into the bedroom, taken clothing from the wardrobe, money from his pocket, all while Carl slept. The guy had skills. Better not to risk rushing a guy like that. Better to bide his time.

'One more thing. My sister died, remember that. So I'm not a guy stepping out of line. I'm doing what any loving brother would do, I'm sure you understand that. So you stay away from my family. I'll pay you. I just want to see where she worked. I don't want trouble.'

Carl grabbed his jeans and yanked them on, quick. He felt more protected now he wasn't naked. Then he focused on what the guy had just said. Had he heard that right? 'Pay me? To show you? How much?'

The guy bent, grabbed a jacket off the floor and tossed it at Carl. His black bomber jacket. Carl put it on, then slipped off the side of the bed and got his trainers. The guy tossed him Carl's baseball cap with NEW YORK stencilled on the front. 'Tuck your hair in so I can't see it.'

Carl did. Now dressed, and wide awake, his confidence grew.

The man said, 'I have five grand. It's yours. You show me where my sister took her clients, and promise not to come after me or my family, and you get it all. Five grand.'

'I promise,' Carl said, arms open as if for a hug. All fear was gone. A minute earlier, the guy had him by the balls – literally. Sixty seconds later and Carl was the man again.

'I have to keep the scissors on you, you understand? Until I've seen the place and I'm safe. When I've seen and I'm in my car, I'll drop my bank card for you, with the PIN number. Deal?'

The guy slipped a wallet halfway out of a pocket in his jeans, as if to prove he had money. 'Deal,' Carl said, smiling inside. Any other day of the week, he'd gladly give a guy a pass for five grand. Not some guy who'd sneaked in his house and put a blade to his balls. In some extreme moment of generosity, he might have overlooked a guy putting a blade to his throat. But the balls? Fuck that. He'd keep half his word: he'd show the guy where his slut sister did her business. But then he'd bury the guy there. Safe and secure it was indeed. A good place for a corpse to lie undiscovered.

Carl kept his calm and let the guy usher him out of the bedroom, down the stairs, and towards the back door. The guy followed close behind, one hand with a fistful of jacket and the other holding the scissors at Carl's neck. Carl felt a blade each side, pressing softly, a constant reminder not to try anything smart. In the kitchen, he saw the busted lock on the back door, where the guy had come in, and wondered how he'd done it so quietly. They went outside and around the house, towards the front.

The man reminded Carl there was a lot of money in this for him. This was by his car, out in the front yard where the world could see, not that any of his posh bastard neighbours would be up at this time. Not that any would race to his rescue anyway. At the car was where the guy knew things might get tricky for him. He had to get two people inside the vehicle, so if there was going to be a moment when his defence was down, when Carl might try to take him, it would be here. But Carl wasn't going to take him, not yet. Couldn't kill a guy in his own front yard, could he? The neighbours would be watching if that happened, for sure. And he was thinking about the money. Five grand. For five grand he would let this guy think he was in control for a little longer.

The guy forced Carl into the driver's seat then got in the back, right behind. There was a moment when he had to take the scissors away, but he was good, he was quick, and Carl wasn't sure he could have turned the tables in that split second even if he'd wanted to. But he didn't want to, did he? Not yet.

So the scissors were back. Left side of his neck, beside the driver's seat's headrest. The guy said something about not trying a trick like hard braking, because the scissors were tight and he'd get his head cut off. But Carl was planning no such silly move. Didn't want to have to spend all that five grand on fixing up his ride, did he?

As he drove, Carl kept checking the guy out in the rear-view mirror. All the way to Barker Street, along a route he figured the guy knew, the face behind him hardly changed, and those steely eyes never left the scissors or Carl's head. But a minute later, as the car entered another section of the estate, those eyes darted about, scanning the area. Carl could tell this was an environment the guy hadn't seen before.

Soon, Carl pulled the car to the kerb on a road between a row of three-storey Victorian houses and a terrace of shops in a low, old stone building. The area was quiet and empty. Lights blazed in the houses, but the shops were dead and shuttered.

Carl pointed. 'Chip shop at the end.'

'Park beside it. Back the car in.'

There was a driveway between the end of the terrace and a tall wall. Carl did as instructed, planning to reverse the car as far as possible to hide it from view of the houses. But a short way in, the guy yelled for him to stop, right now, and he did. The back half of the car was hidden in darkness while the front half poked out, clearly visible under the street lamps.

'Get out. Open the hatch.'

Carl obeyed. He stepped out into the light and moved alongside the wall of the chippy, into the darkness smothering the rear half of the car. For the second time the man had no control over Carl, and this time Carl had a much better opportunity to take the guy, or just run. But again he decided to bide his time. The guy would lead himself to a better place for the table-turning. So Carl did exactly as ordered, and watched as the guy collapsed half of the split rear seat's backrest and crawled out through the car's ass.

Carl knew that anyone watching from the big houses across the way would have seen only a guy in a cap exit the car. It made him grin. *And all they're gonna see is one guy in a cap leave, dickhead.*

The rear of the chippy was walled off, grimy, rubbish-strewn. A large wheelie bin overflowed. There was a wall separating the chippy's back yard from the next, but it had a hole in it. Matt presumed a back route taken by prostitutes.

The chippy had two back doors. One, modern wood, with a window of frosted glass. The other was a small iron door, ancient and badly rusted. It was this door that the pimp dragged open. It opened silently, as if freshly oiled. Matt watched him carefully, ever alert for a counter attack. But the man clearly had his thoughts on money. He stepped aside and waved a hand, like a hotel doorman. Matt stepped forward and peeked inside, one eye still on the pimp. The door led to a kind of small storage unit, an outhouse, but in the brick wall at the back was a great hole, easily big enough for a man to walk upright through. Matt nodded at the pimp to go first. He followed the man inside, then through the hole in the back wall, and was surprised to find himself in a large, open area.

A tubular tunnel of brick with a flat floor of pitted concrete. It was lit by rechargeable portable work lamps arranged by the walls, their powerful LED beams directed at the floor in order to keep the area gloomy. To the right, the tunnel sloped downwards to a sharp turn some seven or eight metres away. Immediately to the left it terminated at a decrepit metal shutter. A rent in the shutter exposed a brick wall. Beyond that wall, the chippy, Matt guessed.

He heard noises down the tunnel; people talking, coming towards them. Two elongated shadows slid across the wall seconds before a prostitute and her punter turned the corner and stepped into view. Both shut their mouths instantly when they saw the two men by the makeshift exit. The guy kept his head down and made a quick exit from the tunnel, out into the night and away. The prostitute approached the pimp. She handed him folded money and looked happy to do so. *Look at how well I did.*

Matt watched with disgust. The pimp grabbed her ass, one quick squeeze, and gave a playful slap in the same spot to send her on her way. Matt thought of Karen. Right here, kowtowing to this guy in the same pathetic manner. Money exchanging hands. A slap of the ass and away. The image put a new rush of anger in him.

'Go, down,' he snapped at the pimp, pointing with the scissors. The woman's face fell. He saw it as she passed him. He saw the look on the pimp's face, too. Hers: surprise that some guy had spoken to him like that. His: anger that she'd seen such a thing.

Down the tunnel they went. They took the sharp turn to the right. He saw the floor was littered with plaster and there were spots on the walls where obstinate bits of plaster still hung. He had worked out where he was before they took the turn and looked down the next tunnel and a new area opened out before them.

He was in an abandoned underground train station. London had lots of them. Their surface entrances were either gone or changed; this one's had become a chippy. The tubular shape and platform were the only clues, though. There was nothing here bar a large cavity in the ground. The station was bricked up at the far end, just past the platform. Spaced along the length of the platform were wooden panels at right angles to the wall, creating private spots, like booths, where the girls could work their clients. Candles arranged along the opposite wall to the platform cast dancing orange light along the grimy brickwork, as if to inject a romantic aura. It failed miserably: the whole scene was pathetic. How terrified of the police must these girls be to come so far from their working area, to sneak underground, to get down and dirty in some tomb-like old station?

And how desperate were their punters for a bit of flesh? Matt had been in some of the worst hellholes on Earth, and even he didn't like this place. How a guy could get hard here was beyond him.

He tossed those thoughts away and got back to the moment. His eyes flicked, his brain working. Where the tunnel opened out onto the platform, the floor was pitted, the concrete churned, as if items planted there had been uprooted. Turnstiles, maybe. That was when he saw the door. In the left wall, right near the spot where the tunnel became a station. It was old iron, like the one they'd used to enter this cesspit. By lamplight he made out an area of new bricks in a square by the door, where a window had once been. A ticket office. Some guy would have been there eighty years ago, smiling out at customers as he unloaded tickets, but now there was only that door. And a room beyond.

Matt moved towards the door. He dropped the scissors and pushed the door. It took effort, but it moved. He opened it a few inches.

'Push this open, I want to see inside,' he said, stepping back.

The pimp looked at him, then at the discarded scissors for a half second, then gave a sly grin. Matt knew the guy was planning to kill him. Knew the guy was thinking Matt was making it easy for him by voluntarily entering some lost room in an old station. So the pimp gladly went to the door and started pushing. Thinking about the bullshit five grand he expected to be paid, for sure. Thinking he could beat the PIN number out of Matt and leave him dead, and no one would ever find the body. So he ignored the dropped scissors and turned his back to Matt and put both hands on the door to push, exactly like someone who didn't realise he was two steps behind no matter how far ahead he thought he was.

'Her name was Karen, by the way,' Matt said, and grabbed him from behind.

Right forearm across the throat, hand in the crook of his left elbow, left hand in the guy's blond hair where it stuck out the back of the baseball cap. A rear-naked choke, they called it. Or the carotid takedown. The guy thrashed. He tried to pull the arms away and he tried to batter Matt's head. His oxygen was rerouted. His brain wondered what the hell was going on. It was asleep before it could formulate a plan.

Matt felt the guy go limp but he didn't let go. This was unconsciousness, but he didn't want that. He turned, put his back to the door, hammered it open with his shoulders, all the while keeping his lethal grip and watching the station to make sure no punter or prostitute emerged from behind a wooden panel and looked his way. When the gap was big enough, he backed through and dragged the pimp with him. Opening the door had scraped away debris and created a clear path, so it closed easily with a single kick. The room fell into utter blackness.

Fifteen seconds the guy had been out. A few more minutes until the brain was dead, but Matt didn't want that, either. The wait, that was. He dropped the guy. Blind, he stripped off the guy's hat and coat and flipped him onto his front. He put his foot on the back of the guy's neck and balanced himself. He could see nothing. It would all be guesswork. He raised his foot and dropped it hard. Raised it again. A second time it fell like a piston. Four, it took. Three times he heard the thump of his foot on flesh and the scrape of flesh and teeth on concrete as the guy's head moved. Only on the fourth stamp did he also hear a loud crack. He squatted and grabbed the guy's hair and wobbled his head, this way and that. No resistance. Neck broken.

～

He moved down the platform, towards the first wooden panel, tense with anticipation at what he might see. Into view slipped what he expected: a woman earning her money. She was on her knees. Her punter was behind her. There was a thick, dark-green rug where they were going at it. No privacy from anyone walking past or even standing at the edge of the platform some way off. But each couple was shielded from view of the next.

The woman had her elbows on the ground, looking at the fingernails on her left hand in the gloomy light, as if bored. Her right hand held a can of Vimto. Empty Vimto cans were scattered around. There was other rubbish strewn about, but there was also the clutter of personal items. There was a book. There was a lidless shoebox with two shoes inside. There was a brick missing from the wall and a small mirror rested in the cavity. Matt understood. The pimp had said some of his girls didn't like the streets: they came here because it was a place they knew and trusted. One way in, one way out, maybe guarded by one of the pimp's cronies during peak periods. The rug. The mirror. The book. The shoes. All suggested a place of relative comfort and safety. But the most telling piece of evidence was the empty Vimto cans. This wasn't just some nook where any girl could bring her punter. It was Vimto girl's spot, her own little home from home. And if she had her own spot, then maybe others did.

Maybe Karen had had a spot.

The woman looked at Matt as he approached. He stopped just feet away. The punter had his head bowed as he thrust in and out of the woman. He hadn't noticed a new arrival. He certainly did when Matt spoke.

'This girl, where's her spot?' he said, showing the photo. The guy jerked, withdrew, fell back, hands going to his groin. He started to protest, but Matt told him to shut up and returned his attention to the girl. He thrust the photo of Karen closer to her.

'You've come out, so that's your lot,' she told her punter. She got to her feet and fixed her clothing. The punter did the same, but with a panic the girl didn't display. His erection had vanished and he followed suit. Alone with Matt, the girl looked him up and down and took a swig of her drink. 'My time costs money, whether it's what that idiot was doing or someone asking questions.'

Matt had expected this, so was quick to produce a twenty-pound note, the one with the smiley face. She was even quicker to snatch and disappear it. 'I ain't seen Red for a while. You a cop?'

She spoke as if she didn't know Karen was dead. Matt's face must have communicated the fact. She changed. The bravado seemed to evaporate. She was looking at him now with a mixture of puzzlement and concern. She nodded deeper into the station. 'Union Jack,' she said.

Matt followed the woman's nod. He approached the next 'spot.' Another rug on the floor. Neater area. No personal trinkets. No prostitute, either.

He continued past more spots, only one of which was occupied. He moved by the romping couple without looking, onward, and alongside the final spot. Fifteen feet ahead was the large brick wall that closed off the station. Newer bricks, like those blocking the window of the ticket office. Installed long after the station closed to prevent people going down the abandoned and possibly dangerous tunnel.

In the final spot there was another rug. This one had a Union flag pattern. Red's. Karen's. He stared at it. There was nothing personal here, he noted. But a lot of trash. Empty bottles, empty crisp packets, empty cigarette packets. The only item that showed any kind of clue that someone spent a lot of time here was an empty coat hanger, dangling from a rusty nail in the brick wall.

He put her there. He cast an image of Karen, standing in that spot. His memory clad her in the last outfit he had seen her wearing: jeans and a white woollen pullover, completely alien to this environment. She glowed like a beacon. She was smiling at him, her hand out to receive his. But then he realised it wasn't him she was smiling at. A man who was nothing but a black shape, a silhouette, walked past him and into the spot, and it was this faceless creature she smiled at. She took his hand. Her killer, in the moments he became so. Matt blinked and the vision popped out of existence.

He turned in a circle, taking in the whole station in the flickering candlelight. His heart fell. His brain froze. He knew his theory was bullshit. He had wasted his time. He had hit a dead end. He went to his knees.

Outside the zone. He had assumed that Karen had been killed *in* the zone, since the girls didn't work outside it, and then been transported to the waste ground and dumped. And so here he was, looking at what he had hoped had been the site of her murder. But he knew he'd been wrong. No way she was killed here. How could a killer have carried a body past the other spots, the other prostitutes, up the tunnel, outside? Unseen? Not possible. *One way in, one way out, maybe guarded by one of the pimp's cronies during peak periods.*

Matt reached into his pocket and pulled out a balled-up plastic bin liner, taken from the pimp's house. He was going to do what he'd come here for, even though he knew he was wasting his time.

Twenty minutes later, Matt left. He made his way up the tunnel and stopped outside the ticket office to grab the jacket and baseball cap he'd taken off the pimp and dumped right there by the shut door. He shrugged on the jacket and slipped the cap on his head. Thirty seconds after that he was back in the world.

In his hands was a full bin liner containing everything from

Karen's spot. He'd swept it up with his fingers. All the debris, all the dust and grime and dirt: anything that could hold a clue. All of it had been collected into a pile and put into the bag. That section of platform was clean. You could eat your dinner off it. The rug had been folded twice to create a neat envelope to hold anything on it. Both went into the back of the pimp's car. Matt slammed the hatch and pulled his baseball cap low. He stepped out of the shadows and into the light. He waited a good ten seconds by the driver's door, exposed to hell, before getting in the car.

Anyone watching an hour ago would have seen a car arrive and a guy get out. Just one guy. Black jacket, baseball cap. Anyone still watching would see the same guy. Black jacket, baseball cap. Guy comes alone, guy leaves alone, no big deal.

3

Matt found a deserted street and parked. He got the stuff he needed from the boot, hit the central locking button and slammed the driver's door, keys left inside. Pulled his cap low again, started walking. As soon as he turned the corner, he stopped and quickly stripped off the coat and cap. He turned the coat inside out, balled it up with the cap inside, and continued the half-mile journey to his Mondeo, parked a street over from the pimp's house. He threw the bag of trash, folded rug and clothing in the boot and took off.

It was past five in the morning when Matt pulled up outside his mother's house. No lights on. He wasn't going to wake her.

He noticed that their wheelie bin was on the pavement. All the bins were. *Collection day,* he realised. *Good.* He got out, got the balled jacket and cap from the boot and crossed the road. The clothing went into his mother's bin, shoved beneath a bag he split so that stinking, slimy trash drowned the evidence of his crime.

He slept in the car. Before he drifted off, he thought about his sister. He'd been close to her body dump site, yet hadn't visited. Why? It had been three days. The police would have long finished their analysis of the waste ground. The area would be back to normal by now. There might be nothing but a bunch of flowers on a tree to show that anything bad had happened there at all. It couldn't hurt to go see, yet he hadn't.

Matt let his mind calm. He did this by imagining what he was very tempted to do. Get up and go back to the bedsit above the takeaway, kick the door in and rouse the big bastard, Dean, from sleep. Make him stand and turn around, and then boot that fat sod right in the ass to return the favour.

He imagined it real-time. He drove the streets in his mind, having imprinted them in his memory. If he'd wanted to see the dream concluded, he should have driven faster, because he was asleep before he'd even reached Alfred Road.

He woke to a loud rumbling. Groggy eyes found the dashboard clock. 7.44. Two hours' sleep.

The rumbling was a large refuse collection truck rolling his way. Guys in yellow hi-visibility jackets were dragging the bins to the back of the truck. All heavy hands and noise and no finesse, as if the guys hated being up so early and wanted everyone else awake as well. Hydraulic arms lifted the bins and emptied them into the back of the vehicle. He watched as a tattooed monster lugged his mother's bin over, waited, and returned the empty bin to the pavement. Incriminating evidence gone. Job done. Matt closed his eyes and went out, instantly.

He woke to a rapping on the window. His eyes flicked open slowly and he saw the clock. After ten. At least he'd grabbed a few more hours. He shivered, cold.

His mother was at the window, smiling in at him. Her hair was bunched up on her head and she wore make-up and smart clothing, ready for the day. She held a cup of tea. He saw the steam rising from it. He wondered how long she'd known he was out here.

He sat up, jabbed the button to run the window down, realised his error, turned the key in the ignition and tried again. The glass whirred downwards.

'Do you want this out here, Matty? You could come indoors.'

There she was again, being cautious with him, as if he was a valuable, fragile ornament. One wrong word and he'd spin the wheels in a screeching cloud of smoke and vanish, that was her worry, he suspected.

He chose indoors. In the kitchen he saw arranged on the worktop the items for a full English breakfast, still in wrappers. One box of eggs, a packet of bacon, a loaf of bread, a tin of beans.

'I can make you breakfast,' she said.

He said, 'Yes please.' Mum always got pleasure out of cooking for people who were hungry. Same as some surgeon who'd removed a tumour from a guy's brain. Equally important in Mum's eyes.

While he ate, she told him a few inconsequential things. How much the neighbours had paid for their extension. Her new favourite TV programmes. She skirted around family affairs until he was chewing the last of his bacon. Then she started slowly.

She mentioned Joseph, Danny's baby boy. The scrapes and hilarity he got up to. How much she liked Lucinda, the woman who'd finally rooted Danny, and how it was a shame they were going through a trial separation.

But not Karen.

She mentioned Danny's good job down in the City.

But not Karen.

She mentioned how her friend's husband had died last year.

But not Karen.

Then she mentioned his old room – storage now for her materials, but better than staying in a car, if Matt so chose. If he was here for another night or two.

But not Karen.

By then he'd had enough. He went straight in: 'Mum, I'm sorry about Karen.'

She held it together, but he saw the effort. She took his empty plate and turned to the sink to wash it. To hide her face.

Matt rose from the table and hugged his mum from behind. It felt weird for the first few seconds because she was stiff, holding back the emotion. Then she relaxed, and he relaxed. They stayed that way and he found himself looking at the taps in the sink while she washed dishes. The taps were the original ones installed with the house, but the handle on the cold tap had been replaced. Twenty-five years ago now. Karen had come into the house thirsty, yelling for Matt to get away from the sink, and Matt had thought it would be funny to tighten the cold tap so she would have to drink warm water. It had been funny until the point when the handle had broken off. He and Karen had both been sent to their rooms, with Karen annoyed at Matt for getting her in trouble.

Old memories, dulled and fuzzy, as if imagined. But they were real, all of them. Thousands of them. And each had this house and this woman at the core. Both felt a little new to him, but they weren't. He'd grown up here and she had made it happen. He just needed time to readjust, like riding a bike after time out of the saddle.

Finished with the dishes, she held his hands in front of her stomach. It felt comfortable. He immediately started to feel content. He glanced out the window, at the yard where he'd played with Karen and Danny, and then at the old clock on the wall near the fridge that was still three minutes fast so that if anyone was ever running a couple of minutes late, they'd get there on time after all. It all slipped into place, like reality in the waking moments after a deep sleep. He hadn't settled any other place he'd been and it wasn't because he liked to move about. It was because he'd left this place too quick, for all the wrong reasons.

'I'm back, Mum. To stay for a while, if that's okay. I'm not running off again.' He wanted to add something about Karen, how he'd stay for her, for the funeral, but felt it wrong to do so, to give specific reasons. Better left as was, with all reasons encompassed but unsaid.

She squeezed his hands again, then moved out of his grasp and faced him. 'Earn your room, young man,' she said, but she was smiling. She nodded at the sink, where his dirty plate lay. Just that one overlooked piece of crockery, as if saved for him. He saluted her and set to washing up.

'And don't break the cold tap,' she said, and he nearly burst into tears.

'Karen got sick of her husband just after you left,' Danny said. He spoke his next few sentences over the course of a thirty-four break. They were at a dim snooker hall full of jobless yobs. 'She used to go out with the girls a lot, and he didn't like it, said she was acting like some kid trying to reclaim her teenage years. So he dumped her. But that was her plan, she told me. Make him sick of her so he wouldn't chase her if she ended it. Make him end it.' He laughed. 'Stopped washing and stuff. Wore shitty clothes that smelled. Worked a treat. Half a year, he was gone. Soon after that she applied to university and got in based on grades from some access course a few years back. She moved into one of those shared student accommodation places and got a part-time job.' He was on the blue. Easy straight into the side pocket. Hit it way too hard, all anger, and missed by a whole foot. 'Some fucking job,' he snarled.

Matt barely spoke for three frames – forty-five minutes. He was happy to listen, to remember, and to see Karen's smiling face in his head. It beat picturing her dead and strangled, as his mind kept trying to. His mother would have that image burned into her soul, because she had identified the body, according to Danny. But Matt would never again see Karen that way, he promised himself.

'We never had any idea she was selling herself at first, Matt,' Danny said as they racked the balls for the next frame. 'She told us she worked in a pub and there were always photos and posts on Facebook to back it up. We never doubted.'

His face was a little imploring, as if he thought Matt was judging him. As if Matt might blame the family for Karen's turn to prostitution.

'Three years she was on the game before we found out, when she was arrested nine months ago. She told us she wasn't like those other ones. Never into the drugs and stuff. It wasn't a life-style for her, she wasn't trapped into it. It was just money. To pay for uni. So she said.'

Matt nodded, but knew otherwise. When he was on Karen's Facebook profile yesterday to print a photo, he'd seen a lot of posts, most sent from a computer at the university. But they were old posts, from more than a year ago. Matt believed she'd quit her course, but hadn't told her family. Prostitutes could make a lot of money. He believed she'd been swept up by bullshit talk from someone like that pimp of hers, or other girls. Talk of riches, whatever. He didn't know about drugs, though. He hoped not. Didn't matter now, though.

'She hid it,' he said. 'Don't feel guilty.'

Danny put his cue down and faced Matt across the table. 'Mum told me to bring you here, Matt. Look, the liaison officer is coming to the house tonight. The woman the police sent us. For support.' He looked awkward talking about this. 'Mum wanted me to tell you you don't have to be there. Do you want to be there? We can stay here until the officer has gone, if you want. That's what Mum wanted me to offer you. So there it is.'

Mum wanted to spare him the gory details. Ever protective, even towards a son in his thirties and a former soldier. He loved her a little bit more for that.

'I'll be there. For Mum. Don't want her worrying about me. We should all be there for this.'

They continued to play. Danny's mood got blacker as he got drunker and dwelled on everything negative. He admitted that he'd found a bizarre form of painkiller: internet forums, where he read about the lives of people who'd had their world shattered by murder. 'It's as if filling my head with so much murder will make me think the world's a living hell and only the immensely lucky ones escape unhurt. That's what my soon-to-be-ex-wife says.'

'You're just reading about how others coped,' Matt said. Danny nodded, but there was no conviction in it.

Danny returned to the liaison officer, but now in a negative light. No longer considering her an angel sent to ease pain, he'd become annoyed about the woman's constant quizzing. Now he was on Mum's page, believing the policewoman was more interested in solving the murder than consoling the family.

'Maybe she knows that's the best way to give us some kind of closure,' Matt said. But Danny shook his head: no. Matt remembered Danny's claim that their mother didn't care about justice, because it wouldn't bring Karen back.

Then Danny shook like a cold man. Throwing off his dour attitude, maybe, because in the next second he was smiling. 'She's coming at six. Three hours. Just enough time for me to demoralise and degrade you on the table.'

Matt launched himself at an opportunity to change the subject. 'Bring it, rich boy. Get the pints in first.'

They played the rest of the game in silence.

~

Before they got in the taxi, Danny got his laminate photo from his car. He kissed his BMW and told it he'd be back tomorrow. Matt used the opportunity to lean towards the driver and tell him they were taking a detour, and to just drive there and not mention it to the other guy.

Both brothers were a little drunk. Matt had decided he needed to be a bit out of sorts for what he was going to do. He didn't think he could interrogate the liaison officer if he was sober, and that was his plan. An interrogation. He knew the police would keep their cards close to their chest with regards to how much they knew. Or didn't know. And it was the 'didn't know' stuff Matt was interested in. To get the information he needed from her, he required two things. One was Dutch courage, because he might piss this woman off, maybe his mother, too, if the conversation turned sour. The other was deeper knowledge of the crime itself. That one he was going to take care of right now.

Matt was in the back seat. Danny got in beside him, handed him the photo. Matt took it, didn't look at it. He put it in his lap and told the driver to go.

'What do you want that for?' Danny asked. Matt just shrugged at him.

~

'Stop here,' Matt told the driver. When the car slowed and stopped, Danny looked out the window.

'What's here?'

Matt told the driver to wait, kick back and read something, and keep the meter running. He got out and Danny followed. And that was when Danny understood where they were. Matt realised that while Danny knew where Karen's body had been found, he had not been here.

'Matt, why are we here? What do you know? You know something, don't you?'

Matt said, 'Nothing. Wait in the car.'

Brewster Street was popular with people leaving or heading to Arkdale Shopping Centre, half a mile north of here. It was past 6pm, yet the street was fairly empty. As they'd driven south, past a junction, the residential section had given way to the walled rear yards of shops on their right and a business park on their left. Out front the shops were shiny and smart to attract the customers, but no such care was needed back here. The yards were grimy, littered with trash and discarded stock, and the gates either broken or jammed open by rubbish. The street lights were too few and too weak and the whole street seemed bleak, like somewhere long-forgotten. Late, when the shops and offices were closed, this was a lonely and deserted place. A good place to hunt prey. A bad place for prey to be.

The other side of the road was neater. The business park had trimmed hedges out front, with shiny glass offices behind small car parks. Light industrial units of metal and brick poked up from behind the offices. They were parked outside the office of a joint supplying animal foods, but the area Matt was interested in was next door. A big square empty eyesore, like a pulled tooth in a healthy mouth. Whatever business had stood there was long gone, even the building. The area, some sixty feet across, was weed-covered, pitted concrete, surrounded by a chain-link fence. With the office building gone, the industrial units behind were left exposed.

'This isn't the way to cope,' Danny said from behind him.

Matt shut his brother's voice out. On the drive to London, he'd listened to a number of YouTube videos dealing with bereavement. He'd done that not for the sanity of his own mind, but to learn how to present the correct image of a sorrowful brother to his family. Keeping mementos, talking to the lost sibling as if they were standing right by you, and making quiet time for yourself – those might be helpful strategies for some, but not Matt. What he needed to do was observe and analyse and unravel the problem. He was not here to view the place where the body had been found simply to try to ease his pain through acceptance. He'd erode his own grief by getting his hands on the killer, plain and simple. Revenge.

A hand clamped on his arm, and he turned to look at his brother.

'The police have already been here,' Danny said, and his tone was almost sympathetic, as if he thought Matt was wasting his time. But his eyes were warm with understanding. Tough army boy Matt was on the trail after all, which pleased him. If only because it proved Matt cared.

'Just give me a few minutes,' Matt said, and turned his mind back to the task at hand.

He went to the fence. Danny followed, but said nothing. Matt took out the laminate newspaper article. There was no avoiding looking at the photo now, but he tried his best to focus intently on the area of ground around Karen, instead of her dead body. There was no fence in the photo, so the photographer had gotten up close, pressed his camera to one of the holes. Matt put his face to the metal and closed his left eye, so he, like the camera, saw no fence. He shifted his feet this way and that, making small movements, minor adjustments, using tufts of weeds and specific cracks in the concrete and a rusted manhole cover as reference, and pausing to check the photo periodically.

And then he stopped. Here. Right here on this spot was where the photographer had stood with his camera phone. Matt had the same angle, looking slightly right and down. He stared at the exact spot where Karen's body had laid.

'Are you looking for evidence, is that it?' Danny said.

No, he wasn't looking for evidence. Video surveillance of the area, any witnesses, any forensic clues – that was the domain of the police, and Matt didn't have access to those things. Instead, he was trying to work out why the killer had picked the waste ground as a dump site. The rotten back yards of the shops were open to the street. There was a hedge that ran the full length of the business park except for where it broke to allow the road to branch into car parks. There were dark little alleyways between the shops. There were a hundred shielded places where a body could be concealed, yet Karen's corpse had been put in the single biggest open spot here, beyond a fence that was driven into the ground and had a locked gate. And the killer hadn't intended to toss her corpse down into the sewers, because her body had been found further from the street than the manhole. That screamed of intent.

The killer had wanted Karen's body to be found right here.

But even that scenario gave him problems. An artist of death, presenting an exhibit, would lay the body in the very centre of the waste ground, or carefully pose it, and neither of those had happened. If exact placement didn't matter, then why take the body such a distance into the waste ground? Dump it unceremoniously over the fence and run. Drag it just clear of the gate and run. Hell, if generating shock and headlines was the aim, why not just parade the body in the middle of the street? Instead, Karen's corpse had been dragged or carried some fifteen feet into the waste ground. Even worse, if the gate had been locked back then, then it would have involved passing her body over the fence, which meant pairs of hands on both sides. More than one killer.

Something about that very spot where the body lay, the senselessness of it, bothered him. His inability to comprehend was forming a headache.

'Matt, don't shut me out.'

The most logical explanation was that Karen had made her own way to the spot where she died. She might have agreed to meet a punter who sought sex outdoors, and who'd been overcome by undeniable bloodlust, no care for where they were. She might have been awaiting a client when a passing lunatic spotted her. But why meet at such a place, with every commercial establishment closed so late and so far from her zone? Also, this theory went against evidence that the body had been moved after death, unless that movement had been just a turning of the corpse rather than transportation. He just couldn't wrap his head around it.

A hand on his shoulder. He turned. Danny, a little angry, said, 'Matt, I'm not some weak little girl. Tell me what you know. She was my sister as well.'

The headache was revving up. Too many theories to process. And he was looking at a naked crime scene long after professionals had processed it and cleaned it. The police would have a better understanding of what might have happened. Matt resigned himself to the fact that he was going to learn nothing by himself. The liaison officer and what she could tell him, that was his only next step.

Up the street, the taxi's horn beeped. 'I told him to read something,' Matt said to Danny. 'Tell him I'll use his head to honk that horn if I hear it again.'

Danny held up a couple of fingers to the driver, indicating they'd be two minutes. He continued to watch Matt.

But Matt was done. Drunk, tired, hungry, cold, and seeking a eureka moment that wasn't going to come. Back in the taxi, his eyes found the photo again, but it wasn't to hunt clues. This time he stared at his sister's corpse, because he needed pain. He deserved pain, for his failure.

Karen was on her back, hips twisted at a right angle, right leg laid over the left, short skirt riding high up to expose her knickers. She wore a fluffy white coat that was smeared with dirt. It was high-waisted and he could see her pale white belly. One arm was straight down by her side, while the other was bent and raised towards her head, fist jammed under her jawbone, as if she were answering the phone. Thankfully her head was pointed away from the fence and the white coat was plumped up at her breasts, which meant her face was mostly obscured from the camera lens. The police believed her killer had strangled her from behind and left her face down long enough for blood to ooze from her ear, run to her lips, and dry hard on her cheek, and he was glad he couldn't see the bruising or the blood. Or the eternal look of horror and pain that was frozen into her eyes as she realised her life was being crushed out of her.

'I failed, I'm sorry, I shouldn't have left you,' he told her.

Matt woke and felt as if his head were in a vice.

He was on his back, looking up at the night sky, and at first full of confusion because he saw four moons. Then he understood: he was in his old room. The ceiling was painted to look like space, with the moons and stars and a spaceship and a comet with its fiery tail. Mum had painted the scene for him when he was eight and mad on becoming an astronaut. Matt used to sit on his bed and pretend it was a space buggy, his bedroom floor the surface of an alien planet. So many years ago, yet the ceiling, although faded, was still the same. He'd thought it embarrassing when he returned from the army, twenty-six years of age, but right now he thought it was cool again.

The ceiling was the same, but that was it. The carpet was different, the green wallpaper now a boring cream. The space buggy had been swapped for a cheap foldaway bed that was closed up and leaning against a wall. His old dresser had gone, and with it the rhymes he had scratched into the wood with a needle. The room was now a storage area for his mother's embroidery addiction. There was a low table overflowing with yarns. Long rolls of material, dozens of them, were leaning against the walls, while others were balanced horizontally across their tops. Matt didn't remember a whole lot of last night after he and Danny had returned home and continued to drink, but he had a vague memory of moving loose rolls off the floor last night, to create space.

The black bag of dirt and dust from the abandoned train station was here, next to a blank sheet of A4 paper laid on the floor. Now he remembered something else. The liaison officer. Louise Tark; tall, forties, slim, sexy, but with an annoying wispy voice. A woman paid to talk to people, with a voice like that and an annoying sympathetic nodding habit. But a nice nose, curved like a ski-jump.

His head was killing him.

He remembered interrogating the woman. Danny and Mum had sat and listened intently, perhaps because he had been asking things they hadn't had the foresight or guts to voice. But in the end she had been the bearer of only bad news. She had confirmed the belief that the body had been transported after death, so the waste ground wasn't the murder site, and that the autopsy had revealed no injuries other than those commonly associated with strangulation. But they knew little more at such an early stage. So far, no witness information had turned to gold, no CCTV footage had shed any light, and no forensic clues had progressed the investigation.

A horrible memory came to him. After the liaison officer had gone, and Danny had also headed home, Mum had tried to engage Matt in conversation. She'd started telling him about her day. He'd figured that, with one child snatched from her, she was trying to take a firm grip of one that had returned. Annoyed that she'd switched off the subject of Karen, he'd sharply interrupted with a claim that he needed sleep, and the guilty burn he now felt wasn't dampened by the knowledge that he'd fobbed her off so he could concentrate on finding the man who'd put a spike in her heart.

More of last night was coming back. After Mum had gone to bed, Matt had sneaked downstairs. He got the black bin liner and folded rug from his car, a handful of whisky miniatures from the cupboard, and got to work in his old bedroom.

He had put the sheet of A4 on the carpet, then grabbed a handful of crap from the bag and spread it on the paper. Laying on his stomach, eyes just inches away, he sifted through the trash. Anything intriguing he put aside, on another sheet of paper. The worthless stuff went into another bin liner, to be thrown. The larger items, bottles and packets and such, were examined for blood, then discarded. There might have been prints on those larger items, but he couldn't analyse prints without scientific help that he wasn't going to enlist.

Now, he looked at the sheet of paper on the floor. Clear, empty, blank.

Later he had worked on the rug. He had cleaned the vacuum cleaner so that nothing would contaminate his evidence, then used the nozzle to suck at the dense fibres. He got a pint of dust and dirt, which then got its turn being sifted through on the sheet of paper.

He had ended up with a good amount of intriguing items.

Then he spent an hour finding fault with each, whittling them down. A lot of fingernail ends, all discarded in the end because he decided their edges were too smooth: clipped or neatly bitten off, but clearly not tipped off in a struggle. Some used bandages, whittled to one that was rolled into a tube, as if it had been around a finger – maybe it had come off a hand that was around Karen's neck. But there was no proof of that, so he eventually tossed it into the bag. Hairs, lots of them, but they got thrown because he couldn't analyse hairs.

He looked at the sheet of paper. Clear, empty, blank.

In the end he had discarded everything because he just didn't know. Nothing was evidence and all of it was evidence. He had no way of knowing. The police and their forensic scientists would know, but that wasn't an option. All he had was guess-work, and it had fuelled his anger. When he studied a potential clue that was probably nothing of the sort, and while he tried to work out the backstory of that piece of junk's journey to the train station, he was reminded of his impotence. And each time he cast something aside because it wasn't a clear piece of evidence, he couldn't shake the fear that he might have just made a critical error that allowed Karen's killer to get one more step further away.

Now, Matt crawled to the blank sheet of paper where he'd chosen to store the good stuff – but had stored nothing. And he saw that it wasn't clear/empty/blank at all. There was a single item there, a tiny blip in a sea of white. It was a sliver of black plastic. He picked it up. He didn't remember finding it. The whiskey miniatures had gone down a treat, fast, and the tail end of his night was blurry, like an object slowly sinking through water, into darkness. The last part was gone. He was lying on his front, sifting through rubbish, and then he was on his back and it was morning and he was staring at the ceiling.

But at some point during the dark part of the night he had

found this sliver of plastic and kept it. The only thing he had kept from all that detritus. Why? A clue, obviously, but how? What had a drunken man seen in it that a sober one now couldn't?

Matt tossed it aside. Nothing, that's what. Fantasy. Maybe he had felt he had to keep at least one thing, just so the whole long night behind him wouldn't be a total washout.

Only it had.

4

___

Mum cooked him instant noodles and mushy peas for breakfast – a combination he'd loved as a teenager. She ruffled his hair, like he was still a teenager. Last time he'd sat here with a hangover, he had been. She left him alone to eat. His phone beeped in his pocket to warn him of a low battery. He realised his charger was one of the many gifts he'd left for his landlord back in Scotland.

Matt took the phone from his pocket, planning to turn it off, save the battery. He touched the ON button to light up the screen, and saw the big envelope icon denoting a new text message. It was from a number, not a name. Not from one of the few contacts in his phone book.

Suddenly he recognised the number. He was good at remembering numbers, especially ones that mattered to him. And seven years ago this one had mattered to him. Christ, he was surprised she still had the same number after so long.

He opened the text message. The battery icon was red, nearly dead, so he read quickly. The text message simply said: RADIO CAMERA. PAY UP!

Puzzled, Matt got into his text messages. He usually kept a

clean inbox but was sloppy about cleaning up the outbox. Over forty messages there, some months old, all to people Peter Jackson, his alias, knew in Scotland, and all to a name. Except one. The same number he'd just been texted from. Her number.

The received message was time-stamped 0607. His sent message was stamped 0344. Clearly, he'd sent it during his dark time, drunk, because he didn't remember doing so, and she'd replied seven minutes after waking. He remembered that about her: a 6am wake-up, like clockwork. Still the same after all these years. The message had arrived while he was sleeping and he might not have seen it for days if not for the low battery beep.

He opened the message he'd sent her. In the years since they'd split, he'd dated several times, but they'd been casual, meaningless and short relationships, and none of the girls had had the intrigue and magnetism of Lisa. And none had really liked his deeply introspective periods, his long bouts of silence when they could be forgiven for thinking he had a mental issue, so they'd quickly moved on. But Lisa, his only long-term girl-friend (if mere months could be called long-term), had never left his mind. Not always at the forefront, but never far back. The split had been amicable, having come about because he'd told her he was leaving the army and thus the country where they were both stationed. They had kept in touch by text for the first three months, until Matt had decided to become an urban gypsy. After that things had quickly petered out. Seven years ago now. He felt a pang of guilt, even so long after, at the lie he'd told her.

But twice since the split, the last occasion over three years ago, he'd gotten drunk and moody and had sent her silly late-night messages in which he'd mentioned how he missed her, how good they had been together, how they should maybe try again. The next morning there was always a reply waiting for him, sent not long after 6am. A gentle shrug-off time, for she knew the alcohol had done his talking. His heart fluttered now with nervous terror. What manner of cheesy crudeness had his intoxicated brain made his fingers type this time?

He relaxed. The message was inoffensive.

Hey, sexy, Matt here. You over me yet? Want to test that techno brain of yours? Guess the object. XX.

A photo was attached. He opened it.

He recognised it as a close-up of the little sliver of plastic he'd found in the bag of crap, although he didn't recall taking the photo. The camera had captured a mark on the little slip of black plastic. A debossed symbol: ZH, but with the H slightly overlapping the Z. At the edge of the sliver was part of another debossed symbol. Part of another Z, it looked like, as if the same symbol was imprinted numerous times across whatever item the fragment had come from.

Radio camera, Lisa's message had said. Seven minutes after waking. Half a minute to open and read the message, half a minute to compose and send her reply. Six minutes of research. A wizard at research, a genius knowledge of electronics: that was the Lisa he remembered. That was why the army had snapped her up.

He sat up now, mind back on track. He raced upstairs so abruptly that Mum called out to him, asking what was wrong. Nothing, he told her. In his room, he hunted on his hands and knees until he found the fragment of plastic. He held it close to his eye.

The sliver was smooth except for the sharp edge where it had broken off, and the tiny debossed ZH.

Camera, Lisa had said.

That little fragment of plastic could have lain in that old station for years, he knew. Maybe some punter had the camera slapped out of his hand when he tried to photograph a girl, or maybe the fragment got trampled inside, stuck in the tread of a shoe. The odds were for it having no significance at all. But Matt saw opportunity where others did not. He now knew that a camera *might* have been at the same spot where his sister *might* have been murdered. And now he could move forward.

~

'You're staring at my boobs again,' Lisa said.

'No!' Matt almost shrieked, but he didn't know if he had been, because his mind had been sent back eight years, to an army base in Cyprus. Drunk, he'd obeyed a colleague's dare to pick a girl for the night purely on how her breasts looked, without even a glance at her face.

'That's the first thing you noticed about me, and it seems you aren't bored of them yet.'

Eight years later, thousands of miles away. This time a greasy spoon in London, not a crowded bar. He stared at her face, willing himself not to look down. He'd sent a drunken message seeking help, and within five more texts they'd agreed to meet that day. Two hours later, here they were. Despite their history as lovers, he'd vowed to stay clear of saying anything sexual in case she was married. So, although she didn't seem offended at catching him glancing at her half-exposed tits, he quickly diverted. 'You got out too, then?'

He noted the hair, long and now natural blonde on top but turning to black at the bottom. He got the impression of a woman letting loose with her appearance after a long period being forced to adopt a certain look in the army. He guessed she hadn't been out for more than a year and a half.

'Sixteen months now,' she said. She tugged her blouse down slightly at her throat, to scratch, and he saw part of a tattoo. A love heart with her name above it. He tried not to imagine a man's name below, but couldn't shake the memory of the time she'd admitted she'd slept around before the army, because she'd hung about with the wrong crowd. 'Redundancies. Automated stuff taking jobs away in every sector, I reckon. I went to the supermarket and saw one girl running six automated tills. The army will have that next. Someone with a keypad, controlling six tanks.' She stopped, as if realising a rant might be brewing. 'I don't mind, really. And I did volunteer for the redundancy. A change is good. I miss the beaches, though. At night.'

Matt grinned. Couldn't help it. Their affair had begun physically four days after that first meeting at the bar. On a beach, at night.

They'd been stationed at RAF Akrotiri, a Sovereign Area Base in Cyprus and the most sought-after post in the British Army. Matt found it to be like a holiday resort, with hot beaches and skiing and tennis and rowdy bars. Lots of families, but lots of single men and women, too. The base was home to the No. 84 Squadron, part of the Royal Air Force's Search and Rescue unit, but Matt had not been part of that squadron and everyone knew it. He was 3 Para, light infantry, with no business there. The story he'd given was a training secondment, but no one had believed that and, suspecting he was undercover to report on whatever, they'd called him The Spy. A detached attitude, never trying to make friends, hadn't helped. Something captivating in Lisa, even upon their first meeting, had prevented him from lying to her.

The truth was he'd had four months left before shipping out to *Civvy Street* and the career transition partnership had arranged for him to study for the European Computer Driving Licence. His commanding officer in 3 Para had set the ball rolling and promised to find him a job back in England. And to make sure his last six months were cushy. Because Matt had saved his CO's life.

'Wow. Did you get a medal?' Lisa had said after hearing his tale.

'Not quite. You're imagining a firefight and old Matt here dragging a legless guy out of harm's way. Don't. My CO was in his billet, drunk. He threw up while unconscious and I cleared his throat. I got a bottle of whisky and this place to see out my time.'

Her eyes had bored into him. 'There's something intriguing about you, Matt Armstrong of 3 Para. You're not exactly the soul of the party, but I see something deeper. Some people give themselves up in ten minutes. Ten minutes, you know who they are. Not you. To get to know you would take more than one night. Give me your phone.'

'Why?' Despite wanting an answer, he had pulled out his mobile. He had to wipe sand off it, because it had been in his left trouser pocket. 'Don't ask. Why do you want my phone?'

'I don't share, and I don't trust too much. Now give me your phone.'

~

'Give me your phone.'

Just like last time, he immediately pulled out his mobile, whose battery he'd managed to replenish with his mother's charger. This time he didn't have to ask why she wanted it. She took it and wiped at the screen. 'Sand? You still don't trust the human animal?'

He shrugged. She started to scroll and jab and flick. He waited. A minute later, she handed the mobile back. Before he put it away, he clicked the key that displayed recently-used apps: she'd been into his text messages and phone book. Years ago, on that day they'd first met, she'd explained that she'd once met and dated a boy who'd continued seeing his girlfriend right alongside her, for months, and now she was forever burned. Things hadn't changed, it seemed. Matt tried not to let his face show his joy, but either he failed or she was too perceptive:

'Don't get your hopes up, it doesn't mean we're getting back together. We just met after years away. But now I know what's open to us. But that's just so jumping the gun, and that's not why we agreed to meet. So, tell me about what's going on. If you remember what I was like, you'll remember I'm the nosiest person alive. Tell, tell, tell. Explain what's going on with this camera thing. And what do I win for guessing what it was?'

'You win dinner,' he said, and immediately regretted it. So much for his tactic to avoid any comments of a romantic or sexual nature. He thought of that heart tattoo, which might or might not have a man's name below it.

But all Lisa did was slap the menu and say, 'Full Monty Big Breakfast, then.' She waved at the men behind the counter. One was a short teenager with a ponytail, while the other was as big and as greasy as one of his breakfasts and looked annoyed that some customer had dared to assume there was a waiter service. He pointed and the teenager came over and took their orders and wrote them on the back of his hand and vanished.

'So when did you become a secret agent?'

Matt fathomed the meaning behind this vague comment. 'So it's a surveillance camera? Tell me more.' Then that word stuck in his head... surveillance. His mind started to fragment like a cracked window, each branch snaking towards a theory. He snatched at the most obvious: in a den of prostitutes, no woman was going to allow a punter to film them having sex, so anyone wanting to record the event would need to do so in secret.

'So where did you find this camera piece?'

'In a den of prostitutes,' he said instantly.

'She couldn't have been that good if you were distracted by a bit of plastic on the ground. Tell me. I know something bad has happened. I know you. I want to help. It's why I came all the way from Manchester at the drop of a hat. I took a week off work to help you, even if it takes that long. Has something bad happened?'

Lisa was onto him. Her intelligence didn't surprise Matt, but it warmed him.

'Something bad has happened,' he said.

Lisa nodded. She reached down and took something from her pocket. Carefully, as if it were fragile. A small black box, half the size of a matchbox.

Matt stared, surprised. Not content with simply discovering what kind of item had shed the plastic sliver, she had gone and gotten herself one somehow. Matt reached out to take it. She let him. He twirled it in his fingers, up close to his eye. He scratched at the debossed ZH pattern with a nail, because he got a better feel that way. The tiny lens was nothing more than a pinprick. What had this item's brother seen? Had it seen his sister's murder?

The teenager brought their food. Matt watched him leave, then caught Lisa staring at him. Her eyes had a pitying quality. He knew she was ahead of him already, and her next words confirmed that.

'The Matt I knew wasn't into trivial stuff. He wouldn't ask me to find out what some piece of plastic was just because he was curious. And that thing is a camera. Whatever has happened, it's something bad and a secret camera might have been used. If you want to tell me, tell me, and if you don't, don't. But I have to ask. And I will help you. Has something bad happened to someone?'

He wanted to lean in and kiss her. Lisa couldn't run off complex mathematics, but she was genius at being able to skip a whole bunch of dots and still see the picture. But instead of leaning forward to kiss her, he leaned back, and he told her everything across a table of food that went cold and untouched.

5

When it was done, Lisa silently handed Matt her phone. She'd loaded a webpage, he saw. He was expected to read, but his eyes watched her over the top of the phone. Her eyes were on her meal as she waited.

Lisa was still the only person he had ever truly felt comfortable around. Everyone else got the cautious Matt, the Matt who didn't fully trust them, who watched what he said, as if always expecting betrayal. Not so with Lisa. Not only was he glad she was here, he wished they'd gotten back in touch earlier, under different circumstances. But maybe a reunion had needed these circumstances.

Forget the past, he told himself. Forget what they once had together. She probably had a boyfriend now, given that tattoo, and she had a life in another city. They were friends, and friends helped each other, and that was all she was here for. It was foolish of him to think they could relight a long-dead flame.

When she looked up at him, he dropped his eyes quickly to her phone and read.

The website was for a company called Zweig-Hofmann, securities experts. Lisa had already accessed the products menu and found the item he was interested in, the ZH micro camera LP46. He began to read.

Zweig-Hofmann specialised in surveillance and security and sold everything from listening devices to burglar alarms. The LP46 was amongst a host of similar cameras. It was the size of a pencil sharpener, and fragile, designed to be crushed in the hand by a spy who didn't want anyone who caught him to know it was a camera. Other cameras in the LP range launched their data to recording receivers that could be located many miles away, but this held the danger of someone locating it. The LP46 was for real paranoid people. Its receiver didn't record, only displayed. To record, you needed the receiver plugged into a computer, and because there was no auto record, you needed to click the record button every fifteen seconds. If you didn't press record, you didn't keep.

He raised his eyes to Lisa. She was watching him. From her expression, he knew that they were thinking the same thing.

If the LP46 camera whose fragment he'd found had been used to record the killing of his sister, then whoever had committed the crime had planned it. Planned it to death. With standard surveillance cameras that recorded remotely, you could stroll around and tape what you wanted and go fetch your hidden receiver and play your video back at your leisure, alone, and no one else need know. But the killer had used the LP46, which meant he had had to have someone sitting at a computer, to click record and then take that recording away.

'This was a conspiracy,' Matt said. Danny had been right all along: this was no sin of an evil punter. 'More than one person was involved, and that doesn't suggest a random act. It says premeditated. Two or more people planned and carried out Karen's murder.'

∼

Brewster Street, half a mile south of the shopping centre. Shops along one side of the road, small industrial complexes and offices along the other. And the waste ground where Karen's body had been dumped.

A good place to hunt prey, he remembered thinking. And to begin his own hunt. He was back here with new information, but it niggled him that he hadn't had that information the first time. Then he wouldn't have had to backtrack. If he'd had that info the first time, where might he be now? How much further forward along the path towards Karen's killer?

When he'd told Lisa to take a trip with him, she hadn't asked where, or why. And now, when he asked her to wait in the car, she nodded without question. He knew she already knew why they were here.

He got out of the car and looked all around him. There were no residences except those above the grimy shops. No way the men involved in Karen's murder would have used those: they'd know the police would knock on all the surrounding doors, seeking witnesses. And the murder had to have been indoors. They'd need time and privacy.

He looked up, over the roofs of the offices ranged along the other side of the road. He turned and looked up and over the roofs of the shops. Then north and south. He couldn't see what he was looking for. The sky directly above the offices and shops was clear. Tension started to creep in and he put his hand in his left pocket, and crushed a fistful of sand. He felt his theory start to unravel. But this was the wrong position anyway.

So he scaled the fence and moved across the wasteland. Stood in the spot. Where she had lain, dead, killed, murdered. He turned a circle, looking, seeking. And then he stopped, with his back to the road.

The position of the body in the waste ground had bothered him. It had been all wrong. What he saw now cleared all that up.

He had moved fifteen feet into the waste ground and at this new position the left quarter of the top four fifths of a tower block was visible beyond the back corner of the office building next door to the waste ground. The bottom fifth was obscured by something white – part of a shed, he thought – just behind the structure. Between the back corner of the offices and a row of large liquid storage tanks painted bright green, there it was, a thin sliver of stone and glass, easily half a mile away. The tanks were to the side and slightly in front of the back corner of the offices, so when Matt moved to his left, or forward, the gap closed. If he moved right, or backwards, the gap widened but the fragment of tower block that was peeking out slipped behind the offices. The high-rise was certainly not visible from the fence, where he'd stood last time he was here.

He knelt and watched the high-rise sink behind the white shed as he lowered himself. Then he lay down, just as Karen had lay. Now only the top eight floors of the tower block, left side, were visible: a tiny oblong strip nestled in the backwards L-shape where the offices and the shed met. He felt his hopes rise.

The only place in the entire waste ground where you could see a distant building was here, right where he lay. Which meant that this spot was the only section of waste ground that could be seen from a distant viewing point.

The spot right where his sister's body was dumped.

6

When he got back in the car, Lisa held up a finger to keep him silent. Her mobile was clamped to her ear. She was nodding as someone spoke down the line. Matt put his eyes ahead and waited. As she spoke, she used her free middle finger to tug down her blouse and her index to scratch at the side of her throat. Again, he saw that heart tattoo, but this time he saw her name printed above and what was below. The name Ray. In that moment, an imagined face popped into his head. Ray: handsome, rich, funny, and a host more things that Matt wasn't.

'I'll try to get down later today, Mum,' he heard her say. 'Keep him warm.' A pause, as she listened, and then: 'No, Mum, I have something on right now.' Pause. 'No, nothing like that. I can't say. But it's important. Look, just give me a couple of hours.' Pause. 'I know.'

She gave a giggle, bid the caller goodbye and hung up. 'My dad. He tried to use his ride-on lawnmower and fell off. He's okay, but I told Mum I'll come back a bit later.'

Matt simply gave a little nod. And he didn't look at her. 'I found a tall building we should look at. It's not visible from here.'

'Where someone watched from,' she said. No question mark: she was simply saving him the time of explaining. All along she'd been on his wavelength. He gave her a direction and a guessed distance and a description.

She touched his arm so he'd look at her, which he did. 'You remember my dad? His multiple sclerosis is a little worse since we were in Cyprus. He has a lot of good days, but he falls quite a lot, especially recently. You could come with me, if you want. When I go back later. After this.'

Another little nod from Matt. He put his eyes out front again. 'I'll go on foot and meet you at the tower block.'

She gave a long pause before saying, 'Fine. Whatever.'

And with that he started the engine for her and got out. He climbed the fence again and leaped into the wasteland. Behind him, Lisa set off.

Her route would be a winding trail through the city, taking corners and roundabouts, tackling traffic jams and traffic lights. His was the path of a bird, or a free runner. He always kept the building in his sights as he moved towards it. Past the storage tanks and the office building. Through the industrial estate. Over a sports field. He climbed fences and walls, crossed roads and gardens, all the while keeping a straight line. He beat Lisa to the building by three minutes.

He climbed over a brick wall and found himself in a car park with a sign that said *Brook House residents only*. Brook House towered above him sixty metres ahead.

Over to the right was the car park entrance, guarded by an automatic barrier. As he stared up at the dark grey building, he caught movement and saw his Ford Mondeo approach the barrier. Without a code to open it, Lisa was forced to reverse and find a parking spot on the street before joining him.

He could see by her expression that she was still annoyed at him, and he knew exactly why. Somewhat cold-heartedly, he had stomped down her attempt to engage him in conversation about her ill father. But no explanation from him would help: it would serve only to push her further from him. He was reminded again of the lie he'd told her, about why he wanted to leave the army, all those years ago.

Neither said a word as they craned their necks and stared up at the top of the tower block. Twenty-one floors. They were focusing on only the top eight, left side. On eight large windows that reflected the cloudy white sky. In some of the windows were curtains and ornaments, and they both realised the significance of this at the same time.

'Residential,' Lisa said, and Matt nodded. 'How do we do this?'

'You should go see your father. I can do this from here.'

He didn't look at her, but he sensed her eyes boring deep into the side of his head. 'I would have gone immediately, Matt, but I know my father wouldn't want me to. He's full of pride. He doesn't want people fussing over him. He'd hate it if I turned up full of sympathy. So he's okay and I'll go see him when enough time has passed that he won't assume I came because he had a silly fall off a lawnmower. So, how do we do this?'

That he'd irritated her hurt, but it was also a good sign. She was still by his side. So he refocused on the reason they had been brought together this day. 'No impatience. Pace ourselves like a distance runner, and be careful not to break into a sprint when the finish line is in sight. Follow me.'

It wasn't advice for her. Matt was warning himself against eager behaviour.

The entrance to the main block was a new addition to the building. Brutalist architecture from the sixties with modern glass doors operated by a card reader. An old trick was to push the intercom for various flats and claim either to have forgotten your key, or that you were a tradesman on a job. Another was to simply wait for someone to open the door, because neighbours minded their own business. Within two minutes, a woman with a pram exited and didn't challenge the two people who slipped in the open door.

In the lift, Matt jabbed the button for floor fourteen then stood back. As the lift rose skyward, he studied a diagram displaying the flat numbers for each floor. He didn't speak and Lisa was content to wait until he was ready to do so.

The doors slid open on fourteen and they stepped out. He turned to face her, feeling he should finally explain his theory.

'If my sister's killer had help, then only one thing explains the positioning of the body. And that camera. Someone was watching out for him. If I was watching out for someone committing murder, I'd need to know what the police were thinking. I'd want to watch them discover the body. And I'd want to hear what they said while they're stood over it. Can't plant a listening device at a crime scene. It would be found. Can't set up a watch post nearby because the police will be knocking on doors. I'd need to be far out of the search area, but still able to see and hear. So you need line of sight, but nothing directly overlooking the crime scene because the police would insist on talking to anyone who might have witnessed something.'

He said no more, didn't need to. She said, 'So here we are. How do you want to do this?'

'You mind?' Matt said as he took her handbag. He started searching through it, until he found an eyeliner pencil and a nail file. 'Let's go. We'll work our way up, floor to floor.'

They quickly found the flat they needed, the lowest of the eight whose windows he had been able to see from a crime scene half a mile away. They heard nothing from beyond the door. Matt hung back while Lisa knocked. There was no answer.

Matt approached. He scraped the eyeliner pencil across the nail file to create a fine dust, then breathed on the door handle and blew the dust across it. Another sharp blow on the handle dispersed most of the dust, leaving little patterns where it had settled on oily bodily fluids. Many hands grabbing that handle over many years had created a mess and finding an intact fingerprint was impossible. But she knew he wasn't after fingerprints.

She grabbed his arm as he made to leave. 'I know the killers needed to use an empty flat, but the murder was days ago. If the owners had been out, they could have come back by now. Are we so sure about these flats that we're willing to interrogate the people beyond these doors?'

'If we have to,' was all he said, and then he was gone, racing away for the stairs.

On the next floor, at the flat directly above the one they'd just visited, someone answered Lisa's knock. Matt hung back as Lisa pretended to have the wrong address. Soon, they were pounding the stairs to the next floor. Lisa was starting to worry that their tactic was pointless.

Here, on sixteen, there was no answer. Matt repeated his dust trick, but when he blew on it, the whole lot came away, leaving the handle spotless.

'I know what you're doing, Matt. This handle looks cleaned of prints. But that doesn't mean–'

She froze in shock as he stepped past her and booted the door open. He was inside before she could object.

She rushed in behind him. They were in a dim, thin hallway with four doors, three in the walls that were closed and one dead ahead that was ajar. She slapped a hand onto his shoulder.

'Slow down,' she whispered.

He shrugged off her hand and stepped further into the hall-way. He moved cautiously, obviously wary of the doors ahead. She stepped forward and slammed her palm onto his shoulder again and this time he stopped.

'Think first, Matt. There could have been a family in here. Not everyone answers to a stranger knocking. There could have been a child behind that door.'

He pulled away and started opening the three closed doors off the hallway. A cursory glance into each, before he bombed into the living room. Again, she was right behind him.

The living room was clean and tidy except for a scattering of children's toys. A large window to the left gave ample light. There was a fake fire with plastic coal in it, and above it a calendar hung from a nail. Also on the nail was a note. He quickly read it as he passed, heading for the window. Instructions for someone to expect a boiler repairman tomorrow between ten and six. The sort of note you might leave for a friend who has agreed to pop by and check on your flat while you're on holiday.

The window had a table in front of it bearing a laptop, some notepads and pens. There was a net curtain over the window. It was a grimy yellowy colour from age, but otherwise clean, except for a spot right at the bottom, right in the middle. A black smear of dirt.

Matt climbed on the table. He hooked a finger behind the middle of the net curtain wire and pulled it an inch from the wall. Up here the wall was dusty, but a spot behind the middle of the wire was clean. He understood.

He grabbed the curtain where the black smear was and tucked a fistful behind the wire. Now there was a triangle of exposed window. Matt knelt on the table and stared out. He saw a school and its sports field down below, a couple of hundred metres away. Beyond the field was a housing estate. He had passed through both on his straight-line journey here. Further still, he could make out the industrial estate where his sister had been found. He ran his eyes slowly over the estate until he found the building and the liquid storage tanks he had had to peer between to see this tower block. From this distance the gap between them seemed paper-thin.

He let out a ragged breath. This was it. Someone who knew the occupants of this flat were away on holiday had entered, somehow without having to break in... had mounted a powerful telescope and listening device on the table and lifted the net curtain, scraping clean a portion of the dusty wall as he tucked the netting behind the wire... had stared through the window and eavesdropped on detectives half a mile away as they theorised around a dead prostitute's body... and had then left and relocked the front door and wiped his prints off the handle.

'What now?' Lisa said from behind him. He didn't take his eyes off the view.

He didn't know. He just didn't know. Dust for fingerprints? Even if a guy cautious enough to wipe clean a door handle had been lax inside the flat, they couldn't access law enforcement databases. There seemed to be no obvious way forward from here, but he didn't want to go back. And even if he went back, there was nothing on the path behind him that offered a fork, a different route.

He looked at Lisa. Her face acknowledged the despair he was feeling. She was fearful that he was going to implode, and he certainly felt that way. Like a man who'd followed footprints to the ocean. His long trek, all for nothing.

He again sought the view beyond the window, but he didn't see the industrial estate now. He didn't see London. He saw the world and felt its vastness crushing his own insignificant mass.

He was beginning to understand that all the detective skills and luck in the world didn't mean anything. Fairness and justice didn't mean anything. People got away with murder all the time. Decent families got their worlds ripped apart all the time. The people he hunted might already be forever out of reach, thousands of miles away. Untouchable. Untraceable.

Matt was still staring out of the window. He had moved the table so he could stand with his face just inches from the glass. His eyes were on the horizon, but his mind's eye was far beyond, taking in the vast planet out there and the billions of people he would never meet. Amongst the billions was one, just one that he dearly needed to find. Those who assisted in the murder would also face justice, but it was the actual killer that haunted him.

'I keep coming back to something my brother said,' he said into the glass. 'If this is about blackmail, about silencing my sister, then who are we looking for? Not someone worried about a wife finding out he'd been with a prostitute. Someone with something bigger than a marriage to lose, and the clout, or the cash, to acquire a good team to help him solve his problem.'

Behind him, Lisa said, 'You said last time Karen tried to blackmail a police officer. But what if this time it was a major criminal? Someone with a gang. If that's the case, my worry is... if these people are willing to murder to protect themselves, and if they find out what we're doing...'

He breathed on the window, rubbed a small hole in the mistiness and peered through, mimicking the view from a telescope. It was all he had by way of putting himself in the shoes and mind of the man he suspected had stood here while another butchered a woman under his gaze. A man he considered almost as culpable as the bastard who strangled his sister. Before, he had sought only the murderer, but now he knew he couldn't rest until he had found that man and his... *watchdogs.* All of them.

'Maybe it's the same this time,' Matt said. 'A police officer again, but someone higher up, with farther to fall.' He rubbed the glass to clean away his iris. He slid the table back into place and let the net curtain drop across the window once more. He knew that trying to cover his presence here was pointless given the busted front door. The Watchdog had been far more careful.

'All we can do now is check the building's CCTV cameras,' Lisa said. 'But I'll go chat to the caretaker. Alone. Wait outside for me.'

They headed down together and she escorted him to the doors. He was reluctant to leave, but knew he was too wired to think straight. The caretaker might refuse to show them the cameras at first, and at that fork in the road Matt would be unable to take the peaceful path. Lisa would. So, under orders to relax and wait, he stepped outside.

But he couldn't relax. She was back eight minutes later, by which time he'd probably paced half a mile back and forth just outside the doors. He stopped and stared and knew from her face it was bad news.

'The cameras, all of them, are broken. The main circuits went faulty somehow.' Her face got grimmer and he awaited even worse news. 'They broke on the day your sister was killed, Matt. I'm sorry.'

'The Watchdog?'

'The caretaker doesn't think it could have been deliberate damage. And I don't see how this Watchdog, as you call him, could have had any role in such a fault. The cameras were down for most of the day.'

He looked past her, through the doors. She grabbed his chin and yanked his gaze into hers. 'No, Matt, he's not involved. Forget it.'

'So what now? We're not giving up. No.'

'Let's go,' Lisa said. 'There's no more here for us. We'll work something else out. It's not over.'

But hearing that word, *over*, hit something home hard. She saw it in his eyes, he knew. It *was* over. Each clue they'd found so far had hinted at another path forward, always forward. But now there was no path. There was no way forward and there was nothing of any use at any point back along the trail. They were stranded.

It was over.

'If you were stuck on a desert island, you'd die in a week,' Lisa said.

'No, I could spear a fish. Easy.'

'And then what, cook it and tear it up with your eyes closed? What if you saw the eyes? Or one eye, mixed in there with a bit of shredded meat?'

He shrugged. 'Fish is different, anyway. But I'm a tuna rather than anchovies man.'

Instead of heading home, Lisa had rented a room at a B&B in Haringey, which was only a short jaunt east from Matt's family home in Muswell Hill. Matt was slumped in a grimy armchair. Lisa sat on the grimier bed. She had convinced him that they had to slow this whole hunt thing down, that he wasn't going to nail the killer in one night, if at all. They would take the night off, relax, order a meal, watch some TV, and see what tomorrow brought. Surprisingly, Matt had agreed. For a couple of hours they had chatted about nothing, just catching up. And soon Matt started to perk up. He even smiled a few times. They were ex-lovers alone in a small room, and that was a million miles from dead sisters and killers. But she knew she had to be careful to keep the conversation away from family.

'What I don't get is why people eat burgers,' Lisa said. 'Ever been near a cow? Covered in shit, stinking. Who first saw that and thought, *yum*? Horses look better. Why did people complain about horse being in burgers?'

'Horses are loved. Horses deserve better than mincing. To some people.'

Lisa lifted a chicken leg still hung with meat and bit into it, hard enough to produce a cracking noise, and then laughed when she saw the disgust on Matt's face. Big grown man, ex-soldier used to blood and guts, and she had had to debone his meal because bones reminded him that his dinner had once walked around. This funny trait of his had sparked their current conversation.

'If you think I'm kissing that mouth now, think again,' Matt said. He looked embarrassed that he had made a flirtatious joke, but she didn't mind. She hadn't come here to rekindle their relationship, but was aware that she wouldn't have made the trip down from Manchester for any of her other friends.

She raised her eyebrows. 'Oooh, like you thought the choice would be yours. Anyway, I think if I offered you a kiss with an anchovy between my teeth, you'd jump at it.'

'Nah,' Matt said, and crunched into a prawn cracker. At the same time, he snapped it with his fingers, so pieces fell into his lap. So he could look down to pick them up. So he didn't have to meet her eyes because he was nervous. She saw right through the cheap ploy.

'Look at me, Matt.' He did. Almost reluctantly. 'You remember what I look like naked?' He turned away, flushing red, and she laughed. Then she got all serious and said, 'I invited you back to my room here, but you need to know I have a boyfriend.'

Matt nodded. 'Ray. I didn't come here expecting anything! The past is the past.'

At first she looked puzzled, then realisation dawned and she touched her blouse, right above that tattoo. Then puzzlement became embarrassment. 'No... that's an old tattoo. I'm with... I'm not with Ray anymore.'

The floor seemed to drop from beneath him. Ray was someone she'd been with long enough with to immortalise their relationship with a tattoo... yet Ray had been replaced by someone else. Was there another tattoo?

She flicked a hand, as if to, not change, but swat the subject away like an infuriating fly. 'What I meant was, don't tell my boyfriend about this.' She took the bone she had crunched and put it between her teeth. 'I will let you kiss me,' she mumbled around the bone. 'Once. If you can take this out of my mouth with your teeth.'

She closed her eyes and stuck her chin out, giggling. Then gasped as she felt his lips on hers. The bone dropped out of her mouth and he pulled back just enough for it to fall away, and then he was kissing her again. And she kissed him back. His hand went to her shoulder, or just below it. Between shoulder and breast. Just where you might place a hand if you were worried what reaction you might get from an outright tit-grab. She didn't mind. She kissed him harder and felt the hand begin to slip lower. His wrist was curving the rise of her breast when he stopped.

'Sorry,' he mumbled.

He moved away. Lisa straightened her blouse, grinning at him. 'Glad to be of service in helping you get over your bones phobia. I apologise, by the way.'

'For what?'

'I'm sorry I got all funny with you because I was trying to talk about my father and you didn't want to hear it. I know why. There I was, complaining about my father having a fall, and you've got a dead sister. It was insincere of me. No, not insincere. I mean... soulless.'

His eyes fell to her chest. It was easier than meeting her gaze, she knew. 'It's okay. Really. Just because my problem is bigger than someone else's, it doesn't mean theirs isn't a cause for worry. The world doesn't revolve around Matt Armstrong.'

'Still, it was wrong of me.'

There was a moment's awkward silence, interrupted by Matt's ringing phone. Glad of the distraction, he listened for a few seconds to whoever had called, then hung up. Not a word spoken by him. His look said their fun was over.

'That was my brother. The police are at the house. They've found Karen's killer.'

When they pulled up outside Matt's mother's house, Lisa said, 'I can wait here if you like. It's a family thing.'

Matt was ready to object, then seemed to think about it. 'If you don't mind.'

'Of course not. I'll be here, no matter how long it takes.'

She smiled to show her sincerity, but he wasn't looking. His eyes were on the windscreen, the world beyond. He seemed to be delaying his exit from the car. Nerves, she guessed. She waited. He checked his face in the rear-view mirror, and checked his phone for whatever reason. Eventually, he could think of no additional distractions, and unclasped his seat belt and got out. She watched him approach the front door and knock, as if he was a stranger to the family home. She didn't see who answered the door because his tall frame blocked it. He went in and the door shut and she put her head back on the headrest. That was when she realised how tired she was. Her eyes started to close.

But jerked open again as the driver's door opened. A man about Matt's age climbed in and sat there as if he belonged. Long hair and a suit – always a suit, Matt had said. *Danny, his brother,* she realised.

'Search and rescue woman, hello,' he said. He looked and sounded a little angry.

'How did you know who I was?' Way back in Cyprus, Matt had had to constantly tell her that he wasn't embarrassed by her – this was because she had complained that he refused to send his family a photo of his new girlfriend. So how did this guy know–

'No offence to old Matt, but he's not exactly a ladies' man,' Danny said. 'I think you were the first proper girlfriend he had. I figured he hadn't seen much action since the paras, either. A woman by his side two days back in London, I figure she must be the faceless search and rescue woman. I don't recall the name, sorry. Why are you sitting out here?'

'It's Lisa. I, er, didn't want to go in. Don't know anyone. This is a time for the family.'

'Good choice. Family thing and all. We get to celebrate because now we have to watch the taxpayers pay for a song and dance in court as Karen's killer tries to defend himself. Didn't know you two were still in touch.'

She had to be cautious here, because she didn't know how in-the-loop the family was about what Matt had been up to since his return to London. 'He said he needed information. I came down from Manchester.'

He flicked on the interior light and took a good look at her. The scrutiny was unnerving.

'Matt doesn't trust anyone in the world, you know?' Danny

said. 'He doesn't like people. He doesn't trust humans, so he keeps them at a distance.'

He was waiting for a response. She just sat there.

'He was always a bit like that, but after the army he got worse. He came back, and he was a bit distant. Not like you'd expect, all traumatised and stuff. He let people think it was the horrors of war that did it, but it wasn't that. I know he didn't see any real action. He was distant in the way you would be if you were at work and around people you didn't like.'

He was again awaiting a response. The one she wanted to give him was anger. She wanted to shout, 'You're supposed to be his brother!' but didn't. She sat there and clenched her jaw and wondered what this ill-speak of Matt was meant to accomplish.

He said, 'Ever been out around a dodgy area of a town at night? That feeling you get, sort of on edge, knowing you might get into trouble for no reason, for minding your own business? That's Matt's world. That night-time dodgy area, that's what he sees all the time. He sees that in a shopping centre on a sunny afternoon, or a bloody village jumble sale.'

She just looked at him.

'Matt's on edge all the time, no matter where he is. Alert, on his guard, ready. Only way he can feel safe and relaxed is alone. He came back to us, and then off he went again. To be alone.' He paused. 'But he's not alone. He's with you.'

She had planned to say nothing again, but felt she couldn't avoid speaking her mind. 'What are you saying to me? What's your point?' She looked past him, at the house. She wanted Matt to return and end this torture.

'He was terrified of spiders when we were kids. I chased him with one. Cornered him, held him down, forced that spider into his mouth, crushed all over his lips and stuff. He cried. Know what he did then?'

'He chewed,' Lisa said, turning to face him. 'He chewed and

swallowed that damn thing and actually said thanks to you. Tell me why he did that.'

Now Danny, surprised by her outburst, refused to respond.

'Bye-bye fear, that's why,' Lisa said. 'All of a sudden Matt knew that his fear of spiders had been just silly. And that's how he did things after that. If Matt got a fear, he killed it instantly. He used to hang out the bedroom window by his hands, so he didn't mind heights. He used to cut himself, so he didn't mind blood. He used to get you, his loving brother, to punch him all over the body, so the pain of physical attack didn't bother him.'

Danny's surprise upgraded to shock.

But Lisa wasn't finished. 'He slept on a pile of bricks outside the house once. He could sit or sleep in any position for hours after that. He wore pebbles in his shoes for a whole day. His feet never hurt again after that, no matter how far he walked. He sometimes starved himself. He always challenged the biggest, meanest boys in his school. He wanted to erase his flaws.'

Danny searched for words, which eventually came. 'You don't know as much as you think.'

'Maybe not. But I know Matt didn't join the army to serve his country or travel, like he claimed. He wanted to see the evil that humans can do. He wanted all the weapons and martial arts training. He was just acclimatising himself to the big, bad world. He doesn't trust the world, he doesn't trust his fellow humans, like you said. That's why he carries sand in his pocket, so if he gets jumped he can toss it in someone's eyes and get the first strike in. There's tough, smart and dangerous people out there, and you never know when some shit's going to land on your doorstep. So Matt thinks the only way to survive this world is to be tougher and smarter and more dangerous than everyone else. Anything else I need to know about him?'

'See. You don't know as much about him as you think.'

What? What did that mean? She was wrong? But Matt had admitted to her–

Danny cut in, his shock suddenly transformed into anger. 'But you're right about machine Matt being tough and strong.' He slapped the dashboard. 'But why does that mean the rest of us have to be weak and useless?'

She didn't understand, but got no chance to say so.

'You say he wanted to erase his flaws, but what he also did was spot flaws in other people. If people weren't as fast and strong as him, he regarded them as weak, in need of help.'

She mellowed, now in line with his point. He believed Matt saw his brother as weak. 'I know he protected you, Danny. There were bullies. You were older than him, so these bullies were bigger than him, but he got them to back off. I know about one boy who lived nearby, a violent troublemaker who was about twenty and you were only fourteen. Matt stalked him for days, worked out his routines, and looked for a chance to get him alone. The guy spent weeks in hospital and the police never knew who attacked him. But I don't understand your anger. Are you upset because Matt helped you? Because by helping, it meant he saw you as vulnerable?'

'I want to know what's going on!' he yelled at her. 'I'm not a fucking weak little girl. I know Matt feels like he betrayed Karen by leaving. If he'd stayed, she wouldn't have gotten into trouble, some shit like that. And I know he's not back to do the grieving family member thing. He's back because he wants to tear the head off the bastard who killed her. But he won't tell me that, because I'm some mere mortal who can't be involved in case I graze my knees. But you're obviously helping him, he obviously thinks you can handle it without crying, so I want to know what you two have found out.'

Now his attitude made sense. He felt cut out, for his own protection. If Matt hadn't told his brother the truth, it was not her place to do so. 'I don't know what you're talking about. We've been catching up on old times, that's all. Remember, I used to be his girlfriend.'

Danny stared out the windscreen in silence. She watched his chest fall and rise rapidly and knew he was fuming. A response was brewing, she knew, so she waited, tense.

Eventually, he threw open the door and got out. But before he shut it and left, he bent down and looked at her and said, 'Yes, you were once his close girlfriend, and you think you know everything. But you don't know why he really left home, and I'd bet the house you don't know why Matt left you, or why he left the army. Or the real reason he joined in the first place.'

The holiday camp feel of RAF Akrotiri had bored him, Matt had told her, and the sluggish pace of daily life there hadn't gelled with a personality that desired action and conflict. The transient atmosphere of the base had prevented a serious bond forming between them, so they'd both known that a day would soon come when they'd be forced apart. They'd assimilated such fact into their relationship, and their eventual split, even though by Matt's choice, had been... easy. His claimed reason for leaving the army, and her, was a fact she'd accepted and had believed for years. Right up until this moment. Now, her head spun and she couldn't stop a pleading question:

'What do you mean? Why did he say he left me?'

'Matt doesn't like to let people get close. You didn't get close back then and he won't let you get close now. If you get close, your pain will become his pain again, and you know what will happen then? He'll just up and go and leave you standing again.'

She sat in the Mondeo and tried to cast aside what Danny had said about Matt deciding to leave once this was all over. But it was hard. Those words bounced around inside her head: '...your pain will become his pain again...' What pain? And what did he mean by *again*?

She cast the dark thoughts aside as Matt emerged from the house, looking grim. His mother hugged him at the door. Instinctively, Lisa ducked out of sight, as if fearful of what might happen if they saw her. Then he jogged back to the car. He handed her his phone even before he'd gotten into his seat. But he said nothing.

There was a picture on the phone. It was a photo of a photo. A mugshot provided by the police, showing a guy with blotchy skin, week-old stubble and short hair going thin and wispy at the front. He had the sort of look that fit different scenarios. Put a white coat on him and a stethoscope round his neck and no one would doubt he was a doctor. Same if you put him in a traffic warden's uniform, or a McDonald's cap. And in the police mugshot, he looked every part the criminal, just like a guy who might have murdered a prostitute.

'Is this him?' she said, with no doubting the answer.

He took the phone back and stared closely at the picture as he told her the story.

Yesterday, the police responded to a loud music complaint in Woodberry Down, Hackney. They kicked in the door when there was no answer and found this guy dead in an armchair. Heroin overdose. Known user. A cursory search of his property yielded evidence that linked him to the recent killing of a prostitute. They also had CCTV footage showing the dead man's vehicle close to the area where her body was found, on the very night she was killed. Name: Declan Barthow.

She watched him bore his eyes into the face of the man he had hunted. The look on his face was as if a void had opened in his gut. Like a space that had expanded and pushed aside organs. She couldn't quite read it.

He dropped his phone into the footwell and rubbed his temples with both hands. 'We read too much into it. Fucking telescopes and listening devices and grand conspiracies about blackmail.'

'Blackmail?'

He sat in silence for a few moments, then explained: Danny had never accepted the theory that some random psychopath had happened upon Karen; he believed her murder had been to silence her, to keep a secret, possibly involving the blackmail of a high-profile figure. 'But this Declan Barthow is just some low life.'

'But if this is him, that's good, Matt. How did your mother take the news? And the police are certain he's the killer?'

He took a long time to answer. She thought the news was going to be bad. A questionable arrest, a distraught mother. She got a surprise.

'The police are convinced. Mum, despite saying she didn't care about the killer being found, is happy that someone will pay.'

He abruptly climbed out of the car. Just like his brother half an hour before, he stood by the open door and bent and looked at her and said something that stung: 'It's over. You should go home now. I need to stay here.'

She watched him enter the house, her mind full of spinning emotions. There was guilt: despite the existence of a blackmail theory, the whole wild conspiracy angle had been boosted by her arrival back on the scene. But there was also confusion: Matt had just learned that his sister's killer had been found, yet he didn't seem relieved.

To the latter, though, she was pretty sure she had an answer: a lone wolf meant no guilty parties running free. Matt had wanted to catch the killer and deliver his own brand of justice. She had tried to help him with that endeavour, but deep down was glad he'd been foiled. His mother wouldn't have coped with attending *two* murder trials. Or the trial of her daughter's killer and her son's funeral.

She grabbed the key to start the engine, then realised she was in Matt's car. Hers was still outside the café they'd gone to earlier. She locked his vehicle, went to the house and posted the keys, and then pulled up her collar, ready for a long walk, followed by a long drive home to Manchester.

7

The next morning, after a night of dreams about Declan Barthow, Matt succumbed to an urge to visit the home of his sister's killer. He set his satnav for the Woodbury Downs estate and forced himself to obey the speed limits.

Barthow's street was lined on both sides with terraced flats on two floors, with balconies for the upper apartments and tiny square lawns for those below. There was a uniformed cop in a raincoat outside the entrance of one of the blocks. He leaned against the entrance doors, hands in his raincoat, looking about as bored as it was possible for a man to get. It was a communal entrance, each door serving several flats. His job, Matt guessed, was to make sure nobody who wasn't a resident entered.

Matt wasn't a resident. But he was family to the dead girl, and maybe the cop had a soul.

The cop stood upright when Matt's Mondeo slipped to the kerb. He watched Matt come up the path, wary.

'Just stop a moment, sir. You live here?'

'The guy who killed my sister did,' Matt said. If he expected some sympathy, he got a shock. The guy shook his head and put up both hands in a *stop* gesture, as if his bosses had shown him a photo of Matt and said: *This is the very last guy on Earth you let anywhere near the flat.*

'You can't come here, sir. Sorry about your sister, but you have to leave.'

'Did he definitely do it?'

'I'm just here to watch the door. You need to just leave.'

'His van was seen driving past the waste ground where she was found. Did–'

The officer continued to shake his head. 'I'm not involved, sir, so I can't answer these questions. Call the police station. Now just please go.'

'Do you know if the CCTV showed him actually in the driver's seat?'

Now the officer gritted his teeth. Clearly, he didn't care about the dead girl or her family, only the trouble he might get into for talking to Matt. Through those gritted teeth, his eyes scanning left and right as if to make sure nobody was watching, he snarled, 'Listen, pal, just piss off.'

As he was driving back to his mother's house, an employment agency made Matt double take. The involuntary action got him thinking: was his brain making background plans to stay in London? Then he drove right past, and wondered what that meant. At a nearby supermarket, he parked and ran laps around the large car park for an hour, more to slow his mind than race his heart.

He was home by midday. His mother was about to head out to see a friend. She seemed livelier today, which pleased him. When she was gone, he fired up her laptop and tried to find out more about Declan Barthow, the police investigation into Karen's death, and what the job market could offer an ex-soldier with – because all his jobs had been cash in hand – a blank work record over the last seven years.

When his mother returned, he was asleep on the sofa. It was early evening. She was standing over him, craning her neck to see what he'd been up to on the laptop. He was glad he hadn't been watching porn. Even so, he jerked awake and slammed the laptop.

'Are you looking for a job?' she said, her face lit up like a sunwashed beach.

He nodded, but then revised that answer because he didn't want to get her hopes up. 'Maybe. Not sure.'

She stroked his hair. 'I'll ask Danny. He's a boss, he might have a space. It'll be good to have you around again. Hungry?'

He nodded again.

They sat down to eat in front of the TV. Matt watched without watching. He waited for Mum to mention Karen, but it didn't happen. Finally, he could bear it no more.

'Mum, you don't talk about Karen. Apart from earlier, when I asked about the man who was arrested, you haven't talked about her. Is that because you don't want to upset me? Or…'

He stopped before he said the wrong thing. There were no pictures of Karen on the walls and he was starting to think it was because of her lifestyle – was Mum embarrassed? But that wasn't a question he could voice – it was too close to an accusation that Mum was trying to forget her, and he knew – or hoped – that wasn't the case.

But he got no answers. Still staring at the TV, his mother started to cry. He said nothing, but he leaned over the back of the armchair to hug her.

'I don't know how to feel, or what to do,' she blurted.

Continuing to squeeze her, he shut his eyes. She was experiencing emptiness and confusion and guilt, and he wished he felt the same. It beat the boiling rage and desire to hurt that consumed his own mind.

He excused himself around about 10pm. He went to his old bedroom and lay down on the foldaway bed and stared into space – literally. The space scene on his ceiling made him think of Karen as a child, and all the fun they'd had here.

Unable to sleep, he accessed the Thanks and Complaints section of the Metropolitan Police website, but he couldn't think how to word his complaint about the police officer who'd told him to piss off. Drowsiness only came when he imagined himself breaking into whatever police station caged Declan Barthow, and he fell asleep as he was tearing away bricks to expose Karen's killer in his cell, screaming for mercy he wouldn't get.

The next day was a blur of useless nothingness. It was one of those days you could wipe from your mind and suffer not a jot for it. Nothing learned, nothing achieved. He got bored, then lethargic, then stale. Bed called him even earlier that night. He stared into painted deep space and decided he had to be proactive tomorrow. Sleep didn't come easily because he was aware that it had been exactly a week since Karen's death. Just a few miles from here, a man had put his hands around her neck and squeezed and hadn't stopped. As his eyelids became heavy, Matt's mind pictured Barthow escaping from his cell, maiming Piss Off Cop in the process, and it was Matt's mother who killed him by running him down in her car.

On Sunday he hit the laptop and created a CV and lied about what he'd been doing the last seven years. Mum got dressed up again and went out, and came back with a long face. Danny trailed in after her, and looked at Matt with something only just shy of anger. He didn't speak until Mum went upstairs to get changed.

'Why didn't you come?' he snapped. Matt raised his arms in a puzzled gesture. 'We just arranged the funeral. It's in ten days, if you can hang around that long. Where the hell were you?'

He was shocked. Mum hadn't mentioned anything about going off to arrange the funeral. He told Danny this, but got no sympathy. 'Well it's in ten days, if you can be bothered to hang around that long.'

He turned to leave. Annoyed, Matt flicked a foot and caught his ankle, tripping him. Danny got to his feet and clenched his fists, like a slighted kid in the schoolyard. He stared at Matt for a few seconds, then turned and left, shouting a goodbye to his mother just before he slammed the door.

He heard a bellow from outside. Danny, shouting at someone. Fearful that his brother's anger was going to get him in a fight, Matt rushed to the window.

He saw Danny running to his car. He saw a guy on a dirt bike tearing away. He didn't understand what had happened until Danny reached his car and plucked a slip of paper from where a wiper held it against the windscreen. Something bothered Matt about this event. A guy dropping an advertising leaflet wouldn't tear out of there like that. He went to the door.

Danny saw Matt exit the house and jumped in his car. He slammed the door and Matt heard the lock engage just as he grabbed the handle.

Matt said, 'What did he give you?'

Danny started the engine. Matt rapped on the window. 'Danny, let me see what he gave you. Let's not be children.'

Danny sneered at him, clearly more upset now following that insult. The car sped away. Matt watched it go. He watched the window come down and a balled piece of paper fly out. Matt retrieved it. By that time, Danny's BMW was turning a corner, then gone.

Matt unrolled the sheet of paper. It was a betting slip, but there was nothing on it. No bet. He turned it over.

On the back was a picture drawn in pencil. It looked like a letter C on its back with a child's version of a cloud inside it: three bumps together.

It was nothing, probably just some coded insult meant for Danny, especially given his brother's angry reaction to it. Matt screwed up the betting slip, cursing himself. What had he expected, a sorrowful confession from a man already dead? Would that have made Matt feel better anyway?

8

———————

Hey, sexy, Matt here. You over me yet? Want to test that techno brain of yours. Guess the object. XX

How was our sex the other night, did you like it?

Very funny. You must be Lisa's boyfriend. I didn't sleep with her when she came to help me.

I'll fuck you up pal if you go near her again.

I just want her help with something else. I don't want trouble.

I know your name is Matt. You'll be seeing me soon, dickhead.

Where is Lisa? Why have you got her phone? I don't want trouble.

It's me this time, Matt. Still prefer anchovies? That prove it? Adrian got my phone while I was asleep. I'm coming down to you. I'll be on the train because he's stormed off and took the car. Loser. I'll text the time and station when I know.

As she stepped off the train, Lisa said, 'Matt, first I want to apologise for making you think your sister's murder was part of a big conspiracy. It haunted me since I left London. I was foolish.'

As they walked out of the station, she said, 'I think you don't want to accept that this dead man they found was your sister's killer. Now, phone your mother and tell her we're coming to dinner. It's about time I finally got to meet your family properly.'

Walking across the car park, she said, 'I put that picture on my social media to see if anyone knows what it is. Tell me about it.'

In the car, he told her about finding the strange drawing, which he'd texted to her, on Danny's car. Like him, she diagnosed it as a letter C on its back with a child's version of a cloud inside it. Like him, she had no clue what it meant.

Driving away from the train station, she said, 'Matt, you look worried. Is it about this picture? I know you think it might be a clue. But what's wrong?'

The train station was still in sight, beyond her side window, and he felt like a line hadn't yet been crossed. Despite being in his car, Lisa wasn't yet fully moored to the inevitable path he was on. Within minutes she could be on another train, heading away forever. He pulled into the side of the road and looked at her. 'I'm worried about you, Lisa. I'm not sure I should have let you come here. If this picture is a clue, then someone out there knows I'm chasing Karen's killer.'

'If it's a clue at all. I have serious doubts, but I'm here to go along with you just in case. And if it is a clue about your sister's murder, there's always the chance it could be from someone wanting to help.'

He shook his head. He could still see the train station, that anchor to her safe life back in Manchester, beyond her head. 'This wasn't a direct note sent to my family by someone who saw the news. It was for me, I just know it. Because I'm hunting a killer. And the vagueness of the picture makes me think someone knows and is playing a game with me. Like I'm a rat in a maze, and they want to see what I'll do next.'

She touched his arm, understanding. But her eyes said she didn't agree. 'Don't read too much into it. It might have no connection to the murder. All you got was a strange picture. Don't start thinking about unknown players out there, watching your every move. I see from your face that that's exactly what you think. And now I know why you're worried for my safety. But I'm not worried, because I'm with you. It's the people against you who need to worry.'

And with that he turned his eyes to the road and pulled into traffic. Soon the train station was lost from sight. Her mooring had been cut, and now they were adrift together.

He pulled up outside his mother's house, but sat for a moment. A good portion of the drive had been in silence, because Lisa failed to find the courage to ask a specific question. Now, with Matt paused, thinking about how this meeting between girl-friend and mother would go, she found it.

'Bonfire night. That was the last text you sent me, all those years ago. I didn't reply for three days, and I never heard from you again after that. I was dealing with bad news and didn't get a chance. Were you upset with me? Was that why we lost contact?'

The 'bad news' was her father's multiple sclerosis, which her parents had finally decided to inform her about. She had been distant, and a little snappy with everyone. But not by text, and therefore not to Matt. For so long she had considered that they'd simply drifted apart, in part because, as she later heard from mutual friends, Matt had decided to leave home. No longer.

And he confirmed it when he deflected her: 'It was a long time ago. Old history. Come on, let's do this.'

He tried to get out before she could respond, but she grabbed his arm. 'I need to explain about something else.'

One foot out the open door, he waited. He looked nervous. But not as much as she felt.

'I went back to my old ways after the army. I had five or six boyfriends in around a year and a half. Ray only lasted a month, but he wanted me and I felt wanted, and I got a tattoo. I still had the lease on a flat with my previous. And now Adrian has asked me to marry him and I said yes.'

He looked away. 'I'm happy for you. You don't have to explain.'

'But I do. I'm not happy with him. He didn't even like my having a job, because we can't sit around all day with his loser mates. I went into the army to get rid of my silly outlook on life, but it didn't work. I started right back where I left off. But I'm not happy with that kind of life. I don't feel right without a man in my life, it's been that way forever, and maybe that's why I stayed. Maybe that's why I jumped in with the next man and the next who showed me attention.'

'It's okay.'

'No, it's not. I attract scumbag men and I can't stop myself trying to get something serious going. I want you to know that I won't be like this forever, having boyfriends for a month here and there before moving on.'

'I understand.'

'But your face says otherwise. I hoped Adrian would change if we married. He won't. And I don't care. I don't want him. Let him be a jobless waster all his life, but without me. I just wanted you to know that kiss we had, it wasn't because I'm the cheating sort. You were always my favourite. The only nice one. Something about you, Matt the dormant volcano, the sleeping lion, intrigues me.'

He nodded, but it seemed forced.

'And I'm sorry for bringing this up when you've got Karen to worry about. I just wanted it said. So now it's said. Let's go inside.'

He paused a moment, thinking. Then he kissed her cheek, and she took it to mean he accepted her words. Or maybe this acceptance was forced, too.

Matt's mother was on her sofa, doing embroidery things. She looked surprised, and then pleased to see Lisa. Both women hugged, then Mum rushed off to make tea – still her main priority for a new guest. Matt thought he could have dragged in a road accident victim spraying blood and she would put the kettle on before dialling 999.

Over tea and biscuits they chatted about Lisa. Mum was genuinely interested in the woman who had made a mark on her Matt and fired questions like an army interrogator, but good-naturedly. Matt was happy to sit and listen because none of it was too embarrassing. He learned a few things that Lisa had been up to since she left the army. He joined in the conversation only when one of the women targeted a question in his direction. Nobody mentioned Karen, but he was glad of that.

Mum asked if either of them was hungry. Ten minutes later Matt was wolfing down egg on toast, while Lisa took her time with sandwiches in order to be polite, and said as much.

'Who looks like they're enjoying it more,' Matt said around a mouthful of food, winking at his mother. Lisa stuck her tongue out at him. She felt her phone vibrate in her pocket and took it out for a moment, just long enough to check the screen.

Soon after that, Mum saw them to the door. Matt hugged his mother, but afterwards she gave him a pained look.

'I'm not running off, Mum,' he said. 'Not again. Like I said, I'll be back in a couple of days.' He had already told her that he and Lisa were popping up to Manchester to meet her parents.

Mum didn't look entirely convinced by this, but did a good job of giving him a happy smile. But she did glance at the bag in his hand. All the stuff he'd brought into the house from his car days before. Lisa agreed that he looked like a man who was planning on being away a while.

'You should go see your brother first,' Mum said. 'He said you had an argument.'

'I'm not leaving, Mum,' Matt said with a laugh. 'Honest. I'm back to stay now.'

A few minutes later, they were in the car. The moment both doors were closed, Lisa said, 'This came in earlier, but I waited because I knew you'd jump to your feet if I showed you immediately.'

She held out her phone. He snatched it. 'What's this?'

'Twitter,' she said. 'It's a social networking site, Mr Techno. I put your picture on, and that caption.'

The caption said: *Guess the logo*. And there were several replies. One user had posted his reply in the form of a photo. It showed a red rose (not a cloud) nestled within a horseshoe (not a C on its back). Below the picture: *Lucky Rose Florist*.

Lisa looked out the window. Mum was still at the door, watching them. She waved when she saw Lisa looking.

'She thinks you'll never be back.'

Matt looked up too and gave a wave. He opened his mouth, as if to refute Lisa's assumption. But no words came.

The Mondeo drew up to the kerb. It was dark.

They were in Peckham, on a road of new blocks of apartments, each one named and coloured after an animal. The twin rows of buildings created a strange rainbow. The one they wanted was called Green Robin House, of which there was no such creature, and they could clearly see which one it was as soon as they turned onto the road.

Things were progressing well, moving forward quickly. Two hours ago they had still faced a dead end. Ninety minutes ago they had had a vague clue in the form of a scribbled image. In the time since, the snowball had gained mass and momentum.

Yell.com had a listing for Lucky Rose Florist in the City of Westminster. Lisa had called the supplied mobile number and turned on her speakerphone. The lady on the end of the phone immediately told them that the advert should have been changed: there was no longer a delivery van to go along with the shop, because she had sold the vehicle two weeks ago. The advertised sale price would, of course, be lowered in respect of this. Apparently, the Yell advert was obsolete, but the shop had been put up for sale on some other website and it was this one the owner assumed they had used to find her. Going along with the woman's assumption that they were calling to buy her business, Lisa had insisted that she needed the van as well as the shop. The van was important, she said.

And it was. At the mention of such a vehicle, especially its sale just a fortnight ago, both Matt and Lisa had looked at each other, their eyes communicating the same thought: a van was a very nice piece of equipment for transporting a body.

'If I can get that van, I'll be interested in the shop,' Lisa had said to the seller.

The seller had said she remembered the name she had to

write on the logbook, if only because of its unusual flavour: Ivor Tchevsky.

'He paid me three point five,' she'd said, 'but don't you go paying more than three thousand. It's only worth that.'

Lisa had hung up and watched Matt. The name Tchevsky, possibly that of the man who killed his sister, couldn't be common, and she'd expected Matt to immediately hit the internet to trace it.

Instead, he had sat and stared out of the window. Was he nervous now they'd entered the endgame? Now that he knew he'd bettered his chances of getting his hands on the man who'd murdered his sister? Their world today was a far cry from the army, where the prospect of killing, and being killed, permeated the very air they breathed. Where killing could result in medals, not sentences.

He hadn't spoken during their drive here, either. Another internet directory listed fourteen people with the surname Tchevsky in the London area, but none called Ivor. However, of the fourteen, only three were of a practical age to own and operate a vehicle. It didn't take long to research those three using the website of the General Register Office and learn that one Petra Tchevsky, 38, of Green Robin House, Peckham, had married a chap called Ivor Peterson seven years ago, and he'd taken her surname. Now, here, watching the building that Ivor Tchevsky called home, Lisa was reminded of the saying, *Be careful what you wish for*. She touched Matt's arm. 'We don't have to do this.'

But what he said next was a shock. Matt hadn't had second thoughts at all.

'I'm not going to assume this Ivor Tchevsky is Karen's murderer. He might not even know anything. This involves more than one person and there will be a hierarchy. We're climbing a ladder and we're at the bottom. We climb one rung up at a time.

I think Tchevsky is just one rung, also at the bottom. So what we need from him is a name. The name of the next guy, the guy on the rung above. We climb that ladder. At the top, when there are no more names above, we'll have the man or woman most responsible for Karen. The one I need.'

If Matt trod the revenge path, he might get harmed. If he killed a man, he would be taken from her. She didn't want to lose him. But that was her only concern. She had no bones about a sick killer getting what he deserved. Just a few seconds after Matt had confirmed he intended to see this through, she was back on track, back on his side. Besides, nobody's appointment with death had been written in stone. Somehow, although unlikely, this could all end without any more violence.

'And how do we work Tchevsky to get that name?' she asked.

He looked at her. 'I know a trick with a pair of scissors. Look, Lisa, I know I've said it before. But I'm going to say it again. You've done enough for me. So if–'

She put a hand over his mouth. 'I'm bored of repeating myself, Matt.'

Three times in the last hour, Matt had told Lisa that he was thankful for her help, that she had done a lot for him, but now it was time for her to leave and let him do his thing. Each time, she had knocked him back. She was in this until the end.

'I don't want you getting hurt.'

She groaned. 'Blah-blah-blah. And I don't want *you* getting hurt, which is why I have to come with you, so you don't mess things up with your big size twelves. Stop going on about it. Now, I think we do this the pessimist's way. First, let's assume Ivor's not there. If we go in there and be nice with Petra Tchevsky, we'll never know where her loyalty lies, until maybe it's too late. Either they're together or split. If split, she either knows where Ivor is or doesn't. If she does, she'll either tell us or not. And if she tells us, she'll either alert him or not after we're gone.'

'So getting this to go our way is going to be like flipping a coin and trying to get four heads on the trot. We need four heads. If we don't fancy those chances, we forget the coin toss.'

Lisa nodded. 'I don't fancy them. So we try a different approach. No threats. Nicely-nice.'

'I'm not much good at nice.'

His grin said he was joking, but she knew otherwise. His comfort zone was in amongst people who might want to do him harm. In that zone his paranoia and suspicion could drive him, instead of taking a back seat. In that zone he got no nasty surprises, like a ghost train rider who knows where all the ghouls pop up.

Lisa said, 'If that door opens and it's Ivor standing there, we do your Plan A: go blazing in. If it's his wife, Petra, then we go with my clever Plan B. Then, when we find out where Ivor is, you can do what you want to get the next name off him. I wouldn't want to deprive you of scissors fun. Agreed?'

'Tell me your clever Plan B.'

They took the stairs to reach flat 12b of Green Robin House, faces cast down to avoid the CCTV cameras. The carpets were green, the walls painted green, and even all the apartment doors were green – not a robin in sight, though. Matt knocked.

A woman appeared behind the opening door. Matt immediately grabbed Lisa's arm in both hands, hard.

Plan B.

The woman was stunning. Tall, slim, elegant, in jeans and a pink blouse, with her dark hair tied in a bun at the back. No make-up, but then she didn't need it. She immediately asked who they were and what they wanted. She sounded European.

'I want my girlfriend's ring back,' Matt snapped.

'What ring?' Petra Tchevsky said, puzzled.

'It's in the back of his new van. His damn lovemobile. It cost me–'

In a flash, Petra Tchevsky bared her teeth and launched herself at Lisa. 'You bitch, I'll kill you.'

Barely in time, Matt got between both women. He held them apart, arm flesh in each of his big hands. Not quite quickly enough, though: strands of Lisa's hair dangled from Petra's fingers.

'I didn't know he had a wife,' Lisa moaned, looking terrified. 'It was one night. In the back of his van.'

'You sick bitch,' Petra yelled, spittle flying from her lips. She strained again to get at Lisa, who moved behind Matt.

'Where is he?' Matt said, letting go of Lisa to use both hands to restrain Petra. 'I'm not going to hurt him, and I don't want to upset you. I just want that ring back out of the van. It cost me a lot of money.'

Petra yanked free from his grip, but didn't try to snare Lisa. Instead, she whirled and vanished into the apartment. But she left the door open. Matt and Lisa looked at each other, unsure what to do next. They had hoped Petra would give her husband up, which hadn't happened – but the door was open…

'So now we hope she phones him and he comes back,' Lisa whispered.

Petra was back a minute later. Lisa took a step back, but Petra didn't even look at her. In her hands was a battered little address book. She had it open at a page, which she tore out and balled up and threw at Lisa. Lisa let it bounce off her forehead.

'This fool friend of his,' Petra said. 'Ivor, that bastard, bought the van for this man. This man works at a casino. He wanted an untraceable van so Ivor bought one cheap and sold it to him. They only know each other because Ivor did some wood-working at the casino. But this fool here, he'll have your bitch's ring. And if you don't want to upset me, break Ivor's cheating nose so I don't have to. You're weak if he fucked your bitch and you let it go. And while you're breaking his nose, tell that bastard he's wasted his last chance and not to ever come back here. Now get lost and take your man-stealing bitch with you.'

She slammed the door. And that was that. Matt snatched up the piece of paper and eagerly opened it.

'The good news is we just skipped by Tchevsky and onto the next rung of the ladder,' Lisa said.

He couldn't drag his eyes from the name on the sheet. 'What's the bad news?'

'You lost your scissors fun.'

9

Matt had a ghost of a smile on his face, had had it ever since they left Tchevsky's apartment. He was enjoying this, she knew. Each metre they travelled, he was getting closer to what he wanted. No more treading water.

Lisa said, 'I always wanted to visit South Kensington. My mum told me my grandfather worked here many years ago, some kind of financial advisor to a French businessman. There's a big French presence here. And money.' She stared out the windows at high buildings and flash cars parked against the kerb. 'And casinos to spend it in.'

'The building is in Harrington Gardens, a right up here on Gloucester Road.' He checked his phone's satnav again. 'Half a mile. Park anywhere here and we'll walk.'

They found a spot and left the car. It was quite dark now but the air was cool. She took his hand, saying they should try to look like tourists, since there seemed to be plenty around. He snaked his hands into hers and she squeezed them tightly, gave him a grin. They walked in silence.

They hadn't found any social media accounts for the name on the paper, Liam Hardy, but he was on LinkedIn as security director of Pegasus Casino. The place was a far cry from what Matt imagined. His knowledge of such establishments came from TV, which invariably showed glitzy places blitzing the night with neon and lines of expensive cars drawing up beneath a vast awning. He expected to see men in sharp suits and women glittering with jewels. But Pegasus Casino was one of several businesses in a long, five-storey building. It was right on the street, behind a tiny pavement. There was a pay-and-display car park across the road. The entrance did have an awning, but it was a simple canvas affair that barely shaded a set of double doors of black glass that bore the name of the casino and an image of a winged horse rearing up on its hind legs. It was hard to determine the size of the interior based on the entrance.

There was foot traffic on the street, but most seemed to be passing through because the casino was the only place open except for a small restaurant along to the left. They watched a man and a woman exit the car park, both in jeans and jackets, and cross the road in the direction of the casino. The guy hauled one of the doors open and Matt caught sight of a foyer, and a portion of a guy in black who looked like security. The noise of electronic gaming machines oozed out. Then the door shut and the street was quiet again.

'How shall we do this?' Lisa said. 'Go in as customers? Not exactly dressed for it.'

The two customers who'd just entered had been dressed casually, but Matt thought it was still risky. 'Let's look round the back first.'

At the long building's rear was a walled garden, raised to the eight-foot height of the wall. On the street running parallel behind the garden they found an iron sliding gate in the wall.

The dark tunnel beyond went under the garden, sloping down, and presumably into an underground parking lot below the casino. The gate was keypad-protected, so probably for staff use alone.

There was a stone stairway giving access to the garden from the street. They went up. The garden had a scattering of benches and Victorian lamp posts. If not for the building looming above them, it would have been quaint. They took a bench close to the wall, overlooking the street, not far from the gateway below them, and waited. Like lovers enjoying the cool night air. Two couples sat on nearby benches, enjoying each other's company.

Like lovers also, Lisa took his hand again. They sat with their backs to a lamp post, their faces in shadow, so they could face the street. It was quiet. Only an occasional vehicle passed along this back road, and the tall building impeded the noise of the traffic on the main road.

They sat in silence for a few moments, then Lisa asked him a serious question: 'Matt, I want to know your plan for when you find the man who... did this. I never planned to ask. I felt obliged to help you, and then I was going to step away and go home and leave you to it. But now I think I couldn't just do that. I will want to stay in touch with you. But for that, I need to know what you plan to do.'

His pause told the story, he realised. Too long for that of a man preparing the correct words. Too long for that of a man asking himself the same question. It was the pause of a man who didn't want to answer, and that told her everything.

'That's very risky,' she said. 'You risk prison. You...' She stumbled here. Threatening Matt with the personal consequences of his actions was not going to be a productive tactic. 'What if we can make it so the killer goes to prison? What if we find evidence, or we can plant some in some way? I'd like you to be a free man so we can chat in places like this again. Not across a prison table.'

'As long as they get punished, I don't care,' he said, and was looking away when he did so, in case, despite the shadows, she saw the lie smeared right across his face.

'This is quaint here,' she said. 'Makes me remember the beach.'

She was trying to change the subject. Knew she had rubbed a nerve with her question. He also tried to get his mind onto something else. Her words threw up an image of the beach, under the starry sky, where, like a scene from a romance novel, they had made love for the first time.

But it was no good: his mind forced itself to return to the here and now. To Liam Hardy. He looked at the tall building housing the casino behind them. Was the man he sought in there, just metres away? Was Matt just minutes away from the only resolution that would satisfy him?

'Did you like sex with me?' Lisa said. Again, he pretended not to hear.

If the florist's van was indeed part of this whole thing, then Hardy was a vital piece and therefore guilty. But how guilty? Was he the killer, or someone tasked with helping another commit the crime? If he was a secondary player, what would Matt do about that? Overlook him as he had Tchevsky? Or, when the ladder climb was complete, would Matt's vengeance send him downwards to mop up those bit players? When asked by Lisa if he planned to find Tchevsky, his answer had been *no*, because that man was a lowly rung, just a stepping stone. But the truthful answer would have been *I don't know*.

He also had to consider that he might be completely wrong about everything. This entire line of enquiry had come from a fragment of plastic and a scrap of paper. The not knowing was eating him alive.

'Car,' Lisa said, jerking him back to reality.

They heard the gate rumble open and felt the vibration of it in their feet. Flowers in a nearby bed shivered. Beyond the edge of the garden, they watched the top half of a black Mercedes-Benz GLS cruise down the road towards them. The GLS drew level with their position and turned left, seemingly right into the wall. It disappeared. They heard its engine below them, muted by the grassy ground.

The engine noise faded, the gate rumbled closed, and all was quiet again. Except for Matt's thudding heart. He had hoped to see a face when someone exited the car to punch numbers into the keypad, but clearly the gate could be remote operated, too. He was wired with tension because he'd prepared for action in the few seconds it took for the car to reach the gate, but the scene had abruptly cooled before it got anywhere near white hot. Now he didn't know what to do.

Lisa said, 'Do we think that was him? Very flash SUV.' He understood her point, because he'd been thinking the same thing: a casino's security director might be able to afford a ninety-grand car.

'Not sure,' he answered, his heart still thudding. Quickly, he thought of a plan, in the hope that it would appease his sense of urgency. 'We should fetch the car and then park on the street. Follow the Merc when it leaves. The driver will have to get out eventually.'

Yes, that was a good idea. Immediately, he felt himself start to settle. Until Lisa torpedoed the plan: 'But if it's not Hardy driving the GLS, then it's a wasted trip. Five cars might come out at the same time and we wouldn't know which to follow. He could leave on foot through the front. He might not even be here.'

He stood up. He had to do something. He was an inch away from storming into the casino when Lisa put her hand on his arm. 'Calm down. I have a better plan for finding out if Hardy's inside.'

He looked at her, almost pleading. Lisa smiled and stood up, and took his hand. 'Let's go check out a blackjack table,' she said.

~

Matt had a case of clothing in the car, but Lisa's extra outfits were back at her B&B, so they settled for what they were wearing. They straightened their clothing, scraped off bits of dirt, and appraised each other in the lamplight.

'Shipwreck victim after two weeks,' Lisa said, looking him up and down.

'Homeless prostitute,' Matt said. She laughed and slapped his shoulder, but Matt wasn't smiling. The mention of a prostitute put an image of Karen in his mind. He shook it out. 'Let's go.'

Pegasus Casino's foyer was a mix of decors tranquil and menacing. The tranquil came from yellow wallpaper, potted plants and colourful paintings. The menacing was a reception desk with three big guys in black suits. They had to fill out temporary membership cards and stare into a camera that would probably set a klaxon blaring if it recognised them as barred players or known criminals. No klaxon. After that they got surprisingly realistic smiles and a bid to enjoy the night. Ornate double doors were pointed at.

The joint was already thriving. Matt had never been in a casino before and he stopped to admire the vast room. Slot machines in rows like a robot army on parade occupied the front of the room. The noises and lights hurt his head almost instantly. They walked down a red carpet that cut the slots arena in half. Beyond them was a stage area. Speakers and lights testified that the stage was sometimes used for shows, but tonight it played host only to a black sports car revolving on a plinth. A prize to be won, probably using the giant slot machine standing alone before the stage.

The people on the slots were not as elegant as Matt had expected. No serious dress code in play here. He saw men in trainers and women in plastic cagoules, and unshaven chins and cheeks devoid of make-up. Their cash was worth the same no matter how glamorous the owner. He no longer felt conspicuous. Lisa said the same.

The red carpet forked at the stage, each new path sloping down to a set of double doors manned by a pair of waitresses bearing a tray of drinks each. He figured the area beyond was for high rollers and expected to be stopped because of his jeans, but wasn't.

Beyond the doors were the gaming tables. Lots of them. As soon as the doors shut behind him, the robot whoops and cries of the slot machines were gone, replaced by soft music coming from speakers high on the walls. It was like another world.

There was another stage here, back wall, between the two doorways. Girls in leotards danced to low music. Before the stage was a bar, effectively barring access to it, with another two girls in leotards serving drinks. Matt found a space and ordered two non-alcoholic beers. He needed a clear head. He sat with his back to the stage so he could watch the room. Here, the females wore a lot of glitter and the men were mostly in tuxedos, although there were enough casually dressed people so he and Lisa did not stand out. Beyond all the tables was a lounge area, with sofas and TVs and coffee tables with magazines. The walls were hung with giant paintings, all of which were crap enough to probably be copies of famous ones, although he recognised none of them.

As he watched, an oblong portion of one painting, including

part of the frame and the wall around it, opened and ejected a woman carrying a tray of sandwiches. A door. His eyes had been fooled. The paintings were literally painted on the walls, frames too. Now that he looked, he could see numerous unmarked doors in the walls, all virtually seamless, reminding him of some giant advent calendar. Some tactic to throw off robbers, maybe? Was there a maze of corridors and stairs beyond the walls?

But there was one door that stood out. It was in a corner and at the top of three short steps, and it was blocked by a big ape in a black suit. The door was plain, flush with the wall, almost giving the impression that the steps went nowhere, but the effect was lost because of the steps. And the presence of the ape indicated that something special lay behind that door.

As he watched the room, Matt's ears caught the conversations of the people sat at stools before the bar. He was able to fade out the overlapping chatter and concentrate for a few seconds on each individual conversation. Some guy talking about his house repayments. Some woman moaning about how insulting it was to have skimpily-dressed females serving drinks. Some guy detailing what he'd like to do to the redhead prancing on the stage.

He sensed an emptiness beside him and turned to find Lisa had gone. His eyes took in the whole room, but she was not here. He cautioned himself about needless panic, rose from his seat while the bargirl was still pouring his drinks, and headed for the door.

He found Lisa in the slots room, staring up at the car on stage as if she'd never seen such a thing before.

'You won't win it,' he said.

'Someone has to.'

'Of course they don't. How did they get it in here? Too big for the doors, won't drive down the carpet.'

'Maybe they built the whole casino around it.'

'Funny. They built the car right here. But either way, that's too much effort for something that luck could snatch from them on night one. Come on, I got you a drink.'

She went reluctantly, after a long glance at the giant slot machine before the stage.

They sat at the bar and had their drinks. Chatting, dawdling and wasting time, but also watching everything. After half an hour, Lisa suggested they should go back to the slots area, where there were more people, more conversations to eavesdrop on. They would not learn anything here.

Halfway to the door, Matt stopped and turned, his attention drawn by a massive guffaw from someone. He watched in awe as a guy was dragged from the bar, laughing, by the redhead dancer. It was the guy who'd lusted after her. Beside him, his mate was saying something, denying something, defending himself, but also laughing. The lustful guy went up on the stage and danced with the redhead. There was a black-suited security guy nearby, watching intently.

Lisa grabbed his arm. 'You jealous? I can get you one of those girls, if you want.'

'Liam Hardy is the security director, right?'

'Sure is. You planning to make a habit of coming here?' Lisa said. 'You want a membership, maybe a tab at the bar, and your own hook in the cloakroom?' He shook his head. 'Me neither. So, you have a plan?'

'Let's tip the 10-4.'

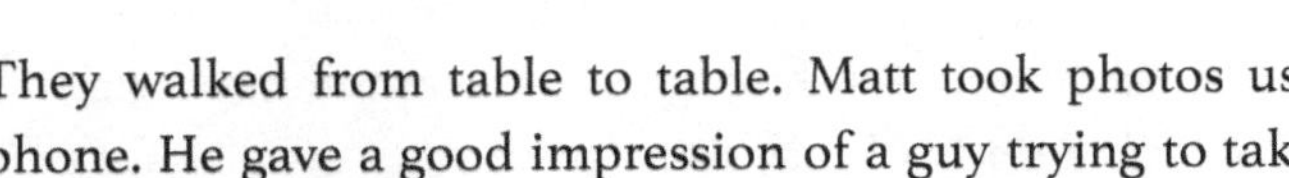

They walked from table to table. Matt took photos using his phone. He gave a good impression of a guy trying to take snaps in secret but being not very good at it. Two croupiers told him he wasn't allowed to photograph the tables. By his side, Lisa pretended to speak into her phone, looking around the club, at the cameras, at the tables and under them. Soon staff and customers started to take offence.

Seven minutes of this game, then they came. Three men. The two behind the one looked like bruisers, bodyguards, because they wore brown suits rather than the black of regular security, but the one looked like he didn't need them. He was at least six-five with thick shoulders straining at the seams of his blue tuxedo. He had a buzz-cut that connected to his goatee by sideburns, making all the hair on his head look like a helmet he could slip off his skull and mouth. And he wore a badge that clearly noted him as SECURITY DIRECTOR HARDY. Matt and Lisa had hoped that the director himself might venture out to see off these two irritating customers, and they had gotten their wish.

'Excuse me, sir,' Hardy said. His English accent was Southern Counties. 'You're disrupting our players, and we don't allow photography of the tables. And you, ma'am, you need to put your phone away, too.'

Matt couldn't take his eyes off the guy. Here he was, the man he needed, the man listed as their top suspect. Just feet away, within grabbing and choking and crushing range. But Matt stayed his hands, held back his rage. He did this by telling himself they would not get information out of Hardy here, now, they would only get subdued by an army of apes and arrested. He had to bide his time, hard as that might be.

'We're not trying to cheat,' Lisa said. 'We're new. Just checking the place out.'

Hardy looked at her, then back at Matt, but didn't seem fazed by Matt's frozen stare. Matt knew he was overdoing the glaring, but he couldn't stop his brain from telling his eyes to soak up every detail of this man. Hardy held the stare for a few seconds, then told them to leave.

'For what? Having technology everyone else has?' Lisa said.

'Let's not have a scene,' Hardy said. He tapped his foot on the carpet. It made barely a sound, but was clearly some kind of pre-arranged sign, because the two bruisers stepped forward, one sweeping an arm like someone saying, *you first*. Leave, in other words.

'This is a joke,' Lisa snapped. 'I was on the phone to my bank manager to get a loan. I was going to put ten thousand on black, but you guys just messed that one up. Where's the manager?'

'Like the tables and indeed every part of this casino, not available to you.'

'Let's go,' Matt said to Lisa. He took her hand.

They were escorted by all three men to the foyer doors. There Hardy stopped while the two bruisers took them to the exit, and there the pair waited until they'd watched their unwelcome guests walk partway down the road.

As soon as the guys were gone, Matt and Lisa split up. Matt went around the back, to watch the rear of the building, while Lisa ran for the car. Twenty minutes later they were both in the car and watching the gate in the wall at the rear of the casino.

They decided to sleep in turns, just in case Hardy worked the entire night shift. Matt chose to watch first, because he knew he wouldn't sleep. Lisa told him to wake her at four, but he wasn't going to do any such thing. He wasn't planning to be asleep when Hardy left the building.

As it was, the GLS left at just after midnight. Lisa was in the driver's seat, so he had no choice but to wake her. She climbed over him so they could swap places. The GLS swung a right once out of the tunnel and drove past them. Matt watched in the rear-view until it reached the junction and swept left, then he turned the car in the road and followed.

'It might be hard to stop them this late,' Lisa said. Matt just nodded. 'Guy like him must expect he might get followed or attacked now and then. Sour customers who lost the house. Sour customers thinking it's all fixed. He may even be armed. What you want to do?'

Matt said, 'We just follow for now, see if we can get an address.'

Midnight, but the traffic was still pretty heavy. Which was good. Enough vehicles to allow Matt to hide the Mondeo when he needed to, and to slow the GLS so that there was never a chance of losing it.

The drive was just a few miles south, to Roehampton. The GLS turned off a main road and entered a housing estate. Matt had to hang back now, because traffic here consisted of one shiny, black Mercedes-Benz GLS and one battered Ford Mondeo and that was it. The Mercedes took a turn, but Matt stopped his car at the corner, allowing Lisa to hop out and peek around the edge of an end terrace. A few seconds later she was back.

'Left,' she said. Matt took the turn and quickly drove to the next corner, where Lisa had watched Hardy's vehicle turn. There, she exited again and did her peeking thing.

'Right,' she said as she jumped back in the Mondeo. He turned left, drove eighty metres along an empty street to the next junction, where the GLS had now turned right. Out she got. Pressed herself against the wall of a house on the right side. Peeked around.

This time when she returned to Matt, she did so at a walk.

'It's parked about halfway down.'

Matt went to look. Here, the terraced housing had given over to semi-detached residences with neat little elevated lawns that made the road seem as if it were laid in a depression, or had subsided three feet. The GLS was at the left kerb, lights off, but he could just about hear the idling engine.

The house it was parked outside was dark except for a light on upstairs. Front bedroom.

The driver's door opened and a man got out, slowly. Hardy. There he was. Matt gripped the corner of the house, digging his nails in. This location was a far cry from a busy casino with cameras and witnesses. No one here to see anything. No one else in the GLS this time. He knew he could cross the distance between he and Hardy in seconds, unheard, and hit the man like a juggernaut. Fight over. But again he told himself to wait. Watch. Stay his anger and bide his time.

Hardy closed his car door slowly, but didn't click it shut. Like his followers, he was trying to hide his presence here. As Matt watched, Hardy walked backwards across the road, staring up at the lit bedroom window. He stood on the far kerb, still watching the illuminated bedroom, and pulled his mobile. He held the device at his ear, but nobody seemed to answer, given how he angrily smacked his phone against his leg.

Hardy crossed the road and entered the garden. Shocked, Matt watched him approach the front door of the house and bend and put his ear to the letterbox. He didn't shout through, which made Matt realise Hardy didn't live here. He had assumed Hardy was locked out and had tried to phone someone to let him in. But if that had been the case, surely he would have shouted through the letterbox. Instead, Hardy was listening and being very secretive about it.

Then he did something even more surprising.

The security director looked around the small garden, lifted a stone the size of a tennis ball, and returned to his vehicle. Standing in the crook of the open door, he launched the stone over his vehicle and then jumped into the driver's seat. By the time the stone had caved in the living room window, the GLS was already tearing away, lights still off.

The crash of breaking glass seemed terribly loud on such a quiet, inert street. No lights came on in other houses, but Matt knew that woken neighbours would be rushing across dark bedrooms to stare out windows.

Lisa raced to the Mondeo, but stopped when she realised Matt wasn't following. 'We're not following Hardy?'

Still at the corner, watching the house Hardy had vandalised, Matt shook his head. 'My turn to have a clever Plan B.'

When an hour had passed, Matt left his room to make it easy for them. No need for the B&B owner to get his place trashed when it could all go down smoothly.

So Matt left his room, left the building, and stepped casually out into the morning sunshine.

The street had a few pedestrians, and he didn't think it would go down here. So he turned left once out of the gate and walked to the junction. Ahead and right, the streets eventually found their way to a town centre. But to his left, the road passed some shops and houses and terminated at a fence with a kissing gate. Beyond that, a kids' playpark. He went there.

A bay window in a charity shop allowed him to bounce his vision backwards, where he saw a blue Audi parked at the junction, just enough of it poking out from behind the corner building to allow the occupants to watch him. Just like the other day, when he'd been following the pimps.

'Keep an eye on this mingebag, lads,' he said to himself with a smile.

He passed the last of the houses and shops and went through the kissing gate. He heard the car approaching. He didn't look round. He heard it brake to a halt not far behind him. He didn't look round. He heard the kissing gate creak like the front door of an old haunted house. Now he turned round.

Three guys. One was by the open driver's door. Hardy. The other two, guys as big as he was, were approaching Matt. He didn't recognise them, so figured they weren't bruisers from the casino. New bruisers. And he noted that the Audi was a saloon, with a separate boot area. Perfect.

'London Street around here, mate?' the closest guy said. Just to explain his presence, just buying time, so he could get closer. They were ten feet away now.

Matt didn't want to get punched in the face, so he turned away from the guys, and pointed, and said, 'Not sure if it's over–'

That was as far as he got. Thick arms wrapped around him. He made a few cursory kicking and thrashing movements, as you would if strange men grabbed you, and then he let himself be taken.

'Someone wants to see you,' the first guy said.

'Little head just got big head in deep shit,' the other guy said.

As he was loaded into the boot of the car, he saw Hardy staring at him, pure hate on his face. And a small pistol in his hand. But no recognition. The guy hadn't placed Matt as the guy from the casino last night.

The boot slammed, shrouding Matt in darkness. As the car pulled away, he thought about trying to memorise the route, then didn't bother. So he just lay back and relaxed, and hoped they didn't take speed bumps too quickly.

He wasn't tired, because he'd gotten a few hours' sleep earlier. After leaving the scene of the window-busting, he and Lisa had hunted out a local B&B and paid for one room in Matt's name. In case the owner was part of Liam Hardy's supposedly vast list of connections, they had decided that it should look as if Matt was alone. He had sneaked Lisa into the room when the coast was clear.

They had spent a portion of the rest of the night lying on top of the bed, fully clothed, talking about Matt's Plan B, before they finally drifted off almost in synch.

Earlier, Lisa had parked the Mondeo outside the house with the busted window, by which time the owner was at the front door, staring out in the street, seeking the culprit who threw a stone. She had looked very scared, but, crucially, not confused.

Lisa rushed over to console her, firing questions, telling her it would be okay. Within minutes, she had been in the living room, helping the homeowner to tape cardboard across the busted window and sharing tea, as if she were an old friend who had popped round in the middle of the afternoon.

Her name was Jenny. Short, pretty without make-up, early thirties, and the owner of a house full of ornaments and photos of family member's kids. Jenny Gaiman, Lisa managed to find out, lived alone, and had done since she split from her boyfriend, Liam. Hardy.

Through careful cajoling, Lisa managed to get the story. Her ex-boyfriend was a very jealous man who wouldn't leave her alone. In the four months since she booted him out for cheating on her, Liam had been harassing her. It started with phone calls at all hours, progressing to unannounced visits at home and then at her place of work. After that she discovered people watching her. People from the casino, where he worked as head of security. They would sit outside her home or work in their cars, just watching. She knew that Liam was trying to find out if she had another man. But she hadn't dated at all in those four months because she feared what Liam might do to either her or her new boyfriend. He had been in prison twice, both times for violent offences. Jenny had no doubt that Hardy had thrown the stone through her window, probably because she hadn't answered his phone call a minute earlier.

This information was beautiful, and perfectly fit with Matt's Plan B.

Now, Matt perked up as the car stopped. He heard a big metal shutter open. He imagined he was at a warehouse.

The car drove in a short way and stopped. He could see a fine line of bright light in the seams where the boot lid didn't fit flush. A well-lit place, then. He heard the men exit the car, heard muted voices and footsteps. He got ready.

But a few moments later there was silence, and then darkness as someone turned off the light. Okay, he thought, this was a tactic to scare him. They were going to leave him here a while, to worry in the dark. Good plan. But he never worried in the dark.

They came for him just a few minutes later. Without warning, the boot slammed open and hands grabbed him and dragged him out. Not a word spoken by his assailants, and the light was still off. If they expected panic, and pleading, he was happy to oblige.

He was carried. Even though it was dark, someone covered his eyes with a cloth that smelled of oil. He didn't struggle, but he did yell questions like *who are you?* and *what do you want?* because that was surely what a shocked man would do. They set him down on his back, and then rolled him.

He felt air, knew he was falling. Before his brain could think of what might be happening, he hit hard, smacking his head, thumping his hip. The cloth fell off his face and he got to his knees, and that was when the lights came back on.

A five-foot LED tube light hanging on chains illuminated a building with a corrugated iron roof and walls, and a shutter with a small, misty Perspex window at head height. The framework seemed to be composed of scaffolding pipes. There were tools and machinery fragments everywhere. He was in an inspection pit in a garage. There was no car above him, but the three guys were. They stood around the edge of the pit, staring down. If they were trying to look intimidating, Matt missed it because the bright light behind their heads cast shadows across their faces. But he put the correct amount of fear and shock on his face, playing along.

'What the fuck were you doing at that house this morning?' Hardy said.

Lisa had managed not only to find out about Hardy from his terrified ex-girlfriend, she had also gotten the lady to agree to let her glazier friend have a look at the window the next morning. So, nice and early, Matt had gone round and knocked on the door, and had been fully aware when he did so that the Vauxhall Zafira up the road had a guy in it who was watching the house. When Jenny opened the door, Matt stepped right inside before he said a word, just like a guy who knew the woman and was expected. It surprised her, and once the door was shut he apologised for his overfriendliness. But hopefully it had projected the desired image to the man in the Zafira.

Now, he said to Hardy, 'What house? On April Road? I went there to see a friend. Who are you people?'

Hardy looked at him, nodding. 'Yeah, she's a friend all right. You fucking her?'

Matt hadn't fucked her, of course. He had talked to her about the window and given a decent quote, and said he'd be back later that day. He had stayed half an hour, which he figured was about the right amount of time. When he left, he made sure that the shirt he'd tucked in was hanging loose. On the doorstep, in view of Zafira Man, he fiddled with the button on his jeans and tucked his shirt in, giving a good impression of a guy finishing up getting dressed. As Matt drove away, he watched the guy follow him. He led the guy right to the B&B and, at the upstairs window, watched him make a phone call. Perfect. He gave it an hour and then left the B&B.

Now, Matt said, 'What's it to you?' He had noticed the item

by Hardy's feet: a petrol can, no doubt not empty. And in the man's hands: a box of matches.

'Maybe that's someone's girlfriend, and you could get in big trouble for going near her. Again, are you fucking her?'

Matt grinned at him. 'Well, you left a sexual satisfaction deficit I had to make up for.'

Hardy flicked the lid off the petrol can and started pouring it over Matt. Surprisingly, he watched his captive sit down and take it. Just sit right there in the inspection pit and just let him pour the stinking fluid all over him. He tossed the can away when it was done. Matt was rubbing the burning fluid from his face. His eyes were stinging. For the first time, he felt a little panic and almost wished he'd gone with a Plan C.

Hardy shook the box of matches. 'Next sarcastic joke, please.'

'For fuck sake, hurry up!' Matt roared. It made all three men pull puzzled faces. Get on with it?

The garage shutter burst open with a screech of rending metal. Torn free of its side housings, it flipped up like a cat flap. But no cat came through. Instead, roaring its way inside, was Matt's Mondeo.

The two bruisers tried to dive aside as the car raced at them, knocking aside tools and a workbench. One made it, but the other guy got caught in the hip and sent sprawling with a scream. Hardy was quicker and more thoughtful about his escape. He dropped into the inspection pit, his head barely dipping below the car as it skidded over the hole and crushed a table with magazines and a kettle against the back wall.

As the Mondeo backed up, it cut a slight curve and hit the doorway, hard enough to shake the whole flimsy building with a sound like thunder. The ceiling light started swinging wildly. Before Lisa could put the car in first gear to rectify her mistake, both bruisers had her doors open and their rough hands on her, laughing and panting like lunatics. But in their haste to have her, one tried to yank her out of the car by her hair and was foiled by his pal's attempt to haul her the other way by her arm.

And then they let her go. They backed away from the car with their hands up and their heads turned towards the inspection pit. What she saw out the windscreen was beautiful.

Matt was standing by the inspection pit, dripping wet, and pointing a small pistol, which Hardy must have carried. No sign of Hardy.

'You were supposed to knock on the door,' Matt said as she got out of the car and rushed to his side. The two bruisers had dropped to their knees and put their hands behind their heads, as if they'd learned compliance from American cop TV shows. She saw Hardy down in the pit, on his back, breathing but not moving. Unconscious. Which was the best result for him, because both of his arms were bent funny, clearly broken, and his nose was oozing blood all over his face and neck. She wondered for a moment if the car had hit him after all. But no, he had jumped into the pit with Matt. Out of the frying pan and into the fire. He would wake screaming in pain.

'I was going to knock,' she said in reply to his query. 'But then I saw through the window. You were in the pit and safe from the car. And they were about to light you up. So I brought it in.'

He handed her the gun. As he moved towards the two bruisers, she shifted into a position from which she could cover everyone with the weapon. In sixty seconds, Matt had found loose cables, tied one of the bruisers to a corner post, and crushed their mobile phones underfoot. The other guy sat by his friend, looking a little perturbed that he'd been left unbound. Matt leaped into the inspection pit and ran his hands over Hardy. When he climbed out, he stood before the two bruisers.

'Where is Hardy's mobile?' Matt said to them.

'He didn't bring it,' the tied guy answered. 'Phone tracking, in case something went wrong. He normally doesn't come along on this sort of thing.'

Matt glanced at Lisa, who shared his disappointed expression. Hardy's phone might have contained valuable information. 'Well, nobody has to worry about the police. Whose garage is this?'

'It's mine,' the same guy said. Unlike his pal, he didn't seem scared. 'Well, my dad's.'

'Is he due in today? Or anyone else?'

'After work, probably. That's when he comes. No one else. So I know what you're thinking. You could leave us here and be on your way. I'll tell my dad a gang of kids tried to rob the place. And we won't try to come after you. No clue who you are anyway. And that's your best option, pal. Wouldn't be wise to go on the run for triple murder.'

'You took the words right out of my mouth, my friend,' Matt said.

'What about me?' the free bruiser asked. 'What are you going to do to me?'

'Nothing,' the first bruiser snapped. 'Stop pissing your pants. He'll tie you up in good time. But first you're going to help him get Hardy in the car, that's all. Hardy's the one they're after, probably because of that woman he's banging. But we don't care why.' To Matt he said, 'So, pal, hurry up and be on your way.'

Matt actually laughed. He liked this guy's balls. 'Yes, sir.'

Liam Hardy woke in his car, alone.

He was instantly aware of his arms, because of the fiery pain. Hot agony that reminded him they were broken. One after the other, the guy had snapped them, which was the last thing he remembered. He couldn't move them. Grey duct tape held them flat against his chest in a cross-shape, like a topless woman trying to hide her breasts. Still disoriented, he briefly thought that the guy had tied his arms to keep him from moving the damaged bones, to keep him comfortable. He realised his error when he saw that his ankles were tied to the brake and clutch pedals by a thick mass of more tape. The awful truth wiped aside the last of his confusion after that.

He tried to jerk free, but his ass didn't leave the driver's seat. More tape was around his waist and wrapped around the seat to hold him in place.

Not just some guy who was shafting Hardy's ex, then. He got the feeling he'd been tricked. Whoever that guy was, he'd planned all this. Planned to kidnap him. Jesus.

He tried to work out where he was, but it was impossible. He could hear a river, but all he could see all around was thick shrubbery, pressing up against the doors and the front of the car. He couldn't see behind, because he couldn't turn and the rear-view mirror had been adjusted so it reflected his bloodied face, but he figured the scenery would be the same. They had driven him into the middle of nowhere. For God knew what.

He looked up. The sunroof was open, and there was a face there, upside down, as if the man lay on the roof with his legs pointed to the rear of the car. It was him. The guy he'd kidnapped. And suddenly Hardy realised that he'd seen this bastard before. Last night, in the casino. He'd ejected this guy and some woman for taking photographs. Shit, this was a revenge thing for being booted out. But where was the woman?

'What do you want? What's this about? I was just doing my job. Get me the fuck out of here, you goddamn lunatic. I know people.'

A hand floated into view, clutching a mobile phone. 'Not a single one of whom is here to help. But it's some of those people you know that I'm interested in. Are you ready to answer questions?'

The man's other hand entered the square patch of sky. This one held a box of matches. Hardy's own matches. Right then Hardy's brain got with it enough to realise a nasty smell, and a wet feeling across his torso. Jesus, it was petrol, and he was soaked in it. His own fucking petrol, probably. And now it was really stinging his nose. He started to struggle against his bonds, despite the stabbing pain in his busted elbows, but the guy struck a match, and that made Hardy freeze.

'Okay, man, okay. Tell me who you are. What do you want? I ain't gonna fuck you around.'

The guy blew out the match and tossed it away. Then he moved. He leaped over the sunroof and thudded onto the bonnet of the car. He sat cross-legged, and now both men stared at each other through the windscreen.

'What I want from you is just a lift, Liam. I'm climbing a ladder. You're a rung on it, right above the guy who told me all about you. I gave him a pass because I got a lift. You'll get the same pass if you get me onto the next rung. All you have to do to make it home tonight is answer some questions. Easy. Are you ready for your first question?'

Hardy considered screaming for help. Help might come running, but if no help heard his shout, the guy might punish him. So he just nodded.

The man said, 'Then here we go. You bought a van a couple of weeks ago. It belonged to a florist. It had a picture of a flower and a horseshoe on it, but you probably had to peel that off. Now, you asked a guy to find you a van, but did someone ask *you* to find one?'

Hardy paused. He remembered the stolen van. The one with the sticker he did indeed have to peel off. Was this guy the owner? Had that little fucker Tchevsky grassed him up?

The pause, it seemed, was too long. The guy struck another match. Hardy blurted, 'Yeah, a van. Blue, a Mercedes Vito, sliding door, eighty thousand on the clock.' In his panic, he spluttered a few more useless facts about the van, because he didn't know what the guy needed to know, how many of the details might be important. The guy held up a hand and Hardy stopped talking.

'That's not what I asked, is it?'

For a second he couldn't remember the question. Then he did and words tumbled out again: 'My boss at the casino, he wanted a van. Needed it untraceable. His name's Anderson Orbach. That's the guy you want. Not me. I don't know what he wanted it for. Was it your van Tchevsky stole? Is that what this is about?'

'Tell me about Anderson Orbach. Describe him.'

'Mid-forties, about six feet, bald. American. Likes golf. Ex-army. Er... I don't know what else to say.'

'Who else is involved with running the casino?'

Hardy shook his head. 'I don't know, honest. Just him, I think. He never seems to need to ask permission to do things in the casino. Never talks about any kind of boss. But I don't know if he owns it or not. Don't know much, honest.'

'How do I get close to Orbach?'

That shocked Hardy, but also motivated him. If this man was after Orbach, a higher rung, as promised, then Liam could still get out of this okay.

'I don't know. Orbach is paranoid about that sort of stuff. He comes and goes by car or bike. Keeps all sorts of different hours. Uses the underground garage at the casino. Half the time he never even leaves his apartment or his office. Got his own apartment in the casino. I don't know what else to say.'

'Who gets to see him? All staff? Who has access to him? To the office and apartment?'

'No one gets in the apartment. I've never been in there. Now and then he calls staff to the office, but it ain't often. He never comes downstairs onto the floor unless the place is closed. You planning to kill him?'

The guy paused. Thinking. But he twirled the matches in his fingers, as if considering lighting Hardy up. 'What was the florist's van to be used for?'

'Orbach didn't tell me that. Honest. Serious.'

'After you got the van, what did you do with it?'

'I left it parked outside the garage, the one we took you to. I left the keys in it because someone was coming to pick it up. That was it. That was the plan. Next I knew, it was gone. Never saw it again, never heard about it. Never knew who picked it up. Serious.'

'But that's not the only van you ever had dealings with for Orbach, is it?'

'Just that one van. I don't know about any other van.'

'You were asked to steal a van the Saturday before last. Or someone you know was–'

'No way, I don't know anything about that.'

The guy tutted. 'I think you do, Liam. Saturday before last. In Hackney. You stole a van from outside a drug dealer's house, and then you drove it past a waste ground. Made sure the CCTV cameras got it. And then you parked it right back where you nicked it. That was the plan and you did it.'

Hardy was shaking his head, wild-eyed.

The man said, 'You deny it, yet I know Orbach made that happen, and you're his head of security, and that means he tells you everything.'

'Does he fuck. He knows lots of people. I'm just one. If he set that shit up, then he did it without me. You need to go see him about that.'

The guy paused again, and Hardy thought his admission

might have been accepted. The anger had done it. Hardy was genuinely angry about that final accusation, because he truly knew nothing about some drug dealer's van or a waste ground or CC-fucking-TV cameras. A liar wouldn't have exhibited the annoyance Hardy felt at being falsely accused – surely the guy could see that?

'Know anything about a guy called Declan Barthow?'

'Never heard that name. Serious.'

'Sure? Sure you weren't told to break into the guy's flat and plant things?'

Hardy shook his head again. 'No fucking way.' He hoped that same incredulous look was on his face, the same tone in his voice, because again he felt annoyed at a false accusation. 'Serious.'

'Stop saying you're serious,' the guy said, 'If I believe you, I believe you, and it won't be because you're promising you're telling the truth.'

'I am telling the truth. Ser... Look, you need to talk to Anderson Orbach about all this, because he's the boss and I'm no one. If this was something Anderson set up, he set the thing up without me.'

'Heard the name Armstrong?'

Hardy shook his head.

The guy didn't look pleased. 'I think you might be lying, Liam. Head of security, yet you claim to not know quite a lot.'

'Look, I don't hear names. I don't know any names. I'm an errand boy, that's what I do. I do the odd side job for Anderson, and there's never any fucking names. I'm not involved in half the stuff Anderson gets up to. Go see him.'

'So tell me about this little line in side jobs, Liam.'

'We do shit on the side as well as the casino, but they're all Anderson's babies, okay? If there's some big shit going down that you need to know about, I'm the wrong man. He just comes to me for little jobs.'

'So tell me about the last little job you were involved in.'

'Three days ago. Anderson told me someone had been moaning about his neighbour's wall. Guy built it overlapping his land. Anderson said he could fix that problem and he paid me a hundred quid to help. I just got a couple of local idiots to take a cut and shut we had out back of the garage and crash it into the guy's wall. That was it. I got a hundred to break some guy's wall. Don't know what Anderson got paid.'

'And you found out about this moaning homeowner how?'

Hardy opened his mouth, but seemed reluctant to speak.

The man said, 'You seem concerned about saying the wrong thing. But maybe it's the right thing. Liam. Maybe saying nothing is absolutely the wrong thing to say. I'll give you five seconds to think.'

He didn't need five. What the hell could it hurt?

'Orbach hears stuff. He has people in the know, or something. That's all I know. Thousands of people come in the casino, and he's the boss, so he knows stuff about people. He's connected.'

Shock seemed to wash over the man's face. And in the next moment, he vanished. And all went silent. Hardy waited a few moments, but heard nothing more. Had the guy really gone?

'In the casino, at the bar, there was a man,' Matt said as he stopped before Lisa. She was sitting on a rusted shopping trolley laid on its side in an area of the wasteland where a sea of junk had been dumped, some twenty metres from Hardy's car. They had agreed that she would stand back, so that Hardy didn't distract himself by appealing to her for mercy. But she had heard the whole thing by phone. 'The man at the bar made a comment to his friend that he liked the redhead dancer up on stage. And soon after that the redhead grabbed him off his stool. Someone had done him a favour, but not his friend. His friend was just as surprised when the redhead came over. Someone else.'

He saw the dawn slowly rise across her face. 'They're listening.'

He started to pace, back and forth across a short distance. 'It's how they do it. It's how the Watchdogs find people with problems. This man who Hardy said had a dispute with his neighbour about a wall... he must have been complaining about it inside the casino, and the microphones and cameras picked it up. And then Orbach stepped in to offer his services.'

She stood and approached him. 'But... do you think these people were involved in your sister's murder? That Orbach and his people overheard someone complaining about her in that casino and... But what problem could she have posed? And to who? I think we should be careful that we don't jump to conclusions, Matt.'

He turned and headed back towards the car.

The lurch in Hardy's stomach as he saw the man return was actual physical pain. The guy sat cross-legged on the bonnet again, preparing for a nice chat. More questions, Hardy realised. And the man still held that phone and those matches. This wasn't over yet.

'These side jobs,' he began, but here Hardy found his sheer sense of outrage.

'Look, asshole, I don't know what you think I'm involved in here, but you can fuck right off and let me go. The boss likes to help his customers, that's all. It's no different to comping someone a room. Keeps them sweet. No one gets hurt. Just a bloody brick wall.'

The guy laid the phone on his knee and struck another match. 'But people do get hurt, Liam. Because this sideline of jobs you and Orbach have isn't always about boundary disputes between neighbours. Sometimes you people do bigger things, things that cause real damage, don't you? Tell me about some real damage. Tell me about one of your biggies.'

Hardy paused. At first he couldn't think, but then he could. He remembered a thing with a boat. It was the first time Anderson had come to him with a side job. And it was something a long time ago and far, far away, which couldn't possibly involve this guy and would be just fine to admit. And that was a fact he'd quickly come to accept – this fucker had been wronged in some way and somehow he'd found out who was involved.

'Yeah. Okay. Anderson called me in the office, told me a story. Said he'd overheard some lady in the casino talking to her brother on the phone. The brother had some problem with his wife, cheating on him or something with a TV star. I took her to his office so he could talk to her, but I don't know what happened, what they discussed, but I remember Anderson got me to find him the phone number of an expert on boats, and I know it had something to do with the cheating wife guy. Something in Haiti, I think. That's all. End of my involvement. So – hey, where are you going? Don't you believe me? Come back here...'

Matt didn't need to ask. Lisa was already typing and scrolling on her phone. He waited. Within a minute, she turned the phone his way. He leaned close and read, only touching the device in order to scroll through an online newspaper article from two years ago. *Haitian Times*, which was a New York City newspaper aimed at Haitian residents. Something she had found through a search using a combination of words such as TV STAR and BOAT and HAITI, probably. She was good at such things.

Haiti National Police yesterday announced the arrest of a man in conjunction with the disappearance of TV star Etienne Frecker's luxury yacht. Investigators clearing the rubble from a collapsed building overlooking the harbour at Cap-Haïtien, where the yacht was moored, found a battered but usable DVD, which contained shocking footage. *Easy on the Eyes* star Etienne Frecker's yacht was believed stolen until police viewed the DVD's footage, which they say showed a man sinking the boat. The video was recorded from a camera on a hat worn by the saboteur.

Police identified Manno Bellile and later arrested him at his home.

According to police, the video shows Bellile, 42, an unemployed bricklayer of Port-au-Prince, swimming out to the yacht during the night and climbing aboard before breaking into the cabin. Despite stringent safety features aboard the high-tech vessel that prevent such a thing, Bellile flooded the ballast tanks to overcapacity, which caused the sinking. Bellile does not deny the crime and claims that he learned how to bypass the yacht's safety features by researching on the internet, where he also purchased a lock-picking tool that the video shows him using to enter the locked cabin of the yacht.

Bellile strenuously denies any involvement in an explosion that destroyed the disused apartment building where the DVD was found – investigators discovered the cause of the explosion in the run-down tenement building to be faulty work by squatters attempting to reconnect the gas supply – but he admits going there to watch the boat sink.

Police discovered that Bellile emptied his bank account of over ten million gourdes in the days before the crime, but the accused denies he was planning to use these funds to flee the country. The money has since vanished. His motive appears to be that Frecker was seen in the company of Bellile's wife at a party, suggesting an affair.

When the man returned and assumed his position on the bonnet, Hardy said nothing.

'I just read about that little side job with the boat. Bellile was nobody. He didn't have the skills to sneak aboard a yacht and bypass security and play around with safety features so he could sink a yacht. But what he did have was life savings. Eighty grand in our money. All gone around the time that boat sank.'

Hardy shook his head, not understanding. 'I don't know anything else about that. I swear.'

'Bellile could have paid the money to sit back and let professionals sink that boat as revenge against the TV star for sleeping with his wife. But he didn't. Bellile got involved. He chose to do that mission himself, with a camera to record it all. Is that how it works? The clients don't hire someone to do a job – they recruit people to help them do the job themselves.'

'I swear, I can't help you with that. I don't know.'

'If you want to sink some guy's expensive boat, you find people who will plan everything, take care of every detail, so that you can do the deed yourself and never get caught for it. That's what you Watchdogs do. You're problem-solvers. The Watchdogs have the event recorded so they know every detail, so they can direct their client. It's also their safety net, to stop him talking. And when they've set it up so that all the client has to do is follow some simple instructions, like painting by numbers, the Watchdogs take up a position overlooking the crime scene to watch everything happen, just to make sure they can cover any problems. Like a disused tenement building on a harbour.' Here the guy narrowed his eyes and gritted his teeth. 'Or a block of flats half a mile from a waste ground.'

Hardy said nothing. The longer the guy theorised, the fewer questions got asked that Hardy didn't have answers to.

The man blinked rapidly, as if waking up out of a trance. 'Okay, Liam, we're nearly done here. Ready? But now you need to work that memory of yours real hard.'

Hardy nodded. A new intensity had overcome the guy, suggesting this whole nightmare had reached its epilogue, the endgame, whatever you wanted to call it. Maybe all the rest had been fishing, or a test. Whatever, the next question was going to be the sixty-four thousand dollar one. The reason why Hardy was tied up and covered in petrol.

'We're back to Saturday before last, Liam. Cast back your mind. You there? I'm there. I'll always be there. A girl was killed. Murdered. A... prostitute. She was dumped in a waste ground in Hackney. Name of Armstrong. Karen. Possibly she was known as Red. Tell me what you know.'

Fuck! Someone close to this guy had been killed, and he thought Hardy was involved. It explained the petrol and the matches. He was suddenly a lot more scared. 'Jesus, I don't know anything about a murder. Seriously.'

'You didn't get a whiff, Liam? Nothing from a series of little jobs that might have given you a clue? No dropped word from Orbach about some punter getting threatened by a prostitute and wanting to silence her?'

'Nothing, man. Nothing. I wouldn't have sat back and let shit like that happen.'

There was a pause. Quite a long one. Hardy lowered his eyes and literally tried not to shit his pants. If the guy didn't believe him, he might not ask again. A flying match might be the response.

Then: 'Who was the last person who went to see Orbach? Of the customers. The last big, important one. Forget people who want cats rescued from trees. The last big one that you were cut out of because you're small fry. Within the last couple of weeks.'

Hardy didn't have to think about this one. He remembered it well. 'There was an old guy, but I didn't see him. He was in the casino. Orbach called him a judge. I don't know what it was all about, but Orbach liked it enough to get me to get the guy's address, but I just passed it on to one of my men, and that's all I know. Look, if this is the guy, I had no idea that he killed someone. But it might not even be connected. That judge could have been anyone. So... was this woman someone you knew?'

But the guy had gone again.

'A judge?' Lisa said. 'That would fit your theory. Judges are old, so I imagine one might have lost his wife. Might have turned to paying for sex.'

'So he seeks a prostitute. But she knows he's got a lot to lose, so she turns to blackmail. When the casino's microphones catch the story, Orbach offers a way to silence her. But these aren't run-of-the-mill hitmen. Orbach's offer has an intriguing twist: How would you like to kill her yourself?'

Lisa rubbed her forehead. 'This is big. I hope we're wrong. But if not... There can't be many judges in London. Does Hardy know where this man is?'

'You still have that address, Liam?'

The pain in Hardy's arms was getting worse. His answer came through gritted teeth. 'No, I never had it. I got someone else to get it. A guy called Cooper. I passed it on to Orbach, but I didn't see it, it was written down on folded paper. I didn't see it, I swear. So... you said a prostitute was killed. Your wife or sister?' Hardy had no idea why he'd asked that.

'My sister,' the man said after a pause. 'And I'm going to get to everyone involved in her death. This man, Cooper, who is he?'

'Cooper is one of the casino security team. But he's nobody. Look, seriously, I know nothing about your sister getting killed. Neither does Cooper. It's all Orbach. I'm low-level, a runner.'

'What about Ivor Tchevsky?'

Hardy didn't want to go down alone, and here he'd been given a means to stick one to that grassing little bastard. 'Yeah, he knew some shit was going on. He stole that van knowing exactly what it was for. I don't know how, but he knew. But I didn't know anything. Please believe me.'

Another long pause.

'I do believe you, Liam. I believe you weren't one of the people directly involved in my sister's murder. But you might have played a role, and I can't be sure you didn't know at least a little of what was happening. And I have to make sure.'

'I wouldn't lie to you, man. Look where I am.'

The man stood up. 'That's not what I meant. I meant I have to make sure none of the guilty get missed.' And with that he struck another match, and leaned over the sunroof, and Hardy stared up at the little flame held above him. And watched it fall.

10

___

Amongst the thousands of people entering London by train that evening was a jolly Scotsman with curly brown hair and a bushy grey beard. Maybe there were dozens such. The beard made him look much older than his 45 years, but it was a look he enjoyed. He thought it got him more respect, and it hid two massive tattoos on his cheeks, put there by drunken soldiers during a drinking game they unimaginatively called 'first to pass out gets their face tattooed'.

He hailed a taxi, then he checked the address he'd written as a draft text message on his phone. He told the driver to take him to a car hire firm.

Once in a rented vehicle, a plain Nissan, he found a B&B and settled down for the evening.

Around ten o'clock, he made his way to the address in his phone. He parked a street away and continued on foot. A hundred metres up the street from the place he wanted was a doctor's surgery with a gloomy car park, and there he hid, watching the building. In his pocket was a stun gun.

A few minutes later, Darren 'Daz' McKinley exited his hiding place and moved towards his target. The sign out front said the door would be locked at 11pm, no admittance after that time, so Daz expected it to be open. It was. He walked right in like he belonged. On his left was a staircase heading up. Past, at the end of the hall, was an alcove with a tiny desk and computer and a register, but no attendant. An open door on the right emitted the chatter of people. He went up the stairs. He glanced into the chatter room as he climbed and saw old circular tables with people eating. A late dinner. No one saw him.

The stairs turned right off a half-landing. On the next floor a thin hallway ran past the stairs. Big wooden doors faced him, each with a cheap plaque boasting the name of a tree. He was after Elm, which was to his right.

He found a light switch, was about to hit it when another door opened. Two camp-looking guys came out, chatting seemingly in fast-forward. Down the stairs they went without even a glance at Daz. Gone. He turned back to the light switch.

The darkness wasn't deep because of the light filtering up from downstairs, but it was enough to show him the glow from beneath Elm's door. Armstrong was not yet asleep.

There was a linen storage cupboard at the end of the hall, door half-open, light off, empty. Stun gun in hand, Daz slipped through the gap. He was ready for a wait to get his man. He turned to shut the door a little further, and that was when he was grabbed from behind.

An arm went around his neck, and another grabbed the wrist holding the stun gun, forcing it down, into his flank. He felt the sting, the painful flutter of contracting muscles. That all took half a second. By the next half of that same second, he was on the floor, out cold.

~

When he woke, he was on a bed and two people were staring down at him.

'You okay?' said the male. It was Armstrong, he now realised. But he didn't know the woman.

He sat up and was offered a cup of tea, which he took in trembling hands. It was lukewarm. 'How long was I out? And what the hell did you do to me?'

'Eighteen minutes,' Matt said. 'Scared us. All this time and we never knew you couldn't handle your electricity.'

'Piss off. Do me again. I need to know that was some anomaly one-off, going unconscious. Who does that?'

'Maybe just little girls.'

'And what would you have done if I hadn't brought that stun gun? Sand in my eyes? Bet you still carry that shit around every day.'

'I would have choked you with tufts of your own beard, or set it alight.'

'Do me again. I'll show you that was a fluke.'

Matt reached for the stun gun, as if Daz had asked him to pass the sugar, but Lisa snatched it from him. 'You children,' she moaned. But she was intrigued by this new buoyancy in Matt around his friend. Instantly she liked Daz because he was clearly someone Matt respected enough to exit his shell for. He was even making jokes.

Matt had told her all about Daz. He had been Matt's commanding officer in 3 Para, the guy whose life Matt saved, who got him posted to Cyprus to finish his last six months serving the country without doing any such thing. And the guy who had kept tabs on the Armstrong clan after Matt left home to reinvent himself. Daz had not been asked to do this; he had offered because he knew Matt would cut all ties and would not even spend a few moments a day checking his loved ones' statuses on the various social networks.

The arrangement had been that Daz would only contact Matt if he had bad news, and only by text. It seemed wrong to offer such a tragic update so impersonally, but Daz understood Matt's reasoning. So Daz had sent the text and gotten on with his life. But he had understood that he had set unstoppable wheels in motion and that a time would come when he'd get a return text message or call. Part of him had expected to hear that Matt had gotten himself arrested, or killed. He hadn't expected a text asking for help.

'I told you to come tomorrow morning, but I expected some trick like this,' Matt said.

He had also told Lisa about the stun gun game played by his ex-army comrades. Any man who managed to stun another in the back got rewarded with half a day off from menial chores. It was Daz's way of making sure his men stayed alert at all times, so he claimed. But part of it was the practical joker in him. Daz had been the only man never to receive a shock, and the cleverest at finding ways to distract his men so he could load them with electricity. Even now, years later, Matt had figured that Daz would come early to their meeting and try to test Matt's state of alertness, and that he might even bring a stun gun for old times' sake.

Daz put out a hand. 'Can I have my toy back, please?'

Lisa was about to hand it over, but Matt snatched it. 'No, he'll do himself, he really will.' He put the gun in his pocket. Both men laughed and Daz rose from the bed to hug his former subordinate. It was a show of emotion that surprised Lisa.

'Good to see you, though, Daz. Been a long time.'

'Sorry about your sister, Matty.'

'It's fine. Don't mention it. By that I mean, really don't mention it again.'

Daz nodded, understanding. Matt didn't want to talk about his sister. The plan to solve the killing, sure, but not Karen herself. Daz went to the window, pulled the curtain a chink and glared out. 'So, tell me what's upsetting my old friend.'

Lisa looked at Matt. 'He's here to help but you haven't told him yet?' She had assumed Daz was in the loop.

'I didn't want to mention it until we were face to face.'

Daz laughed. 'What he means is he wanted to wait until I was here, so it would be for me to say no to a suicide plan.'

Matt winked at him. 'Got me.'

'No worry,' Daz said. 'I'm in whatever, as long as this ain't some Insane Jane madness about trying to hunt down your sister's killer or something like that.'

Matt's face fell, but only for a second. That was as long as Daz could hold back his laughter. 'Just kidding, pal. I ain't stupid. As soon as I sent that text to you, I knew that obsessive brain of yours would be on the trail. Five minutes after that, I had a bag ready for when you asked for my help.'

'That's very good of you, Daz,' Lisa said.

'I wouldn't be here if not for Matt, literally, not on the planet, so I owe him. I will still owe him even after this, unless it gets me killed. So, soldier, why don't you tell me what dangerous shit I just volunteered for.'

When Matt woke early the next morning, Lisa was already up and doing sit-ups. Daz had not stayed the night. They showered – separately – dressed, ate, and then drove to Daz's tacky B&B. They were getting used to such places. He was waiting outside, smoking at a plastic table in the tiny garden. He waved, didn't speak, tossed his butt into a plant pot loaded with them, and then led them upstairs.

His room had only a single bed and an armchair, which Lisa took. Daz went to a single unit that served as a kitchen and put the kettle on. 'I just left a luxury apartment for this, you know.'

'Much appreciated,' Lisa said. 'He's told me all about you, by the way.'

Daz raised his head to look at her. 'Sniper bullet or chunks of carrot?'

She got his meaning. She remembered the story of Matt saving a commander who nearly choked to death on his own vomit. 'Sorry, carrots.'

'Yeah, cheers, Matt.'

'I didn't want to lie to her,' Matt said. 'It was years ago, in Cyprus, and I was trying to impress her.'

'You were trying to get your leg over, you mean. I should have sent you to Alaska. Anyway, we're looking at over four thousand judges on our little island.'

When told that the man they hunted might be a judge – Hardy hadn't been certain – Daz had offered to get an internet whizz he knew to do some research. Daz had agreed that a judge was someone whose career could be seriously damaged by a tale of seeking prostitutes. And a judge was someone who could know dangerous people, or at least have the funds and the clout to find such.

'There's all manner of different roles and ethnicities,' Daz continued, 'so if you could have gotten him pinned down as a mixed-race tribunal judge, for instance, we'd have less than thirty to look at.'

Matt shook his head. He hadn't thought to press Hardy for such details. He convinced himself Hardy wouldn't have known. But it was still an oversight.

Daz poured three cups of tea. 'I have my man compiling names and hunting addresses, but let's put that on the back burner for now. All along I thought you brought me here for my skill and expertise, when really you're just after my money.'

He was referring to a plan the two men had come up with last night. Matt said, 'If the Watchdogs decide to check on you, they'll see a successful businessman. Born and bred in Scotland. As long as they don't look back far enough to learn you were in the army with one Matt Armstrong, brother of one of their victims, it'll work.'

'So what's the score with the drug guy you say they set up as the killer?'

Lisa spoke now. 'It doesn't help the Watchdogs to have the police still looking into what they're doing. So now and then they probably help the police close a file. They packaged up a dead drug dealer, some nobody called Declan Barthow, and they made it look good. So unless the police have a real close look, or new evidence is dropped in their laps, Barthow will go down as Karen's murderer.'

'Shocking. And this name, Watchdogs, where did you hear that? Some newspaper advert they put out?' He was joking, of course.

'Just something we came up with for them,' Lisa said. 'Maybe they don't call themselves anything.'

Daz stroked his beard. 'Always knew you had the killer instinct, Matty. But shit, two dead guys now and more planned.'

'Backing out?' Matt said.

'Hell no. Go back to my office and the daily grind? This is a holiday for me. A Thai massage, a scenic cruise, a bloody orgy on the beach – not my thing. You ain't getting rid of me. You said you wanted us together when you told your girl the plan. So here we are. Tell her.'

Lisa was watching Matt. He knew she might not like what he was about to say, so he approached the window and spoke while he stared out at nothing.

'In a casino, it makes sense to record and listen in to what people are saying down in the bars or at the card tables. Helps them work out what freebies to give, or to see who's vulnerable, or who's about to get too drunk to be allowed to stay. And people must moan about all sort of things while at the bar or slot machines or card tables. So one day the microphones catch some guy moaning about, say, his wife's ex-husband. The ex is always coming round, hassling her. Maybe the new guy has noticed that the ex-husband drives a flash motorbike that's his pride and glory, and the guy would love to see it go up in smoke one day.

'Orbach knows the guy has money, the way he gambles, so he thinks he can take some more of it. He sends someone down to have a word. "Hey, we overheard what you said. Tell you what, slip us five grand and we'll arrange for you to steal and burn the bike, and we'll make sure no one ever finds out. No big deal."

'Or how about a guy who wants to sink a boat belonging to a Haitian film star because the film star stole his woman? No big deal.

'And then one day they overhear a man talking about a prostitute trying to blackmail him and how he wants her dead. Again, no big deal. Just another day at the office for the Watchdogs.'

Matt turned to face Lisa and Daz. 'And then rich Daz here walks in with his girl and his bodyguard, and starts talking about his big problem, and the cameras and microphones are rolling.'

Lisa looked at both men, back and forth, as if awaiting someone to say it was all a joke. No one did. She looked a little horrified. 'No wonder you didn't want to tell me this, Matt. You two plan to pretend to have a problem you need help with? What problem?'

Daz quickly outlined it, but he didn't sound convinced. Lisa looked even less impressed than before. 'That's not a problem. It's more like a rich little boy's fantasy.'

Daz looked a little hurt. 'It is actually a fantasy of mine. And no innocents get hurt. I see problems, but it could work.'

She still looked unsure, so Matt said: 'It's the only way to get into Orbach's office.'

'It's madness,' she said.

Daz sucked his teeth. 'I agree there. It seems like a long shot, sergeant. We just perform an act and hope they offer their assistance? What if it takes weeks?'

Matt shook his head. 'People's problems might have ironed themselves out by then. I don't think they'd wait. If they hear of our problem, they'll react quickly. You run your own security firm, Daz. There's no boss to beg for time off. But if you can't spare the time, no problem. You can go home.'

'I didn't say that. I'm doing this. But can you do this? Maybe these people know your face. Maybe they checked out Karen's whole family, just to see who might cause a problem afterwards.'

'I doubt they did that. My face would have registered by now. I've been in that casino. And Hardy was a big player, but he didn't have a clue who I was. I don't think they expected any real scrutiny after they set up Declan Barthow. Besides, Karen was just some lowly prostitute, remember? Who'd miss her?' He hated saying such words. 'But just in case, I'll disguise myself. I'll get some nasty face fungus like yours. You still got that lovely artwork on your cheeks, by the way?'

Daz glanced at Lisa. 'Shrapnel scars or embarrassing ink?' he said to her, eyebrows raised. At first, she didn't respond, perhaps still worried about their bizarre plan. But soon she started laughing.

'I told her everything,' Matt said, laughing too. But his was mostly relief that Lisa had jumped on board the plan.

Casino. Daz had to join. Camera, no klaxon, temp card, enjoy the night and ornate doors. No problem for Matt and Lisa, either, so Hardy hadn't officially barred them the previous evening. Done. They were in. Matt took the rear, playing the part of a bodyguard, while Daz and Lisa walked on slightly ahead. They moved amongst the slot machines, noting where the cameras were. Despite believing it would be too noisy here for microphones to pick up the sound of people quietly talking, they started their act.

Daz wore a red suit and Matt a black one. From the same respectable high street retailer, Daz had also splashed out for a black dress with a slit up the thigh for Lisa. To pull this off, Daz had said, they needed to look like they oozed money. Or Daz did, at least. They certainly stood out amongst slots players in jeans, T-shirts, trainers, pullovers, and even baseball caps. Seemed the brass didn't care what you wore, as long as you brought money in the pockets.

Matt was supposed to watch Daz, as his professional body-guard, but he could hardly keep his eyes off Lisa.

'You two back on then?' Daz had asked as they watched her admire the dress in a mirror earlier.

Matt's response had been: 'Honestly, I don't know. Not sure she could handle my emotional baggage.'

'Ye jest. She's watched you beat and torture and kill a guy. I don't think she's going to run because you live in your own head at times.'

'We'll see. I'd certainly like to maybe rekindle something.'

Now, Daz slapped his shoulder. 'I'm a rich idiot with para-noia and you're being paid well to make sure nobody mugs me, even in a flash London casino.'

Matt got the point: act the part. He tore his eyes off Lisa. They swaggered around the casino. Daz took Lisa's arm in his: they were supposed to be boyfriend and girlfriend. Matt trailed behind. Daz had also paid for new haircuts and Matt's head was shaved short, to emphasise his strong jaw, give him the mean look you wanted from a bodyguard.

They left the slots area and headed down the slope to the table room, where the real money was to be lost. They pushed into a crowd near a table where some guy was pissing off the house by having some luck.

'Well, some might think a million is enough money,' Daz said to Lisa, and not quietly. 'But once you've got that first mill, you just want another. And then more. Humans are greedy.'

They headed for one of the bars and sat, aware again of the proximity of cameras and unseen microphones.

'I get bored, you see. I always need a new adventure, something cool, not just crappy stock-car racing. Not just holidays in the sun. I'm bored of that stuff. What's the point of being so rich if you can't buy fun and adventure with it?'

A few minutes later they moved again. Table to table they went, spending a little here, a little there. Daz kept up his monologue, berating his boring jet-set lifestyle. Lisa listened intently, keeping up her act of being impressed by an older man with money. And Matt followed them like an obedient dog, head slightly down, not fully trusting that his shaved head and stubbly chin and cheeks would be an adequate disguise. They had discussed at length the possibility that the Watchdogs might know who he was, or that a facial recognition system might flag up his and Lisa's faces as a pair that had been evicted from the casino recently.

After three boring hours, during which Lisa won six hundred pounds and Daz lost eleven hundred, they left the casino. Out in the car, now a flash Mercedes-Benz S-Class rental befitting Daz's jet-set lifestyle, they reviewed the night. They had seen seven or eight security guys, no bald boss-type, and they hadn't gotten the sense that anyone was worried about the disappearance of their head of security. Or that they'd been recognised. Matt had watched every face carefully, clientele included, and his inner alarms hadn't jangled. And of the pair of bozos Hardy had been with: no sign. Maybe they weren't casino employees. Maybe they had heeded Matt's warning to take a holiday far away. Maybe they were still tied up.

But on the negative side, no one had approached them, and they put this down to one of three reasons.

One, no one had been listening. Maybe they didn't listen every night.

Two, no one had cared, because Daz was just some rich guy moaning.

Three, there was nothing to intrigue the Watchdogs, because Daz hadn't mentioned a problem he needed assistance with.

They decided to try again the next night.

Daz had rented a suite at a plush hotel, just in case anyone was following them. A high roller couldn't be seen in a crappy B&B. There were two bedrooms, but all three of them stayed in the same room. Daz took a comfy sofa while Lisa and Matt slept clothed on the bed.

Later, while both Lisa and Daz slept, Matt got up and went into the living room. He was finding it harder and harder to relax, his mind constantly turning back to the question of who had sent him the clue on the betting slip. And why.

As well as the clothing, Daz had purchased groceries. Matt had specifically wanted a bag of apples, which he now retrieved. In the living room, he took the apples and a new belt he'd bought, and got to work. The tension soon slipped away.

❧

Night two was again unproductive. Daz and Lisa walked arm in arm and Matt trailed behind. He now wore sunglasses, but not to enhance his bodyguard image. His head remained still, but behind the tinted lenses his eyes roamed, seeking, analysing.

Some guy at the bar was talking about his new car and Daz got chatting to him. Loud, to make sure hidden microphones didn't miss it. Daz expounded upon speed and power and how back home in the misty Scottish Highlands he often cruised at over a hundred miles an hour. He cursed down London and its CCTV and speed bumps and one-way streets and traffic jams – how anyone could enjoy driving in such a city was beyond him.

They moved on. Dawdled some, talked some, spent some. Nothing came of it. Burly security guys came close and they stiffened, got ready for action, but always the guys walked on by, heading somewhere else. Eventually, Matt called it a night.

Back at the hotel, Lisa asked Matt about what she'd found in a waste bin: battered apples, many with smile-like slices. Matt had bought another bunch of bags of apples that afternoon. What was he doing, juggling with them?

Matt didn't answer. But once again when his partners were asleep, he hit another room with another bag of apples.

11

———

In the morning, they split up. Matt drove off in his Mondeo while Daz and Lisa, arm in arm, went shopping.

They talked and laughed like a regular couple, in case of stalkers. Matt's paranoid idea: maybe the Watchdogs watched potential clients for a period before making a move, to be sure of their sincerity.

At one point Daz looked in a shop window, but Lisa saw that his eyes were on the world reflected behind them, so she looked, too. Across the street, a man was watching them. Just some guy, nothing memorable or strange. He stood out only because they were seeking such people. He watched them watch him and briefly put two fingers up to his eyes.

They walked on. 'So you have people watching for people watching?' she said.

Daz looked at her, surprised. 'Smart girl. Matt chose well.'

'I guess that means we struck gold. The Watchdogs are interested in us. Unless your secret watcher is wrong.'

'Time will tell. Now, I'm just going to play with my balls for a moment. Excuse me.'

He slipped a hand into his trouser pocket. His fingers started to play in there, but Lisa knew he wasn't fondling himself. All three of them had practiced this trick. Daz was manipulating his mobile phone, texting by muscle memory.

Without moving her lips, Lisa said, 'I hope you took off predictive text, or you could be saying anything.'

He smiled at her.

He took his hand out of his pocket for a moment, then went back. That puzzled her. It suggested he was sending more than one message. Both to Matt? Or one to someone else?

Her own phone rang. Daz shot her a warning glance, and she knew why. The use of phones could spook any watchers. But she pulled the phone and put it to her ear.

'Mum. How's Dad?'

Daz's tense shoulders relaxed, she saw. She'd put the conversation on speakerphone and her mother's condescending tone was just too good to fake. Nobody would assume this was a chat loaded with secret messages. She made sure she mentioned multiple sclerosis, and that she was out shopping, which almost enraged her mother. When it was over and the phone was away, Daz patted her shoulder. For the watchers. But quietly he said, 'You should find time to head back and see your father.'

'I will.'

'But don't mention your father in front of Matt. Definitely don't get upset about your dad in front of him.' Louder, he suggested a shop and pulled her towards it. She went willingly, and thought hard about what Daz had just said.

In the shop, she couldn't keep her worries to herself. 'There's something else I'm not sure I should tell Matt. The man we told you about who employed the Watchdogs to help him sink a boat. Bellile. I read more on the story. Bellile had been in prison only a week when another inmate killed him.'

Daz's concerned expression matched her own, and she knew he understood. If the Watchdogs worried about loose tongues ruining their glorious events, they might have orchestrated Bellile's downfall to stop him talking. Had Karen's murderer warranted the same concern? In Matt's eyes, a killer already dead, no matter how painfully, how gruesomely, would have escaped justice. The only justice that mattered to him.

'But that's not my main worry,' Lisa said. 'You and Matt are now in their sights.'

Daz took a long time before answering. He simply said, 'Don't worry, we'll keep that in mind. And no, we do not tell Matt about Bellile.'

Only one of Daz's messages had been to Matt. He read it and smiled. They were being watched. So, they had been right. The casino was the place. They had found the Watchdogs. He almost shook in anticipation.

Then he cursed. If the Watchdogs were watching Daz, they might also be watching Matt. He was driving to his mum's house, but now that would have to be postponed – if the Watchdogs knew where Karen's mother lived and he, a potential client, suddenly turned up there...

He made a turn, then another, and pulled up outside a massage parlour. It would look too suspicious if he abruptly went back to the hotel, perhaps alerting the Watchdogs that he was onto them. So he went into the massage parlour and paid for the cheapest, quickest item on the list. A pretty girl took him into a candlelit room, but he didn't accept her touch. Instead, he said he just needed to make a call first. She was happy enough to wait, playing on her own mobile phone in the other corner of the room.

He called his mother's landline, but got no answer. Next he called Danny, who answered amid a cacophony of shouts and chatter.

'Hello?'

'What's going on there?' Matt said.

'Matt! Where are you? Jesus, we thought you'd run off again. Ignore the noise, just a palaver at work. The funeral is on Wednesday. Tell me you won't be missing it. Don't let your last memory of Karen be ash.'

His heart sank. If the Watchdogs followed him to the funeral of one of their victims...

His pause must have gotten the message across. Danny said, 'That's not good, Matt. Not good at all.'

His brain tried to think of the best response, but again the pause let him down.

'Are you investigating, is that it?' Danny asked.

He said nothing.

'Good man. Blackmail, remember that. Do what you have to do, but don't miss the funeral, okay? That would probably tip Mum over the edge. Look, I have to go. Mum wants to talk to you, so I want you to ask her where the funeral is being held. Give her a call.' He hung up without a goodbye. Matt held his mobile to his ear for a long time afterwards, as if there was still a way he could resolve this.

Had he imagined it, or had Danny sounded a little relieved that Matt was investigating Karen's murder? If so, it meant he didn't buy the story about Declan Barthow being her killer. Did he believe Matt would find the truth?

He didn't want to think about such things.

Six miles away, Daz and Lisa were still shopping. But Lisa was getting bored and wanted to go back to the hotel.

'Ten more minutes,' Daz said. Eight of those minutes passed. Then there was a moment when Daz broke away from Lisa and entered a newsagent's, pushing roughly past a young black man in jeans and a pullover who was exiting. The black man sneered at Daz then vanished. Daz was in the shop for just a few seconds, and he returned with a chocolate bar.

'Suddenly developed a sweet tooth?' Lisa said.

Daz shrugged. They walked on. Lisa scooted round to Daz's left side, put her arm around his waist, and pressed up close. It was the side the black man had passed on. Her hip pressed hard against his. And she got concerned.

When they got back to the hotel, they found Matt in the smaller bedroom, sitting on the bed, holding his new belt, doing something to it, although Lisa had no idea what. The belt didn't draw her attention, though. The apples did. They were all over the floor, mostly scattered around a six-foot upright lamp that had been placed in the centre of the room. They were all battered, some split in half, some with great rents in them. Again.

'What the hell's going on here?' she said.

Matt stood up and put the belt back on his trousers. Strangely, he didn't need to thread it through the belt loops. The loops had gone, as if cut away and discarded.

He ignored her question. 'Just in case they're watching us in this suite somehow, it's best if we separate. The bodyguard should get a separate room. But how sure are you that they're watching us?'

Daz explained what they had seen while out. It should have been good news, but nobody's face said that. Daz sensed tension and scuttled off to make tea. As soon as he was gone, Lisa stepped close to Matt.

'Daz is your good friend, right?'

He was puzzled.

'But how well do you know him now?'

The puzzlement deepened.

'I'm not sure what he's up to, but it's something.' She explained about the black man in the shop. About sliding up close to Daz after the interaction between the two men and finding no lump in his pocket where there had been one before. 'He told me he has friends watching us, but I asked him if that man at the shop was one of them and he said no. So Daz passed something in secret to a man he claimed not to know.'

Matt shrugged. 'He knows a lot of people. It was probably a personal thing, not connected to this. So he was correct to say the man wasn't one of his people.'

'He knows people? He's from Scotland, Matt. He doesn't know London that well. And he didn't say it was some old friend. He said he didn't know him.'

'Daz is okay, Lisa. It was nothing, or he would have said so. So don't worry.'

But Matt's explanation was weak, and he wasn't nearly as puzzled by Daz's behaviour as he should have been. And so she did worry.

That night Daz's Merc tore up to the front of the casino with a screech of rubber. Daz jumped out and ran up the steps while Matt went to park. Daz spoke to the doormen, telling them to fob off any police who might be looking for a guy who destroyed the speed limits and blew a red light.

An hour later he was at a roulette table, trying to encourage the other players to join him for a road race later, fifty grand to the winner, claiming the London streets would be great for a car chase by police. Matt wondered if Daz had overdone it, but liked his proactive attitude, although they couldn't be sure if it wasn't all a waste of time. The idea that the Watchdogs approached people in the casino to offer their services was beginning to seem unlikely, despite the story Hardy had told them in the minutes before he went crispy.

It remained an unlikely notion right up until the point when a black Range Rover pulled them over on a darkened side street as they drove back to the hotel.

The vehicle had more than one man inside, but only one got out. Black suit, black shirt, black overcoat and black hair. But a bright white face, which gave him a ghoul-like appearance, and with that shiny black car by his side and darkness all around, the scene looked like something out of a Tim Burton movie. They half expected him to flap his long overcoat like wings and fly towards their car.

He didn't fly. He strode quickly to the front of their vehicle and flipped open a cigarette case, a gesture designed to relax, to show he was harmless, a friend just wanting a chat. Daz rolled down his window and stuck his head out.

'Seen that trick before, mate,' he said. 'I take a fag and thirty seconds from now I'm smoking it on my ass, no car or money.'

The ghoul didn't have a friendly face, though. He continued to proffer the cigarette, but now his posture seemed to say, this conversation is going to happen, so why not get comfortable?

'Stay here,' Matt told Lisa. He flipped his door open and Daz copied. Both men stood behind their doors.

'What do you want?' Daz said to the man. 'And you stay right there. Put your cancer away.'

The ghoul flipped his case closed and lost it in a pocket. When his hand withdrew, it held a little black bag, like something you'd carry diamonds in. But he didn't offer this bag. It stayed clutched in a fist that hung by his side.

'I work at the casino,' the ghoul said. He had an American accent that was barely there.

'I'm no cheat,' Daz said. 'So shall we just be on our way.'

The ghoul flicked his head to the other side of the car and took in Matt. Matt tried to look perplexed, and a little scared. That was the normal reaction of someone pulled over on a dark street by such a man in such a car.

'You showed a love of fast cars tonight, sir,' the ghoul said. 'You like to race?'

Daz eyed up the black Range Rover. 'I can't beat that machine, if you're thinking of a bet.'

The ghoul smiled, shook his head. 'You shouldn't drive so crazily around London, because you might get stopped by the police.'

Matt and Daz looked at each other. Matt got back in his seat, a cue for Daz to do the same. Daz copied. But neither man shut his door.

'If you want to race around London without the police catching you, you need luck,' the ghoul called out. 'Or you need to control luck.' Then he tossed the black bag onto the bonnet of their car and got back in his vehicle. It moved off, dissolving away as smoothly as if it were part of the night itself.

Matt exited, snatched the bag off the bonnet and got back in his seat. He opened it and tipped the contents into his hand. Daz flicked on the interior light. Lisa leaned through the gap between the front seats to see.

In Matt's hand was a single casino chip. He could see

PEGASUS stamped on it. It was not stamped with a monetary value, however. Not a normal chip at all.

'That's for the one-armed bandit,' Lisa said. Both men looked at her. 'The big machine where you can win that sportscar.'

Daz punched Matt's arm. 'They want us back there. We're on.'

In the very early hours of the next morning, Lisa found out what the apples were for.

She woke to a rhythmic thumping, light, the beats ten seconds apart. She wrapped her bathrobe around her and went into the living room.

Matt was there, and the standing lamp was in the centre of the room again, and there were apples on the floor again. But this time they were all in halves. From the doorway, she watched Matt lay a fresh apple on top of the lampshade, just under head height, and step backwards four or five feet. His eyes darted down and up as he shifted his position slightly, working for the correct place. He put his hands on the front of his belt, like some cowboy. Intrigued, she watched as he yanked the belt free by one end, right hand, a backhand swing, flicking the length of leather like a whip. The buckle end caught the apple and cut it right in two. Both halves leaped away. Matt immediately stepped forward, took another apple from a bag on the floor, and was about to place it on the lampshade. But he froze instead. She figured he'd smelled her, or heard her raised heartbeat. He turned, looking as guilty as a naughty child.

Lisa walked towards him. He didn't move. She took the leather belt from him and he didn't object. The looped metal buckle had been filed into something sharp, like the curved end of an axe. She dropped it on the floor.

'So that's your plan,' she said. 'We can't get into Orbach's office with weapons, so you made one? What, the apples are Orbach's throat? You plan to slice his throat with that Hollywood trick?'

He didn't respond, which gave her her answer. Lisa moved to the sofa and sat. Matt just watched her.

'You plan to kill the man right there, in his office?'

He cleared his throat. 'You watched me kill a man the other day, and you're surprised that this was my plan?'

'I thought your plan was to ask him questions. Matt, we don't even know if he's involved in this. Not for sure. We don't know if any of the dead ones really are.'

'There'll be questions for sure. Before I do it. I'll make sure.'

'You killed Hardy, and you killed a pimp, and you plan to kill Tchevsky, and here I still am. So this is not about your morals.' She got up and stood in front of him.

'I'm not going to kill Tchevsky. Hardy believed Tchevsky stole a van for him. But it was bought legitimately. Tchevsky lied to Hardy, and he wouldn't have created a paper trail to his doorstep if he'd known what that van was going to be used for.'

'So he dodges the Armstrong bullet. Look, I'm on your side. The Watchdogs are not people the world should miss. Your sister was killed, and I think you have a right to take an eye for an eye. What goes around comes around. Tit for tat. All those things. It might throw doubt on my own morals, but I'm a fan, I'm on board, I'm sold. My concern is not your desire to kill the guilty. It's your safety. What's your plan for getting out of the casino afterwards? You know, that place full of security guards and cameras? What's your plan for making sure you don't get a twenty-year prison sentence?'

'Look, I don't think you should be there tomorrow, Lisa.'

'So you have no plan?' She threw up her arms.

'Everything will be fine.'

'I don't want you to go to prison, Matt. Or get killed by macho security guards. I care about you, if you haven't worked that out already.' She kissed his lips, but he pulled away.

She stepped back, shocked. 'And that would be the defensive Matt before me. The one that doesn't like to get close, in case he loses people. The one that would rather run away. Is that your plan, then? You have no care about whether or not you get caught?'

He didn't answer.

'Have you thought he isn't the only one, Matt? Orbach hasn't done all this alone. It's too big for one man. If you go to prison for his murder, you're finished. How will you get to the other Watchdogs?'

'I just want Orbach,' he said. 'And the guy who actually put his hands around Karen's throat.'

'Bullshit. There's a dead pimp and a dead security director, and those guys were super low-level. You needed to kill them, and I don't see you being content once Orbach is dead. You'll start to think about all the others, and you won't stop. But by then you'll be in prison and they'll be out here and you'll have no way of getting to them.'

He seemed lost for words.

'The escape is planned and we're getting them all, don't you worry,' said another voice.

Lisa turned to see Daz in the doorway. He had been listening.

She looked between both men. 'What are you two planning? Daz, who was that black man you passed a package to in the street? Tell me what's going on.'

Daz didn't answer, and Matt repeated his assertion that he didn't want Lisa at the casino tomorrow.

'So we're keeping secrets? To keep me safe? Oh, sweet. Well it's not happening. Tell me your plan or not, doesn't really matter. But I'm coming with you tomorrow. And you're not going to stop me.'

~

They had to queue for the slot machine.

It was a three-seater, with three big reels, one for each player, and a bigger bonus reel up top. Matt knew nothing about slot machines, so Lisa explained how it worked. On the smaller reels were many symbols, some fruit, some £s, Xs and os there, too. Three os got you nought, three Xs ten pounds, and combinations of fruit and £ signs awarded various payouts. There was also a car on the reels, and three of those got you a spin on the big reel. This one was virtual, with 256 different symbols, according to a customer that Lisa had spoken to. He even gave her the odds: 16,777,216 to one. Nigh on seventeen million to one that your single spin on the big reel would display three sports car symbols, thus winning you the vehicle that posed on a pedestal behind the machine. A black Aston Martin One-77, sleek and beautiful. It didn't have the science-fiction looks of some cars Matt had seen, but there was a spec list hanging above the vehicle that screamed its brilliance. Lots of numbers, but he understood only one of them: £900,000.

'Bloody half a year's wage, that,' Daz said. It got him a few dagger stares.

'I'm going for a drink,' Lisa said. She kissed Daz's cheek and walked away. But she didn't go for a drink; she went looking for answers. She found one at a roulette table. Her eyes alighted on a man in a blue suit who was waiting his turn in a seat. It was the black man she was sure Daz had slipped a package to. Her heart started racing. She moved closer and stood behind the man as he finally got a seat vacated by another house victim.

Back at the Aston Martin, a guy in a sheepskin coat cursed the slot machine and got out of his seat, and the lady in front of Daz and Matt literally ran forward to take her turn, holding up a chip as if it were an offering to God. She shifted her butt a little on the leather seat and cracked her fingers, as if she thought skill and mental readiness might get a sniff here. And still held aloft her chip like it was THE ONE. Matt was surprised by her confidence. Fifteen minutes in the queue and not once had he seen anyone win a spin on the big reel. Not once had someone earned their shot at the seventeen million to one chance.

Lisa followed the black man to the bar. She hung back and noticed him nod at someone as he took a seat. The second guy, who was white and about the same age, got up and went to the toilet. Lisa followed him inside.

The man went into a cubicle, so Lisa went to the washbasins and rinsed her hands. In the mirror she was aware of the closed cubicle door and the guys at the urinals craning their heads round to look at her. Most looked perplexed and embarrassed that a woman was in the male toilets, but one guy drying his hands was grinning at her. When he came towards her, she told him to piss off because he couldn't afford her, and he quickly veered away.

The white guy exited the cubicle after flushing the toilet. Lisa quickly scuttled inside and shut the door.

Meanwhile, the lady at the slot machine kissed her single purple chip, trying to bring herself some luck. Matt remembered what the ghoul had said. *You needed luck, or you needed to control luck.* He stared at the machine, using the glass to watch the room behind him. He tried to distinguish a recognisable face amongst the glittering dresses and obsidian suits that morphed and swirled and danced in the reflection. He expected they were under surveillance, but the Watchdogs didn't need faces on the ground for that. They had electronic eyes.

So he concentrated on the machine. The woman spun the reel, got nothing, and sat there as if in disbelief. The guy on her left seemed to decide Aston Martins weren't for him and got up. It was Daz's turn. He took the seat and Matt stood behind him. The shocked lady was still just sitting there, maybe trying to work out what had gone wrong with her tarot cards or whatever.

Control luck, Matt thought. He was getting a funny feeling. The chip had been given to them in a plush bag, by casino staff. *Control luck.*

Jesus, he thought. *We're going to win.* The eyes were watching. The chip was blessed in some way, but unlike the lady's it wasn't under God's charm: it contained a microchip that could trick the machine, or the watching eyes were connected to hands on magical buttons. Whatever, the chip they had been given was designed to win. Something striking was about to happen.

Lisa strode through the bar and found a free armchair. She watched the white guy who'd been in the toilet cubicle. The black guy had gone. She saw the white guy give a nod to a new player in this game. That made five co-conspirators, including

Matt and Daz. The new guy gave a sly thumbs-up to someone else, but Lisa's eyes failed to catch who. So now there were six, and counting. Her heart was really thudding now.

~

'That was quick,' Daz snorted. Matt jerked himself back to the real world. 'Thieving bastards.'

So much for a magical chip. Another victim claimed. They left the machine and their seat was quickly snatched by a man in a suit who carried a chip in his teeth and a bunch in his hands. Not 16.7 million, but more than one, and so he had a better chance than they'd had.

They found a quieter spot, near a pillar surrounded by tall, fake potted plants.

'Now what?' Daz said. 'For a minute there I really thought they'd given us that chip so–'

'Excuse me,' cut in a voice. They turned to see a man in a grey suit, middle-aged, bulky up top but with thin legs. One of those guys who lifted weights with just his torso and arms in mind, probably a vanity thing, just for looks. 'I'm Mr Carter, here to inform you that the casino manager would like a word. Nothing sinister, nothing wrong. Would you like to follow me to his office?'

Bingo.

'Stay behind me,' Daz said to Matt, who nodded like a good robot bodyguard. Off they went, single file, guy in grey leading, Daz in the middle, Matt bringing up the rear, each man five feet away from the next. The guy in grey walked purposefully and didn't even check that his guests were following. The cameras, of course, knew they were, and the guy had an earpiece that put him in contact with whoever was watching.

They aimed a straight line for the door Matt had seen the

other day, the one in the corner that was guarded by an ape in a suit. This was it. They were going in. For sure such an important door would lead them to the manager's office. To Orbach. Matt touched his belt, just to reassure himself. Five minutes from now and–

'You bastard,' shouted a voice from behind them. There were a hundred people talking, laughing, sighing, cursing, but decorum insisted on low volume and the loud shout cut through it all like a bomb blast. Heads turned, even that of the stony bull in grey. Daz turned. Matt turned.

Lisa was right there, her face full of anger. But that anger, surprisingly, was directed at Daz, who looked shocked.

'You cheating bastard,' she yelled again. 'Who the hell is Jane? I told you that would be the last time you bloody fucked some other woman behind my back, you asshole!'

Daz opened his mouth, but nothing came. He didn't know where to look. The guy in grey vanished, but into the mix came men in black, three of them. Standard security. To escort them out. *Game over,* Matt realised. Lisa stormed off as the security guys arrived.

Matt and Daz were told to leave, please, and a finger pointed at the exit, just in case they thought they should climb out through the roof, and the apes followed them all the way to the doors, and held them open, and thanked them for not raising a scene, even though they had. Lisa had vanished, but once outside in the dark, standing there like lost children, they saw her. She was across the road in the car park, lurking by Daz's vehicle. Waiting.

'She may not shag you tonight after this,' Daz said.

They approached. No one said anything. Lisa slotted herself behind the wheel. The men took the back seat.

Lisa moved the rear-view mirror slightly so she could see them. She flicked something over her shoulder, which landed between both men on the back seat. A little oblong packet wrapped in newspaper, no bigger than a cigarette case. A second package landed beside it, but this one bounced onto the floor.

She held out her hand for the keys and they were slapped into her palm. She started the engine and pulled away. They were free of the car park before she spoke. Both men were willing to wait. They knew what the packages were.

'Bombs, you bloody idiots?'

Matt stayed silent. Daz said, 'Where did you get these?'

'I saw your men, Daz. A lot of them. I followed two and found those things planted. One in a toilet. One moron planted one under a gaming table, right where people were sitting.'

'They're just smoke and noise,' Daz said. 'Subterfuge. For the escape. Which we won't need now you've ruined everything.'

The look she gave him in the mirror was pure disgust. 'And your men? They were still there, still lurking. They didn't leave. No, Daz, it was not all subterfuge. They planted those things and then conveniently placed themselves near all the security guys. For a takedown, once the so-called smoke and noise started. You better explain to me right now.'

It was Matt who spoke. He no longer sounded meek or embarrassed. And he wasn't. Lisa had just ruined his chance to get answers, and he was growing more and more angry about it the further the car took them from the casino and Orbach and retribution.

'We know damn well that Orbach hasn't done this thing alone. There were a number of them involved in Karen's murder, and I don't have names and addresses.'

'So, the great plan revealed. You kill Orbach and Rambo here sets his dogs off and they kill all the security guys?'

'Damn right,' Matt spat. 'I want them all. Every single one of them. So why did you ruin it?'

'Listen to you. All of them? There's no chance a few of those security guards are innocents? Not one of them could actually be someone hired to protect a casino? Why the security and not the waitresses or the croupiers? That seems like a better disguise than being a doorman. You really think all the men involved in Karen's death are conveniently packaged up in black suits and waiting in that casino?'

Matt didn't speak. Daz watched both of them.

Lisa was driving fast now, but she watched the mirror more often than the road. Half a mile passed before she spoke again. Now her tone was softer. 'You were doing so well until today, Matt. So well. You did research and you took no real risk. Tonight was just wading in with giant boots on.'

Matt's anger was gone, too. 'So what do you suggest?'

'Find out for sure who's involved, Matt. No innocent casualties. Do some more research.'

He said nothing.

The car pulled up back at the hotel car park. Without a word, Daz scuttled out and into the building. It was obvious he felt awkward in the middle of what was essentially a domestic. Alone with Matt, Lisa clambered into the back seat.

'I understand what it's like, Matt,' she said, taking his hand. 'You're so near the end, and you're impatient. But that'll make you take risks, and we can't take risks against these people. So, tomorrow, let's continue the research. We know Orbach's probably involved, and we can use him to find the others.'

He grabbed her, hauled her close, and kissed her. She responded with equal vigour. He tore at her dress, yanking it up, over her thighs. She responded again, tearing away his belt with ease and pulling down his trousers. She sat astride him, but he pushed her off, then yanked her legs so she lay flat, head bent awkwardly against the corner where the door met the seat. She pulled him close. He entered her slowly, but quickly built up momentum like a runaway train.

There was something about his intensity that she didn't like, and it wasn't because there was pain, because there wasn't, and it wasn't because she wasn't enjoying it, because she was. What she didn't like was that he wasn't fucking because he wanted to fuck: he was venting anger. But the intensity didn't diminish, even when his stamina started to wane. The drive was still in his eyes even as his thrusting started to lose power.

'Let it go,' she moaned at him. It served only to intensify his wild eyes. This was some kind of bloodlust expressed as sexual lust. She lifted a leg, slid it across his chest, and pushed him away, hard.

He hit the door and sat there, panting. He thumped his fist against the back of the driver's headrest.

Lisa sat up, fixed her underwear and smoothed out her dress. 'I want no part of it. It's suicide. You won't get away with it. I won't watch you throw your life away.'

'What if this isn't about blackmail?'

She said nothing, but waited for him to continue.

'What if Karen didn't make a dangerous move? What if she did nothing, Lisa? What if she overheard something, or saw something, just by accident? What if she did nothing wrong, and it was just unlucky chance that sealed her fate? That makes it so much more unfair.'

She said nothing.

'She didn't deserve this, and it'll kill me if I think even one of those involved escapes.'

And right there, with that line, her suspicions got solid, immoveable confirmation. Ever since the start, Matt's desire to find his sister's killer had grabbed him by the scruff of the neck and never let go – as Daz had said to him earlier, *I knew that obsessive brain of yours would be on the trail* – but it had been so much more than that. A need to feel needed, or important, or just mighty, combined with a revenge that could hardly be sated. The idea of a murder conspiracy had appealed to Matt because he could strike a guilty man down and targets would remain; the notion of a single killer, who already lay dead by his own hand and thus beyond justice, had abhorred and angered Matt. And now it seemed that he was forcing himself to justify his actions by laying every single modicum of blame upon his targets – and completely exonerating his sister of any wrongdoing.

Revenge was hardwired into everybody, but in Matt the compulsion had become mania and he was overrun. Had been for a long time, for even Danny's tales of his childhood brother had hinted at a boy consumed by winning against those who wronged those close to him. She knew Matt could kill everyone in that casino, and that night his dreams would become nightmares as he worried that one, even just one, survived, escaped.

'This could destroy you, Matt. If you were a bad man, you'd become a monster written about in true crime books. But you're a good man, although your obsession threatens to outgrow your ability to contain it. What if, afterwards, it's not enough? What if this crusade causes someone innocent to be hurt? You'll have both worries. They'll tear you both ways. Tear you right down the middle like two wild horses. You have no way of knowing who is innocent and who isn't. Don't do this.'

He closed his eyes. He was already torn two ways, that much was obvious. When he opened his eyes again, she saw immediately that his mind was made up. There was no sitting on the fence on this. He had come down on one side. It was the side he'd already been on.

'I want no part,' she said again. 'Maybe that will be easier for you in the long run, because you won't know about my father's deteriorating condition. You won't have to sit in dark corners, seething over the doctors who didn't cure him.'

She got out of the car and retook her place in the driver's seat. And waited. She still hoped Matt would come around to her way of thinking, that he might at least ask what she'd meant about her father, and one of the two looked like happening when he got out and stood by her door and looked ready to say something. But in the end he said nothing, and she drove away certain that she would never see him again.

12

———

Matt and Daz slept late, past ten, and woke fresh and vibrant, and sure of what they needed to do. Matt had come too far to give up now. Last night, Daz had aborted the plan, but now he called his men and told them they were on again for tonight. Same deal. 'This time,' he said, 'don't get watched as you plant your devices.'

A short while later, Daz ended a phone call and announced that he'd bloated his bank account by an envy-inducing amount.

'Flash sod. Sold some assets?' Matt said.

'Lawsuit,' Daz said. He saw Matt's frown and added: 'Something I won't go into. Business thing. A company offered a deal that I threw back in their faces. I just peeled it right back off their faces and stuck it in my pocket. Quick cash settlement. Assets take too long to turn into cash. We need it tonight, right?'

'Hopefully.'

'Better do, because my lawyer promised me close to half a million dollars. I just got about a hundred and seventy. So this better work. Hey, you listening? Or mentally masturbating over knowing the Watchdogs are going to die tonight.'

Matt wasn't listening, but not because of the Watchdogs. Any thought of them brought up horrible images of dead innocents in the casino tonight, and he shut the whole thing out of his mind. Instead, he was thinking about Lisa, who was probably safe at home by now. And in bed with her boyfriend. That thought, though, was equally unnerving.

Later they went out to put on a performance for the Watchdogs. At a fancy restaurant, Daz ate a fish meal alone at a table, while Matt stood nearby, alert, watchful. Other guests looked and pointed at Daz, perhaps figuring he might be a film star or powerful politician because of the Terminator-like bodyguard. The image would have been blown away if they had seen the car the pair arrived in – a battered Mondeo. Daz had been told last night that Lisa had gone home, but it wasn't until the morning that he learned of her mode of transport. An empty space in the car park told the story. It hadn't gone down well, but it had given Daz an idea.

Out on the street, he'd pretended to make a call to Lisa. Angry, he'd yelled into the dead phone that he was sorry, but that didn't excuse her taking his beloved Merc, and then he stared at the phone, hoping it would look as if she'd hung up.

'Bitch,' he yelled, before uttering a whisper to Matt, 'Sorry, dude. Anyway, let's go eat.'

After the restaurant, they visited a Porsche showroom. The salesman took one look at Daz's scruffy grey beard and told them the price of their cheapest model with a grin on his face, as if he expected them to scatter. When they didn't, he followed them around. And each time they stopped to admire a car, he cut in with the cost. They made sure they admired the models nearest the large windows, for the benefit of watchers. Back at the Mondeo, Daz made a show of pointing at the car, flapping his hands in annoyance, and pretending to wipe dust from it. A fine presentation of a man embarrassed to be near such an eyesore.

The pantomime was a wasted effort, though: both men had kept a careful watch for suspicious characters and nobody had tripped their internal sensors. But it wouldn't do to break routine, so, before they went back to the hotel, they performed one last act. On a quiet back street with a forty limit, Daz got Matt's Mondeo up to ninety miles an hour and practiced drifting around a corner, just to remind hidden eyes and lenses that Daz was a speed buff.

Lisa hadn't gone home at all. That intention had evaporated as she was driving away from the hotel. She was in Daz's Merc, watching the front of the casino. Earlier, she had watched the rear of the casino, but something told her Orbach might have a different way out than the sloping road into the underground car park. He had an apartment in the casino, according to Hardy, but she had also checked out a nearby residential block because he was the big dog, and such a man might want to have a second residence close to his baby. But she had seen nothing of interest, no one who might match her man.

The front, then. The establishments in the bottom half of the edifice belonged to various companies, but the upper half of the building was entirely uniform windows, maybe a single office space. There might be an apartment in there, with access from the casino. She scanned the windows, looking for movement, but there was nothing. She tried to empty her mind, focus on nothing so that movement behind the glass would draw her attention, but street activity kept breaking her trance. Cleaning staff had come and gone. A food delivery truck had been and gone. A postman had made a cameo in this production. Extras by the dozens went to and fro, just getting on with their lives.

There was a high fire exit on the side of the building, and

below was a forecourt boasting second-hand Japanese runabouts, amongst them, near the fire exit steps, an expensive-looking motorbike. The flank wall and the car lot were shabby, worn, old, yet the bike and the fire exit were new, and they stuck out like diamonds in mud. Their shiny skins shouted a bond, a connection in the same equation.

Hour after hour, her tiring brain had tried to convince her she was wrong, and it was becoming harder to ignore the voice. Even if her theory was correct, it didn't mean the man she sought would show his face. Knowing she couldn't sit here all day, she started the engine. She would get some food and return. It was as she was turning into the main road that a glint of sunlight stung her eyes. Across the road, the fire exit had opened. Quickly, she hit reverse and backed into the side street. A driver who'd paused to let her enter the traffic flow flashed his lights in annoyance.

She watched a man emerge from the fire exit and come down the switchback steps. Her hands trembled. Bomber jacket over a white suit. Carrying a sports bag and a crash helmet. Bald.

Orbach.

Back at the hotel, Matt swept a bug finder around their room. Daz had bought it earlier. He came out of the shop with it in his pocket, and a video watch in his hands. He proudly showed off the watch to Matt, just so any observers would think it was all he'd bought. Rich guy spending.

The bug finder didn't scream at them, so the room was clear. Daz called someone from his mobile. When the call was done, Daz gave Matt a thumbs-up.

Matt said he needed a bath. If this all went wrong tonight, he wouldn't get another nice soak for a long time.

Sitting back in the bubbles, he thought about what was to come. Daz's company, MacSec, provided personal security for C-list celebrities with a bloated sense of their own popularity; for corporate parties; and for people seeking another kind of backup. The latter were the kind of people who made up his crew. They were all former street thugs, drug dealers, car thieves. Daz had hired the ones he thought were led down the criminal road only because they had nothing better to do. On the straight and narrow now, but willing to veer for their boss.

While Matt and Daz faced Orbach across his office, Daz's mob would position themselves within a few feet of the casino's security team. When Orbach's blood flew across his walls and Daz gave the signal, those reformed characters were going to explode half a dozen flash-bang bombs, causing panic and disarray. In the mêlée, Daz and Matt would make their escape, but escape wasn't the primary reason for the gang's presence there tonight. As Matt had said many times, he wanted all the people involved in Karen's murder, top of the chain or not. Anyone and everyone who contributed to the performance of her death. Every cog and wheel and component. Every piece of wiring without which the machine of murder would not have worked. And he had to be sure. Liam Hardy had died for that reason. And the security team at Pegasus Casino would die for that reason. Amid the smoke and stampeding gamblers tonight, Daz's security team would pull blades and slit throats. Matt would lie low for a while, then review the situation, find out who had escaped the net, and hunt them down.

But: the note that had been delivered to him. Someone had wanted him to see this through. Someone who knew that he was hunting his sister's killers. He had reached a dead end and that someone had stepped in to help. That person had known information Matt hadn't, which made him wonder how much of the truth they knew. Was he being led by someone who knew everything, maybe a traitor amongst the Watchdogs' crew? Or followed by another enemy of the Watchdogs who had also hit a brick wall? The possibilities were boundless and headache-inducing.

Whoever it was, he had to find that person, after this was all over, or it wouldn't really be over at all. But for now he had to shut down his running mind, or the spiralling theories would spin out of control and he'd probably end up connecting Karen's murder to JFK's assassination. He sank low in the bath and let the hot water soothe him.

Orbach rode past his own casino without a glance at it, turned south, and ninety seconds later stopped across the road from the red-brick academic wing of Boston University. Lisa parked some way back and watched Orbach carry his jacket and helmet and head towards the university. She was wondering if he was a mature student when he walked right past and vanished into the building next door. A swimming pool. She followed.

The interior looked like it had once been a school. She bought a swimsuit and entered a changing room that looked like a former classroom. The place was quite busy, but she didn't see Orbach.

She found him in the pool, a former assembly hall. The ceiling was vaulted like a cathedral, and the walls were old tile, and there were murals depicting sunny beaches, as if the swimmers were supposed to pretend they were in the cool waters of the Mediterranean. Orbach's age and bald head made him stand out against a clientele of young, lithe and noisy student-types. The young female bodies made her feel old. She got in the pool close to his position.

He was floating on his back, hands free of the water and

holding a mobile phone. Lisa swam past to get a good look at her quarry. He appeared completely hairless except for his eyebrows. Sinewy and tight, but not thin, like a long-distance runner who'd recently taken up powerlifting. The water was beaded on his tanned skin as if he'd applied an oil-based moisturiser. His face was round and baby-like, especially because of his hairless head. She had the random, bizarre thought that he could play an android in a sci-fi film. Not her type of man, but she could sense that some women would think him beautiful.

So, she knew what he looked like, but now what? For the next half hour, hour, whatever, Orbach looked like doing nothing, just floating and playing some video game on his phone. She could swim and waste time and follow him after he left, or she could assume that her pursuit was going to yield nothing and try something else. Nothing here was going to help Matt, unless Orbach made a call. But he was content to float and play. He was just here to relax. Her plan was to get out of this place.

Instead, without a clue why, she splashed him.

He jerked, planted his feet on the bottom, and glared at her. After just a second, that angry look turned into a smile as he took in her pretty face.

'Sorry,' she said.

'That's fine, miss,' he said. He had an American accent, quite thick, although she couldn't place the location. 'It is miss, is it?'

A blatant come-on. She ignored it. Started to swim away, quickly. She was desperate to get to a computer. When Orbach had stood up, he had exposed his chest, and she had stared in shock. And known right then that she might have a chance to set everything right.

13

One final time, Matt closed his eyes and visualised it all in his head. Orbach standing five feet away, chin up, neck exposed; the belt ripped free in a backhand motion, uncurling like a slingshot. He didn't need to understand the forces and physics involved; he'd felt the weight of the belt buckle, and he knew his own power. Whipped around with speed and precision, that sharp metal would find no obstacle in flesh and muscle and gristle.

When his eyes opened again, he was surprised to see he had already arrived at the car park across from Pegasus Casino.

'Who knows what life will bring after tonight,' Daz said. 'This might be the last time we see each other. One final chance to back out. Just say the words, *I have pissed my pants like a terrified little boy*, and we'll abort.'

Matt's answer was to open the door and climb out. They left their phones behind, and their identification. No interruptions. Nothing carried that the Watchdogs could use against them if things went wrong. There was no more to do to delay this thing.

~

Lisa dumped Daz's Merc behind two others in the car park, blocking them in, and pelted across the road and thumped through the doors, nearly knocking down some woman who was leaving. The guys behind the counter looked up from their screens. She calmed herself, rubbed her arms as if she were cold, and walked up to the counter to give a tale about the dog eating her membership card.

Once past the inner doors, she scanned left and right, but Matt and Daz were nowhere to be seen. Again she called both their mobiles, but got only voicemail. She quickly walked past the hypnotised slots players, headed for the tables room.

And there she saw them. Walking with a guy in a grey suit. Headed for the nondescript door in the corner, the one guarded by a man in a black suit. Different ape this time, but same stern pose that said, *you ain't getting in here unless invited.*

She thought about calling out. Should have. She did not care about embarrassing them: she had done that last night. She just needed to stop them. But she waited too long. Only a couple of seconds, while her brain cycled through other options, but by then it was too late. The guard stepped aside and opened the door, and in a moment Daz and Matt were gone and the ape was back on station, as if he had never moved.

She scanned the room and saw a face she recognised. The black guy. He was here. The others of Daz's team would be here. She moved around the room, watching, thinking. She knew she could interrupt Matt's plan again, easily. A bomb scare, for instance. Ironic for sure. But if she caused trouble, it would not go down well. Matt would simply try again, and the next time he might be hastier, might forgo a plan and just dive in and make a mammoth mistake. Worse, if she got herself on Orbach's radar, the Watchdogs might get suspicious and do some deeper research and find out things that could spell Matt's doom.

She watched the black man approach one of the security guys and say something. Maybe just some bullshit line like, *Nice night, eh?* The words weren't important; the man's placement was. She looked at the other security guys and saw shady characters lurking near them all. It was going to go down, then. The bombs were planted, and the men were in position.

Now what? she thought.

She looked over at the cage, where a guy was cashing in some chips. The woman behind the counter was speaking into a radio. An idea formed.

Beyond the simple black door was a hub turned brilliant white by strip lights. A corridor ran off ahead and another pair left and right. The walls were bland, grey breeze blocks, the floor scuffed concrete. The man in grey led them ahead, to another hub with doors in the walls and a staircase that they took. At the top was a security door with a keypad. The guy in grey shielded the keypad with his body and tapped a code, and a click announced that the door was open.

Beyond was a corridor more worthy of a plush hotel than the back offices of a casino. Thick carpet, red walls, ornamental vases on plinths. More doors in both walls and one at the end with a plaque that simply said ZE BOSS on it. Matt was reminded of a penthouse apartment. He had assumed that by 'apartment' Hardy had meant a room with a bed crammed in, a TV on the wall and maybe a small drinks fridge – but no, it was looking as if Orbach had a luxurious home here.

The guy in grey had a fist raised to knock the door when his radio squawked. He hauled it and jammed it to his face.

Daz and Matt heard nothing more than garbled words amid

white noise, but the man in grey was obviously quite used to the sound quality because he nodded as he listened, with a finger raised to pause his guests. Then he put the radio away. He spoke to Daz with a grin on his face.

'I have a message for you. Apparently, your girlfriend has found the perfect cakes for the party. She says you no longer need to waste money buying too many.' He clearly found it humorous to be party to someone's personal affairs.

Daz and Matt glanced at each other, and then Matt broke character. 'What did she say, though? What was the exact message?'

The guy in grey shrugged. 'She just said to tell you she has found the ones you need.'

He turned to knock again. When Daz glanced at Matt for a second time, his pretend bodyguard jerked his eyes, as if saying, *Let's go*.

'Wait,' Daz said to the guy in grey. 'I need to speak to her. Where is she?'

He told them she was downstairs. He huffed. 'The manager has a strict timetable. Are cakes really that important?'

'I can't piss her off,' Daz said. 'You don't know what she's like. Women.'

He clearly didn't like his time being wasted. He led them back down, and got on the radio and ordered someone else to give Orbach the news that his guests would be delayed by ten minutes.

He left them outside the black door after pointing across the room. They saw Lisa at the cage, talking to the woman sitting in there. When Lisa saw them, she jerked her head towards the entrance. They met her halfway, but said nothing. Lisa remained silent, too. Ears were listening, of course.

Outside, a safe distance from eavesdroppers, Lisa said, 'I

know who you need to kill to avenge your sister. Get in the car and I'll explain.' They crossed the road, to the Merc. Lisa took the front and Daz and Matt the back. And then she told her story.

'We've all heard of the Ejection Tie Club, right?'

Both men nodded. It's an exclusive club, although there are thousands of members. To qualify, you have to be a pilot, and you have to be sitting in a Martin-Baker ejection seat when an emergency forces you to bail out. Oh, and you have to survive. Your reward is a membership card, certificate, a patch and a tie and a pin, or a brooch if you are female. Members often wear the ties and pins so they know each other. You get invited to dinners and air shows.

'Anderson Orbach is one of them.'

She had their attention fully now.

'I followed him today,' she continued. 'He went to a pool. That was when I knew, because I saw his body. He had a scar along each collarbone. Very faint, the sign of good surgery, but I saw them. Sometimes men die ejecting from aircraft, and sometimes they get out unscathed. But there are injuries. A common one is, upon launch, the shoulder harnesses cut so tight they often snap both collarbones. Same time, same type of break. Hardy already told us Orbach was ex-army, and the odds were too high a soldier could receive the same kind of break – to both collarbones – some other way than by ejector seat. I'm certain Anderson Orbach got those scars because of an ejector seat. But the Ejection Tie Club has no member called Anderson Orbach.'

Here, both men furrowed their eyebrows – hadn't she just said that Orbach was in the club?

'He must have cast aside his old identity,' she answered. 'But if that were the case, then when Anderson Orbach came into being, someone else must have disappeared off the face of the Earth–'

Matt understood that notion perfectly well, having left a series of identities in limbo as he skulked around Britain over the years.

'–so I did some checking based on Orbach's rough age, when he was likely to have served, and cross-referenced it with similar-aged tie club members with whereabouts unknown. There were a few ejector seat survivors who were later listed as missing in action, but only one man's story jumped out at me. He was Lieutenant Colonel Teddy Riley, 3rd Infantry Division. He ejected from an F-16 over United States army base Fort Stewart in Georgia, in 2001. He healed up and later he was in Iraq, and that was where he went missing...'

'...In Fallujah in June 2003, attacks on American soldiers were down. The role of the 3rd Infantry Division was turning to peacekeeping, although they weren't happy about this, being an offensive unit. They were helping with trash collection, electricity maintenance, water supplies. Attacks were still occurring, but there was no record of such an attack in the case of Lieutenant Colonel Riley. The Defense POW/MIA Accounting Agency listed him as missing, but they had no idea what happened to him. On June 21st he was in a vehicle, manning a twenty-four-hour guard post in the city, when he simply vanished. The vehicle was where he left it, untouched. No damage to the guard post, no evidence of weapons discharge...'

'...He simply did not respond to his radio and was not there when they went to look for him.'

On her phone, she showed them the English language website of a news agency called *Al Bawaba*. June 23, 2003. Page 4 of a section entitled simply, 'Your Area'. Each man read.

In the Jolan district of Fallujah, a local man called Mulik

Ralik was found dead in a juice bar he ran with his brother. The windows were barred due to the volatile environment and the doors were locked from the inside. A noose hung from a rafter. Ralik was found on the floor, under the noose, dead by strangulation. Yet the death was no suicide, because around Ralik's neck was one of his own belts, tied tightly.

The prime suspect was Ralik's brother, Abdel Maslih, who was missing along with all his savings and most of his clothes, although he left behind a wife. It was common local knowledge that the brothers did not get on, for Maslih often accused Ralik of some underhanded trick in their past, usually something to do with ownership of the juice bar.

Matt looked up at Lisa, none the wiser. She said, 'The day before Lieutenant Colonel Teddy Riley went missing, soldiers from the 3rd Infantry were working on electricity problems in that portion of the Jolen district.'

Here she paused again before her final sentence: 'Lieutenant Colonel Riley was with another soldier when he went missing from that guard post, and neither man was ever found. Lieutenant Colonel Teddy Riley and Sergeant Damon Mason. Two soldiers from the same unit, both vanished at the same time.'

She was done. There was no more to say, but then she didn't need to. Matt understood what she was getting at. He needed to pace, as he often did when things were tumbling and forming in his mind, but stuck in the car all he could do was fidget.

Matt said, 'So it's not a leap to assume this is how it started. Two guys, good friends, fellow infantry soldiers, are doing their civic duty in a war-torn city when they learn about a local man and his bastard brother. Maybe they overhear him, or maybe he just starts complaining to the nice fellows from America who are rewiring his kitchen. Maybe he's seen how tough and merciless the soldiers are, or he just feels they have nothing to lose in a city full of so much violence. Surely, he thinks, these nice American men who laugh and joke with him and drink his tea will help him. They have guns, and he's seen some of them kill men before. What will one extra kill matter? It's nothing to them, but for Maslih, he will have his revenge against his evil brother.

'So Maslih offers them money. Maybe they agreed only to help him commit murder, or Maslih insisted on doing it himself. Two soldiers made good money for a day's work and realised they could be on to a profitable enterprise. So they do it again, and again. By now Riley and Mason are missing in action, but they don't care, because they can hide in Iraq. Money gets good, it becomes a business, and business blooms, to the point where these guys leave that country and set up here, and open a casino, and load it with microphones and cameras that aren't just for player safety.'

Lisa reached over and grabbed his hand, squeezed it tight. 'Which means you now have a number, Matt. Maybe Riley and Damon employ a hundred people to help with the dirty work, but they are the bosses, the ringleaders. Riley and Damon are the only two you need. Two men.'

It was almost a plea, and he gave her theory deep consideration. Two men, former soldiers. And the guy who paid to kill a prostitute. Three men. No more wires or cogs. It seemed unlikely right now, but once those men were dead, it might just satisfy his hunger. For her sake, he hoped so.

A pause. She watched both men. 'So what do you do now?'

'We go back in, pick up where we left off,' Matt said. He saw Lisa about to object and added, 'But we stand down the bombers.'

Daz nodded and pulled out his phone.

When he got out of the Merc to make the call to his people, Lisa clambered across into the back seat. Matt looked at her in equal parts puzzlement and apprehension, as if he feared a repeat of the last time they'd sat together in a vehicle. But she positioned herself against the door, with a clear two-foot gap between them.

'Your brother said to me, "Your pain will become his pain again".'

He knew she was awaiting a reaction, a question, so she could explain. But he was already on her page. He knew this conversation was past due. So he did not question; he explained.

'The army was a brotherhood. My brothers had problems in their lives, and they shared them. But it was all as a backdrop to the threat of war. Somehow, that made it easier. Made it acceptable. I didn't fret for those brothers.'

'But you worried about everyone else in your life. You can't deal with people close to you being hurt. It tears you up inside, and you can't control it. You get consumed by the urge to fix their problems. You didn't join the army because you felt you were a burden after your mother found a new partner.'

It wasn't a question. 'Yes. I'd been unable to leave her because she needed me. But when John moved in, she had someone else to protect her. I was able to convince myself that she'd be okay. Plus, John was an extra person to worry about. So I cut contact. With everyone. I joined the army.'

Daz had finished his call, she saw. But he was keeping his distance, aware of their conversation.

'It got worse after I left the army,' Matt said, staring at the headrest in front of him. 'How's this for a bizarre story. My mother ran a shop. She complained about a customer she'd not been paid by. I got upset for her, far more than she did. I wanted to do something about it. One night I sat outside their house in my car, waiting. Thankfully nobody came out. But it scared me. I needed out, and, in a blink, I fled my life again.'

She waited, her eyes urging him to continue.

'But even moving away was only a temporary fix. I tried not to socialise with people in whatever city I settled in, but even so I started to warm to co-workers, and then I started to worry about them. And when it became unbearable…'

'You ran again. And again. City to city, over and over.'

He nodded. 'Empathy, sympathy, care, those are normal things. But not to this degree. This need to even the score, to get back at those who've done wrong… it's not normal. I have an obsession with revenge. I dream about everyone who's ever wronged me or someone I know. I dream myself hurting them. And there have been times when those dreams… aren't dreams.'

'The army was a comfortable place for you. The brotherhood. The only time you've ever been happy. But you left.' She took a deep breath. 'You left because of me.'

He knew she was aware he couldn't deny her claim. He couldn't lie. He chose silence, which was answer enough.

'I was puzzled by your attitude whenever I mentioned my father. You'd never met him, so what could be your problem with him? Even Daz warned me not to talk about him in front of you. But now I know why. You left me because my father was ill. I felt pain. And that pain became your pain. It was easier for you to run than deal with it. It still is.'

Again, he confirmed with tight lips.

'My father will die at some point, Matt. I will deal with that in the typical way. A lot of sorrow. A lot of pain. I might need someone like you around me when that happens.'

'I wouldn't be good around you. Like you said, I'd blame a doctor for not finding a cure. Or the lawnmower manufacturers for faulty equipment. Just like you said, my revenge desire is outgrowing me.'

'So you'd rather run away again? Did you think about what that might do to me? My boyfriend runs away when I need him the most.'

He stared at her, shocked.

'Yes, I just called you my boyfriend. How could you not be, with how we feel and our history and why we're in this car park? I want you with me. My father will die, Matt, but I want you there when it happens. My pain will become your pain, but we can deal with that. Maybe with me around, we can... keep you stable. Maybe after this, you will have spent so much time boiling with revenge that it'll burn itself out. You threw me away when you learned about my father's multiple sclerosis. You will not throw me away again. Leave me if you can. I almost dare you. Try it.'

She was grinning, and he forced a grin back. She took his hand. 'What happened to your sister was the worst possible pain you could have endured, and one that you can't run or hide from, but it hasn't killed you. You're functioning normally. You're the same Matt I always knew. Maybe, now that you've experienced the worst possible offence someone can commit against those you care about, you're finding it easier to control this obsession. Maybe, one day in the future, I'll stub my toe on a crooked kerb and you won't feel the desire to burn down the council offices.'

He gave a nod, but this gesture wasn't totally forced. She pulled him close, to whisper into his ear:

'But sometimes revenge is totally acceptable. So let's go and do this.'

Anderson Orbach's deep tan gave him a Hispanic look. He was stood behind his desk in a pale-green suit and a black tie, a friendly arm extended over the mahogany desktop. There were two chairs in front of the desk. Daz shook the offered hand and sat. Orbach did not offer the greeting or the second chair to Matt, obviously aware that he was nothing but a bodyguard.

Matt stood behind the free chair, upright, stern, playing the role. He got a glance that was long enough only to register his size, but after that the casino manager's eyes never left Daz. Behind his shades, Matt tried not to look at Orbach. The very presence of one of the men who might have orchestrated Karen's murder was unsettling. He put his gaze on a wall safe behind and above Orbach's head. Tried to clear his mind. It was all he could do to avoid leaping over the desk and grabbing the man by the throat.

Orbach wasn't one for small talk. He got straight to business. 'You need my help, so would you like me to explain what I can do for you, Mr McKinley?'

Matt flinched. Orbach knew Daz's real surname, somehow. Daz, though, remained motionless, as if he might have expected this. There was nothing to worry about. Any look into Daz's life would reveal exactly what they wanted these guys to know: that he was a Scottish businessman down here for a mini holiday. As long as their scrutiny had been cursory, it should remain a secret that Daz had once served in the British Army with one Matt Armstrong, brother to one of their victims.

'Your men, when they rudely accosted me last night, mentioned something about, shall we say, making luck. Now, in my mind, that sound like a veiled accusation of cheating. Is that what this is about, Mr Orbach? I have a little lucky run here at your casino, so of course I must be cheating?'

Good. Matt was impressed by Daz's performance. They had discussed their tactic for this meeting. Orbach's men had at no time mentioned why Orbach wanted to see Daz, and nobody was supposed to know about the little side business Orbach operated. So they had decided that complete ignorance was the way to go. Daz would assume, as anyone would, that the matter at hand was a casino one.

Orbach leaned back in his chair. The monkey in grey who'd escorted them here was beside and slightly behind his master. Now each powerful seated man and his standing protector looked like a strange reflection of the other pair. Matt noticed that the monkey was glaring at him. It wasn't mistrust. Matt gave him the same stare back, turning his head to point his nose directly at the man, so he would know Matt was looking. Two alpha dogs sizing each other up.

'Cheating?' Orbach said with a laugh. 'No, Mr McKinley. If you were a cheat, you would not be in this room. You would be in a room far less cosy.'

Daz laughed too. 'So why am I here?'

Now Orbach leaned forward. Matt tore his gaze off the monkey. The urge to do it now was hard to resist, but resist he did. He could step forward, grab the belt, yank, whip, and send the buckle into a fast and lethal arc into the throat, tearing it open, spraying blood everywhere. But the image was a fancy. The distance was wrong, and he needed Orbach standing. He had trained his eye and hand for that exact height and range until it was imprinted upon his muscle memory, like driving, and he couldn't trust himself to achieve a killing blow if he had to move his feet and aim for a sitting man. So he would wait.

'Mr McKinley, do you know how many people last year were actually imprisoned here in Britain for traffic offences?'

Daz laughed. 'Mr Orbach, you are not cold-calling at doors selling double glazing. Drop the sales pitch. I'm sitting here because you clearly have something to offer me that I'm interested in. Why don't you get straight to the point? Let me help you. Some of your men gave the impression this is about cars and driving fast. I've made no secret of my love of such things over the past few days. What are you offering me? A race? For money?'

'A chase, Mr McKinley. A chase.'

'Tag with cars, you mean?'

'London has more CCTV cameras than any other city...'

He stopped when Daz, with a laugh, held up a hand. 'Sales pitch, remember? Tell me what you're offering me. And since you aren't a charity, what it will cost me, too.'

'A hundred and fifty thousand pounds.'

'You're offering?'

Now Orbach laughed. 'That's what you'll pay. For that, you'll climb into a fast car and drive fast around London.'

'I do that anyway, Mr Orbach. All for price of £1.30 or so a litre.'

'You'll weave in and out of traffic. You'll jump red lights. You'll mount pavements. You'll turn heads. It'll be a thrill-a-minute the likes of which you have probably already dreamed of. You'll take up space in the local newspapers.'

'And I'll take up space at Her Majesty's pleasure.'

'All you'll ever see of the police is their flashing lights in your mirrors, Mr McKinley. That's what I'm offering you. Blunt and simple. A police chase around London, with no comebacks. That's the thrill you desire, right?'

'And you control the police, do you? You'll arrange it so they just chase me, make it look real? Is that really the same thing? That's like having sex with a blow-up doll, Mr Orbach. Excuse the foul imagery.'

'It will be real, Mr McKinley. I will not pay the police off, I will not dress up my own men in their uniforms. They will be real police officers and they will really try to throw you in jail. I will make sure they do not catch you.'

'And how could you do that?'

'If I told you, it would probably sound like a sales pitch. You don't want that.'

'And if it goes wrong?'

'It never goes wrong, Mr McKinley.'

It went bad for Manno Bellile, Daz almost said, meaning the Haitian man that the Watchdogs had failed to protect – and then possibly killed to ensure his silence. And that would have ruined everything. And then there was Matt, who should never learn that the man he hunted might also have been eternally quieted.

Instead he just nodded as if liking the idea.

'So you have men who can fool the police? Drivers who will throw them off? Men who can arrange it all so that I'm untouched?'

'I have experts at my disposal, yes.'

'Is this your side business, Mr Orbach? Do you always bring your guests up here and offer to solve their problems?'

Orbach gave a little laugh. 'Actually, I usually conduct my business in such a way that my casino isn't involved. So feel privileged that I chose to meet you here. And this isn't a problem you have, Mr McKinley, it's a desire, and I also make fantasies come true. I prefer to think of myself as in the business of... satisfaction, guaranteed.'

'You guarantee? Then I'm in. But if the police grab me, I might have to mention your name. You understand? Your promise is not fit for purpose if I end up in a cell. Giving your name in that situation would be akin to complaining to Trading Standards if a toaster does not toast.'

'It will not go wrong. That wouldn't be *satisfaction guaranteed.* But if the police capture you somehow, I will compensate you five times what you paid. That shows my confidence.' He smiled. 'I always toast.'

'Then let's do it. Right now. I'm game.'

'Two days, Mr McKinley. This needs to be set up. I need to

arrange the arrival of my expert. He's a plane ride away and will not perform if suffering from jet lag. Surely two days is adequate?'

Daz laughed. 'One expert? I thought you meant a great team. Men with radios at every corner, men with binoculars on tower blocks, men in cars to block the police and clear a path.'

'No. One man can do wonders these days with a computer that has sway over other computers. There will be other players in this production, of course, along the lines of what you just said. But they are worker ants. I require my expert. So, two days?'

'I want to meet this superman.'

'You will not meet him. No one meets him. He is not a sociable chap, I'm afraid.'

'Two days? Okay. I was being rash. I need time to think about this anyway. So what do I do?'

'Go away and think. I'll be in touch.'

'Got a pen?'

'No, Mr McKinley. I don't need your number or address. Please go and hide. My finding you will at least partly prove my skill.'

Daz paused. Here it was. The moment. He had agreed, in part, to the deal, and now they had to do what businessmen did after a deal. Daz stood and stuck out his hand, for a shake.

Orbach rose. Daz felt Matt shift, moving directly behind Daz. Orbach circled the desk, stood before it, and stuck out his hand. Daz shook.

'One more thing, Mr Orbach,' Daz said, and then, as planned, he sat. He removed himself from Matt's line of sight. Five feet between Matt and Orbach. 'My man here.'

Orbach's face grew puzzled, and maybe a little suspicious – or did Daz imagine that part? But his eyes rose from Daz, to Matt, with a slight movement of the back of the head, to uncover the throat. Perfect. Daz put his eyes on the goon in grey, who was still behind the desk. Daz would be over that desk and on him before Orbach's body hit the ground.

Orbach leaned forward and stuck out his hand, and Matt shook it right over Daz's head. Then Orbach returned to his chair and the goon in grey came towards them, one hand raised and open as if to say it was time to leave.

Daz looked at Matt as they turned to go, shocked. He saw nothing on that face that said fear, reticence, cold feet. The chance to kill Orbach had passed, and Matt had allowed it.

14

———

'The car we'll be in will have to be destroyed or abandoned, and wherever that happens will become a crime scene,' Matt said.

They were sitting in Daz's Merc, Daz and Lisa up front, Matt alone in the back. As he spoke, he stared out the side window, a smile on his face. It was the smile of a man at peace with developments. He had worn the same expression since they'd left the casino, although he hadn't said a word until they were in the car.

'The police will swarm all over the car, and the Watchdogs will want to know what they say,' he continued. 'The expert Orbach mentioned will be watching them from somewhere nearby. It's him, it's the same man. Sergeant Damon Mason, the other Watchdog. He's the man who watched the police at Karen's crime scene from a tall building. He's the other man I need. If I had killed Orbach in his office, we would have lost the chance to ever get this expert. But now we know where he'll be, and that's why we're going to do the job. We'll do the job and we'll find this expert, and I'll kill him, and then I'll go back to Orbach's office and slit Orbach's throat.'

When he returned his gaze to Daz and Lisa, he caught them

exchanging a worried glance. 'Go through with the job?' Daz said, watching Matt through the rear-view mirror. 'Pay the Watchdogs to arrange a car chase across London?'

The confidence in Matt's smile was also in his eyes as he returned Daz's look. Yes, he was sure, Daz realised.

'Okay,' Daz said. 'It's your show, so we'll do it. We'll wait for them to contact us. But they want a hundred and fifty grand, Matt.'

He knew it was the wrong thing to say the moment the words left his mouth. Did he really expect Matt to give up because of the cost? He got the response he expected.

'I'll pay you back. It's on, it's fucking on. I'm going to get them all.'

Again, Daz and Lisa exchanged worried looks.

The next day Daz got a message from an unknown number. Puzzling. It gave simply a postcode and said NOW. The postcode was in Surrey, thirty-odd miles away.

Daz and Matt drove there, while Lisa went shopping. The location turned out to be a former airfield now called Longcross Proving Ground. It was a racetrack, where you could get a day's insurance to drive a fast car around. The place was busy with drivers who'd got a gift experience for their birthday. Their car was stopped at the gate by a guy in a tracksuit. They expected to be asked for a membership card or voucher proving they were allowed access here today, but instead he directed them to House Thirteen. He appeared to know exactly who they were.

One of Orbach's men, no doubt. Matt committed his face to memory. Just in case.

The Houses were actually a row of garages in a long building backgrounded by woodland. Some were shut, but many were open. Cars were pulling in, their time here done, while others were exiting and joining the racers on the track. The vehicles were mostly fast breeds like Porsche and Ferrari, but there were a number of drivers bombing standard production cars around. Men in oily coveralls milled about and made-up girls sauntered here and there, maybe seeking someone rich and single or just awaiting the return of a partner.

House Thirteen was in the middle, and when they pulled up outside, the door immediately rumbled open. Another guy in a tracksuit came out, and a guy in a suit jacket and jeans. Jeans carried a briefcase. Matt and Daz got out. Lisa stayed in the car.

Inside the garage was a Suzuki Swift in red. It was a hatchback, quite cool-looking, and Daz and Matt exchanged a look. If this was the car they were going to drive, it made sense. Small and nippy, just right for London's crowded streets.

They knew why they were here, but Daz said, 'Why am I here?' He was careful not to say *we*: this was meant to be all about Daz, of course.

The Tracksuit pointed at the car. 'Mr Orbach wants to whet your appetite. You get to try out your car. But first you need to go with the doctor.'

The man with the briefcase – the doctor – waved Daz into the garage.

'Why do I need a medical?'

Tracksuit said, 'We have to pronounce you fit to drive.'

Daz laughed. 'You mean Orbach wants to make sure the thrill won't give me an embolism and I can't pay?'

'Something like that.'

Daz went with the doctor. There was a table at the back of the garage, grimy and oily, and there they did the blood pressure and other tests. Matt waited with Tracksuit. He saw another man, or just his legs. He was under the car, on his back.

'This thing had work?' Matt asked.

'Sure has,' Tracksuit boasted, then launched into a list of enhancements given to the Swift. Matt nodded approvingly, although he didn't really know what the guy was talking about.

The mechanic slipped out from under the car and came over. He wiped his palm and shook Matt's hand. He was middle-aged, short, stocky, but had a wiriness to him that showed fitness. A guy who didn't look like much, but Matt knew what to look for and he knew the guy would be able to handle himself in a fight. His eyes captivated Matt. They were different colours, a condition known as heterochromia. He tried not to stare.

'Name's Jenkins,' the mechanic said. His accent was English, but nothing Matt could place. He handed over a business card. It said that Antony Jenkins sold fitted kitchens. 'Get you a good deal on anything you want.'

'Not here for kitchens, I'm afraid,' Matt said. 'So they hired you to make sure this baby runs well?'

'That too. They called me because they said they needed a driver. Word of mouth, I guess. I do rally racing in my spare time. Although I have no idea who I'm working for or what exactly is the job? Better not be a bank job. Not a getaway driver, I hope.' He gave a laugh.

At the nearby table, Daz looked up. 'Driver? For me? No, my man here is the driver.'

Tracksuit looked a little puzzled. 'No, I was told we supply you a driver.'

'Not happening, pal. My man drives me.'

'Er... I'll have to consult the boss about this.'

'Go do that.'

Tracksuit left the scene, possibly to find a phone. Into the uncomfortable silence that followed, Jenkins, the mechanic, gave a little laugh. 'I'm good, guys, really am.'

The doctor declared Daz fit for the job and quickly vanished, work done. Jenkins got in the car and reversed it out of the garage. With a moment alone, Daz stood close to Matt. 'The doctor took blood and prints. They might be giving me a thorough checking out.'

Matt nodded. 'So no lies. We tell them exactly how we know each other. They won't connect us to their last job unless they're looking for a connection.'

They walked out into the pale sunshine. The Swift was waiting, the driver waving them over. Matt climbed into the back and Daz took the front passenger seat. Jenkins looked at Daz and said, 'Sorry. Do you mind having the back seat?' His window was open. He whistled into the air.

'Up front,' Daz said. 'I'm paying.'

Just then, there was a knock on Daz's window, and they saw a boy standing there. He had green snot dried under his nose and wild blond hair. He was no more than four. He started trying the handle.

'That's my boy, Bobby. He loves the front.'

It turned out that Jenkins' son, Bobby, loves to join his father during any car-related jobs. Daz reluctantly got out, once the boy had realised he needed to move away from the door. He slipped in the back, while Jenkins pulled a booster seat from the passenger footwell. Bobby clambered in and waved and said hello, full of joy, but he was crying five seconds later when he couldn't put his seatbelt on. Jenkins helped him, soothing him. Matt could see that Daz thought the boy was cool – but he had a role to play.

'Is this a joke?' Daz snapped. 'How can we see what this car can do with a child inside.'

Jenkins said, 'My boy's not scared of speed.'

'That's not what I meant. Don't you think it's a risk? What if we crash? Get him out, please.'

'I don't drive without my boy.'

'Then you don't drive, pal. We don't need you anyway. My

man is my driver.'

It became a full-blown argument, right in front of the boy, who was captivated. Matt was happy to watch Daz work, but things got tense when Daz said, 'You don't give a shit about his safety.'

Jenkins raised a hand and Matt got ready to intervene, but instead of a strike the mechanic yanked down his sleeve and showed a tattoo. Latin writing.

'*Filius est pars patris*,' he said, angry. It was meant to be a poignant moment, maybe, but Daz didn't think so. He just laughed. There was a moment's silence, broken by the little boy.

'Can we go now? Daddy's good at drivering.'

That made Daz laugh again. 'Okay, fair enough. The boss has spoken. Let's just do it.'

Daz and Jenkins shook hands to show there were no hard feelings. Then they got to it.

Afterwards, the car was shut in the garage. Jenkins made an exit with his boy, but Tracksuit was back. With bad news. 'The boss says no. It has to be our man driving.'

Matt gave a slight nod to Daz. 'Fair enough,' he told Tracksuit. The man then handed over a tiny slip of paper. It had bank details.

'Half needs to be paid before the job. This account number is good until midday two days from now. After that, if the seventy-five thousand pounds isn't there, Mr Orbach will take it as a no and the job is off the cards. You do not contact him again, even if you change your mind. One chance. Understand?'

Back in their own vehicle, they updated Lisa, who afterwards said to Matt, 'You agreed to let that man Jenkins drive. Which you definitely don't want. So I imagine you're working on a plan to get in that car come the day?'

Matt nodded.

'Good to be back,' Daz said as he walked into the hotel room. 'My feet are killing me. Make tea, Matt, please.'

'Sure thing, Mr McKinley.'

Daz put the TV on and sat with Lisa on the sofa while Matt made the tea. They chatted about the great day they'd just had. They chatted about Daz's desire to take the guys up on their driving offer, but he would have to think about it for a while. They chatted about the weather and other bullshit. All of it innocent and designed to tell the Watchdogs that there was nothing to worry about.

They'd strung one of Lisa's hairs between the door and frame to see if anyone had entered their room while they were out. The hair was broken. It might have occurred naturally, but they couldn't risk that and now had to assume the room was bugged. They couldn't use the bug finder this time in case there were cameras.

But while they talked, text messages flew between them. By written word they discussed the impact of having their room bugged, if indeed it was. Clearly the Watchdogs still needed to make sure they were on the level. If the room was bugged, then surely they were still being watched while out and about. Neither would be problematic if they made sure they said and did nothing suspicious. But Matt was concerned about his sister's funeral, which was tomorrow. He could not attend. He could not risk being followed. If Matt was spotted at the funeral of one of the Watchdogs' victims, it would undo everything. So he definitely couldn't go.

But he definitely had to go.

Eventually, he put such dire thoughts aside and retired to his room. He lay on his bed and read a book, but could not concentrate on the story. He couldn't shake Karen from his head, and he couldn't shake the knowledge that a hidden lens might be recording him right now. And in the brief moments that he did clear his mind of such worry, the void was filled by an image of the person who had left Matt the clue on a car windscreen. He had no description, so in the visions the subject was a black shape, like a computer avatar for a user who had uploaded no picture. Matt imagined the faceless person on street corners, at high windows, lurking in cars, eyes on Matt constantly, following his progress, like a parent watching their baby trying to solve a simple jigsaw. His clenched jaw and shoulders soon started to ache.

Around 10pm, he turned off the light and lay still. He could hear the TV from the adjoining room. He could hear Daz and Lisa talking about inconsequential things, still playing a role. He wondered what would happen at bedtime. Daz and Lisa were supposed to be lovers – would they share a bed to keep up the pretence now that their one secret place, this hotel suite, had been compromised?

He got his answer half an hour later. Raised voices. He sat up. Daz and Lisa were arguing.

'I'm clearly not enough for you if you go sleep with some other woman, you asshole,' Lisa shouted.

Daz's reply was quieter and Matt didn't catch it. Lisa told him she should end it, he wasn't worth her, even said she would probably have dumped him ages ago if not for his money. Matt smiled as he realised what was happening.

'I'm going to sleep in the other room, away from your stinking ass,' she yelled.

'Yeah, good,' Daz yelled back.

The door opened and Lisa came in. 'Matt, I need space, I need time away from that cheating fool, so I'm going to share this room tonight.'

With effort not to grin, Matt said, 'I don't know, ma'am. Mr McKinley is my boss and...'

'Sod him, the twat.'

Daz had overheard, clearly: 'Matt, let the silly mare stay in there and cool down.'

'Yes, sir.'

Lisa shut the door. She turned the light off and slipped into his bed. Matt started to object, but she laughed and whispered, 'Strange things happen behind closed doors.'

He got her point. He imagined men in a stuffy room, wearing headsets, staring at monitors that showed two black humps under the covers, dangerously close. Not calling Orbach about suspicious activity, but gossiping and laughing to take the tension off a long night shift.

'Don't worry about the funeral,' Lisa whispered. Then she kissed his lips and put her head on his chest. He started to grow hard at the thought of her so close and began to panic, sure she would notice and be appalled. He tried to think uncomfortable things to beat it down, but nothing worked. By the time he was fully erect, desire overrode everything else and he decided to go with it, but then he heard the deep, slow breaths of one already asleep.

The next morning, Daz and Lisa *made up* over tea and toast and then said they were going out. Daz needed Matt to drive and he should wear his black suit. Matt asked where they were going. The answer was: a picnic. He waited for a text to reveal the real location, but nothing came through. In the lift riding down, he asked aloud, and all he got was the same answer. A picnic. This answer puzzled him, because for sure there was no bugging device in the lift or on their clothing. But he didn't question it.

There was a hire car awaiting them outside the hotel, parked next to the Merc. A sleek limousine with tinted windows and side-facing bench seats in the back. Matt drove and was directed towards Lee Valley Park. At the very first set of red lights they hit, Daz quickly told him to swap places. Daz took the driver's seat just as the light turned to green. Facing Lisa in the back, Matt gave a smile.

Later, the limo took a turn near East London Science School and drove alongside the Channelsea River. Matt barely noticed, his mind on Karen's funeral, due to take place anytime now. Lisa talked about the nice weather today, which just pissed him off, although he didn't say so. He was about to bring up the funeral when the car drove through an arch in a low brick bridge over the river and stopped in semi-darkness. Daz turned to him.

'You've got three hours.'

The door was yanked open, and there stood a guy in a black suit, like Matt's. Matt clicked on. The two men quickly swapped places and the car continued on its way.

There was a motorbike leaning against the brick arch, a leather jacket and helmet dangling from the handlebars. He watched the limo drive another hundred metres and then pull up in a riverbank car park filled with vehicles. There were sight-seers at picnic tables. He watched Lisa and Daz exit the back of the limo. Daz had swapped places with the other guy, because the driver's window came down a portion and a black-suited arm dangled out.

Matt smiled for the first time that day. He grabbed the helmet and the jacket, and ten seconds later turned the bike around and got the hell out of there.

But where to? His brother, Danny, had told him to call Mum to get the location of the funeral, but Matt hadn't made that call. He badly regretted it now. He figured Karen had probably not been a churchgoer, so the funeral director would have contacted the vicar of a local church to arrange the service. The nearest church to his Mum's house was St. James's. But even if the service was there, it was doubtful the vicar would permit Karen's burial in the grounds. This in mind, Matt parked his bike outside some nearby shops in case he quickly needed to follow the coffin to the burial site after the service.

Unfortunately, there was nobody in the church. No early bird family member he recognised, no vicar awaiting the group. No sinner begging forgiveness or homeless guy passing time or janitor sweeping the floor.

In a rising panic, Matt pulled his phone and scanned Google for nearby cemeteries, figuring the service would be held at a chapel in one of–

Then he remembered something Danny had said: *Don't let your last memory of Karen be ash.*

Cremation.

He rushed back to his bike, still searching Google even as he dodged pedestrians. By the time he started the engine, he had a list of crematoria on a map. He picked the nearest and aimed for it. Twenty minutes later he was in the right area, but couldn't find the crematorium. He was about to stop and ask someone when he spotted a BMW like Danny's at the side of the road. Across the road was a florist's and a place that sold headstones – dead giveaway. A thin gate in a high hedge bore a simple plaque that told him he was in the right place.

He bought flowers and entered the gateway and followed a thin path alongside a road. Both led to a car park outside the entrance to a wooden, single-storey building. Outside the doors stood four men in suits, one of whom was Danny. They were all smoking. Ten feet closer and he recognised another face. His uncle, Josh, Mum's brother. And now all their faces and names flooded into his head.

Danny spotted him, looked shocked, then happy. He fished his wallet out of his jacket and waved it.

'They prefer donations these days, mate,' he called over. The other three guys turned to look. Matt felt a wave of nerves, like a shy person thrust into a group. But he washed it down with the thought that many of these people would not have seen Karen for years, either. Theirs had not really been a fractured family, but they weren't exactly the Waltons, either. He would not be viewed as some outcast or black sheep.

He shook hands with men he hadn't seen in years. They were sorry for his loss. He said he was sorry for theirs, while not believing a word they uttered. Inside, he was introduced to other faces he knew, and hands were shaken. They treated him like a loving brother who had been by Karen's side every day. He didn't correct them. But he was aware that this meant they hadn't been informed of his seven-year vanishing act. Or they knew and also knew the correct things to say at a funeral.

After doing the dutiful family member thing, he excused himself and went to the toilet, just to compose himself. When he returned, recorded music was playing and the vicar was approaching the pulpit. Everyone was standing before a chair. The coffin had entered the room and was sat on a catafalque. He had no idea who had brought it in. He half expected everyone to sneer at him because he'd missed something important.

The music ended and the vicar bade everyone to sit. Matt saw Danny on the front row, next to a woman in purple. His mum. He couldn't bring himself to approach them. He chose a chair at the back and rushed to sit before he was the last to do so.

The vicar began a sermon in which he talked as if he'd been in Karen's life to fill the void Matt had left. But Matt grew tense as he stared at the coffin. He needed to see Karen's face. He realised he hadn't seen her in the flesh in a long time and didn't even know how she wore her hair these days. But the coffin was not open. He feared a viewing would not take place, and was tempted to speak up, or just get up. He was scared about his mind. How would he react if he didn't see her? Would this spoil his mind, turn him insane? Or would the same happen if he did see her, pale and dead?

He got up and left. He didn't know why. He felt Danny's eyes on him, and a quick glance back confirmed that his brother had his head turned and was watching him. He realised he hadn't seen his mum's face during this entire event, and unless Danny told her he'd made an appearance, she was going to assume he'd missed yet another important day in their lives.

He rushed out into the car park and took a deep breath. His mind was in turmoil. He was not good at dealing with this type of emotion. But a moment later he saw something that turned his brain to something he was more in tune with. Something he dealt with easier. Danger.

There was a man in a parked car watching the building. He was twenty metres away, far side of the car park, but even at this distance and through a windscreen cloudy with reflected sky, Matt recognised the man.

He should have turned, gone inside, or just hidden his face. But he froze for a second too long. He saw the man's expression change. Saw recognition, then surprise, then shocked realisation.

The ghoul from the other night, the one who had given them the casino chip. One of the Watchdogs' men, watching the committal of one of their victims. He was here and he had seen Matt.

The ghoul started his engine and pulled away.

He got to his bike and turned a left at the corner just as the car was reversing out through a set of open double gates about forty metres away. He was prepared to give chase, but the car reversed away from him as it entered the road, which meant it was going to drive right at him. He pulled in behind a parked van. He heard the screech of tyres as the car shot forward. His head worked out the time frame, based on how fast a car would pick up speed, and at the desired moment Matt gunned the engine, max revs, first gear. The bike leaped out into the road, pulling a wheelie that became a somersault as it threw itself out from beneath him.

To the man in the car, the bike pounced from behind the van like a cobra and he had no time to avoid it. Bike and car collided with a screech of metal, and then brakes as the car skidded to a stop. The bike bounced away. By the time it had cleared the shocked driver's windscreen, Matt was already pulling open the passenger door. The ghoul was still transfixed by the view from his window and that gave Matt all the time he needed, which was about one second. He slammed a hard fist into the ghoul's temple, which propelled his head into the driver's side window hard enough to crack it.

Matt grabbed the man's hair with his right hand, yanked the head back, and drove his left fist hard into the exposed throat. Matt heard the crack of the hyoid bone giving up. One could choke to death with a busted hyoid, which Matt helped along here by yanking the ghoul's head forwards and down, chin onto chest, and rising to put his weight on the guy's shoulders. Trapped in the seat, seatbelt on, jammed between his door and Matt's legs, the ghoul had no chance unless some heroic passer-by intervened.

But Matt had already determined that there were just a handful of people nearby, and they were staring at the bike lying fifteen metres away in the road. By the time their attention turned to the car, a few of them running towards it, the guy was done. Not dead yet, but no more threat.

Sitting astride the gearstick, which was in second, Matt stuck his foot on the clutch and twisted the key to start the stalled engine. He got into a position to work both feet on the pedals, still sitting with the gearstick between his legs. In second gear, he slowly accelerated away, building up speed, passing the heroic pedestrians before they got close. He stuck his hand between his legs and jumped straight to fourth gear, holding the wheel with one hand, still crushing the unconscious man against his door just in case he woke with renewed energy.

He found a quiet side street and stopped. Yanked the guy over into the passenger seat and climbed into the driver's zone. That was when he saw the mobile phone in the footwell.

The battery had come loose, thankfully. But the device had clearly been dropped or banged during the crash, which probably meant the guy had been calling in his discovery. Telling his boss that one of the guys who'd just hired them had attended the funeral of someone they killed. Hopefully the call had failed before anyone had answered. Because if the guy had gotten a warning out, it was game over.

Driving again, Matt used his own phone to call Daz.

'Good news, Matt,' Daz answered. 'An hour ago my watchers just watched two of our watchers pull their Watchdog-ordered watching.'

'That's confusing.'

'I know,' Daz said with a laugh. 'I worked on that line for comedy value. What I meant was Lisa and I had two separate guys following us. My guys saw them take phone calls at the same time and then leave. I think they've seen enough to think we're legit and they've ended the surveillance. We're good to go. No need for you to sneak back through a bloody sewer.'

'Well, that would be fine timing, because they wouldn't have liked seeing what I just did.'

'You're like a two-year-old. Leave you alone for five minutes, you get up to mischief. What did you do?'

'Put it this way: I need your guys to get rid of a body,' Matt said. 'And that bike you gave me.'

Silence. He laughed as he realised what Daz must be thinking. Matt had gone to a funeral and now he was asking for a body to be disposed of. He quickly explained what had happened and laughed again when Daz sighed with relief.

'Look at you, loving this. Freak. Is the man actually dead?'

'No, but he needs to be. Or we will be. Queen's Wood is near here, so I'll go there. Send some guys and shovels.' He gave the location of the bike, still lying in the road. 'The police will race you to the bike. Don't lose. And don't tell Lisa that I killed another guy. I don't want her to think...' What? He didn't even know.

Daz laughed. 'That you're a serial killer? Three makes you one, according to the FBI.'

'Piss off, Daz. Anyway, this was an accident. Sort of.'

'Ah. One of those. Okay, go to a spot in Queen's Wood and call me so I know exactly where to send my guys. Listen, you think this guy was following you?'

'No, not by the shock on his face when he recognised me. I think we're good, like you said. I think he was sent to watch the funeral. Not us. Maybe see who turned up. A precaution thing. After-sales service or something. Or maybe the guy was just morbid. Don't know.'

'You know this makes two of the Watchdogs' men you've put down, right? They could start to get suspicious.'

'Well, both men are missing, so they don't know anything bad has happened yet. And guy two might not be missed for a while. Maybe he's only to report in if he sees something he doesn't like. Or maybe Orbach and Mason will assume the guys went AWOL to go do other things. They know all about going AWOL, don't they?'

'We'll see,' Daz said. 'But just in case they still are watching, I'll pay them their seventy-five thousand pounds right now and see what happens. A way to know for sure. Until I call back, you just stay hidden.'

Well, with a body in the car, he wasn't about to go cruising round London.

~

Matt didn't have to wait long. Seven minutes later, he got a text message:

we're on! get ready for a memorable day. will call day after tomorrow at 6pm. be ready to go.

Daz then called to explain. He'd forwarded a message he'd been sent by the Watchdogs, which he'd received just seconds after dispatching his electronic payment to the account number they'd given him.

'Matt, my boy, if they were watching, it would have looked very suspicious that we killed one of theirs then immediately paid the money. So they don't know about your dead man. He didn't warn them and nobody saw you do him. I can't promise the police won't nab you for it in days to come, but the Watchdog surveillance has gone.'

Matt wasn't that convinced. 'Maybe they watched and have decided to have us killed. Let us do the job, then wipe us out.'

And now Daz wasn't convinced. 'They'd be Insane Janes. Too risky. We could turn up at the job with an armed mob, or the cops. No, they know nothing.'

They decided to give it another two hours, just to make sure. Daz and Lisa roamed London, and their watchers watched for watchers, but reported nothing. Matt met two members of MacSec at the edge of Queen's Wood and left them the car and the body and walked away without a word. He hailed a taxi and went back to the crematorium, but by then the funeral was all over. And the bike had gone. Pedestrians were going this way and that as if nothing had happened. There were no cops talking to witnesses. The scene looked inert. Good. He moved on.

That evening, they didn't leave the hotel. Because Daz was paying for the job, he insisted that Matt should treat them all to dinner in the restaurant. Matt was short of money so Lisa paid. Afterwards, they returned to their rooms. Again, wary of surveillance equipment, they kept conversation safe. Later that evening Lisa and Matt stayed together in Matt's room, leaving Daz alone to watch MMA videos.

She called Adrian.

She was in the bathroom, using the phone, talking quietly. Matt couldn't help himself and lurked by the door, listening. He couldn't make out anything she said, her voice just a low rumble through the thick door, but there was a moment of laughter that pulled at his heart.

He scuttled into the bed as he heard her finish up in the bathroom. She came out and looked at him, but he closed his eyes and pretended to be asleep. She was still on the phone. 'I'll be there in a few hours,' he heard her whisper. 'Can't wait to see you again.' She hung up.

He continued to pretend to sleep as she got dressed. And as she left the room quietly.

Matt got up a few minutes later, dressed and left the hotel.

He drove to his mother's house and shut the car off. All the lights were off in the house. He didn't know why he was here. He felt like an immature child running home. Why was he so upset that Lisa had scuttled off back to her boyfriend? They had separate lives, cities apart. If she felt her role here was done, she had no reason not to go home.

He tried his mother's front door, but it was locked, of course. He didn't want to wake her, so he cranked his driver's seat back and got comfortable. In the dark, and the cold, his mind returned to Lisa. She was part of his upcoming plan, so he hadn't wanted her to leave. But that was only part of the reason. The rest was jealousy. He wanted her all for himself.

Matt woke hours later, staring at the roof of his car. His phone said it was seven in the morning. He considered waiting until his mother was up and talking to her, at least to explain why he'd left the funeral early. To make everything good between them before he left again, maybe for the last ever time.

Instead, he started the car.

He drove around London until the rush hour traffic of office rats became too annoying to allow mellow thought and so he parked and put his seat back and cleared his head. Or tried to. But he couldn't shake Lisa from in there, and knew if he did that Karen would appear instead. Or the blank avatar man. He worried about Lisa and he was upset with himself for running out on his mother, and he was still torn up inside about Karen. His life was consumed and ripped at by the women in it.

He drove on. Found a petrol station and bought a map of Britain. Ran his eyes over it, seeking to attach them to some place that sounded tranquil but might also be cheap. After this, if he wasn't in jail, he'd need a new place to live. And a new job. And a new name. But it was a cursory glance, because so much could go wrong before then.

Eventually, around ten, he drove back to the hotel.

And found Lisa waiting for him.

There was a suitcase on the bed.

'Where the hell have you been?' she said, as if she hadn't been the one who crept out last night. Still in shock, he pointed at the suitcase. Told her he'd overheard her conversation with her ex-boyfriend.

'Silly idiot thought I was coming back to him,' she said. 'I only pretended to so I could pack my things. I'm gone for good. I'm yours for good.'

He didn't know what to say.

She stepped closer to him. 'Matt, I'm a phase kind of girl. I obsess and then I forget. It's why I don't keep jobs for very long. It's why I left the army. It's why Adrian, although fun, was never going to figure in my life for long. But around you I feel different.'

His mouth opened, but all he made was a noise, as if something had shorted the circuits between brain and voice box.

'When you contacted me the other day, it was the first time I've thought about my future in a long time, Matt. Know when the last time was? The only other time?'

Of course he didn't. 'When we dated back in Cyprus,' she said. 'I'm beginning to think that must mean something.'

Now she touched his face. And he found his voice.

'I didn't see my sister's face at the funeral, Lisa. That's going to haunt me, I'm sure. And I didn't speak to my mum there. And I pissed off my brother. I'm awful at social things and because of that I messed up, and I don't know what to say to you, and I'm worried that whatever I do say might just go ahead and do the messing things up thing again.'

She stepped past him and locked the door. 'We'll sort all that. But for now, let's not worry about it.' She took his hand. 'And we don't need words for what happens now.' And then she pulled him towards the bed.

Two phone calls came to Daz's phone in the small hours of the next day. The first was from Matt. Matt's phone alarm woke him at four. That day he'd napped quite a bit because they'd stayed in the hotel room, staring at maps, imprinting London on their brains, so Matt was all full up on rest and jerked wide awake almost instantly when his phone trilled. He turned off the alarm, called Daz, heard it ring in the next room, then heard Daz groggily speaking into his ear.

'Send your men now,' Matt said. He hung up and was asleep before Daz had finished the call he made to a man a few miles away.

The second call came at just past seven. A voice he didn't know said, 'Mr McKinley, I've been asked to tell you that the appointment needs to be delayed. We'll be in touch in a few weeks on this number–'

'Wow, no, why?' Daz moaned. 'I paid my first half. What's the problem?'

The man didn't want to say, but Daz pressed, and eventually he spoke to someone else who'd got back to him and explained. The driver had had an accident and couldn't drive. They were seeking a replacement, if he cared to wait a few weeks.

Well, he didn't. 'We'll use my guy,' he said. 'Guy's good. He can drive like a pro. You give him the orders, he'll come through.'

The man went off again. Daz listened to faint voices as he spoke to someone far from the phone but in the same room. Then he was back. 'Okay, we'll use your guy.'

'So what happened to your driver?' Daz said.

'A fall,' the man said, then hung up.

No fall at all, Daz knew. He had called his men after the episode at the racetrack and one had followed the driver, Jenkins, once he'd left. They'd followed him home, to a simple, bland house in an urban maze, and a few hours ago four of them had paid him a visit. They had tried to break into his car, but used no caution, no finesse, just a healthy dose of clumsiness. The noise had woken the driver and down he had come to ruin their plan, but of course his appearance had been part of their plan. They'd attacked him in his own driveway.

A few bumps and bruises just to satisfy themselves, and one broken elbow as per instructions. 'Don't go overboard,' Daz had ordered. 'Just make sure he's in no state to drive a car.'

More hours spent going stir crazy in the suite. Matt stared at maps and consumed energy drinks and slept again. If all went to plan, this would be over in just a couple of hours. But he was prepared for a long, hard night.

Daz left the hotel for a period and sent his men out to check one final time to make sure he wasn't being watched. The report came back positive, as in negative. At four he, Lisa and Matt went into the hotel's rear car park to meet MacSec.

There were seven of them, all hard, young individuals in a variety of gear, everything from a lady in a trouser suit to a guy in a tracksuit to a girl in a long dress to a chap who looked like part of a road construction crew. A snapshot of London's typical make-up. In a crowd none would appear linked to another, and at any location you put them at least one would fit in like part of the furniture. A tool for every job.

Matt applauded their logic. He had expected a motley gang in torn jeans and sleeveless tops and tattooed to hell.

A girl in a black skirt and white shirt who looked like a clothing store assistant stepped in front of Lisa, who had looked her up and down and clearly was surprised that such a sweet-looking girl was part of this crew. The girl looked Lisa up and down and blew her a kiss. Lisa mimed knocking it aside.

'Meet the fine girls and boys of MacSec,' Daz said. 'All ladies and gentlemen who would be in coffins or cells if not for me.'

They started disputing this, some with colourful language, and Daz laughed. 'Shake hands with the toughest man you'll ever meet and his equally tough friend,' he told his crew. And their hard looks mellowed as they all shook hands with Matt and Lisa. Then they all got down to business.

There were four off-road bikes, so each rider would carry a passenger. Matt memorised the plates because the bikes were bland and typical, nothing that would draw attention in any city in the world. Each vehicle had a pair of black leather outfits draped over the seat, so the riders would be inconspicuous once on the road.

The four bikes would shadow the red Suzuki Swift containing Matt and Daz in a box-pattern, meaning they would create a square around the vehicle. One ahead, one behind, and one each side. Each pair of riders would carry a radio and a map.

Lisa was to ride with Judd, the gang's unofficial leader. He was the black guy Daz had passed a package to seemingly an age ago. He was wearing a suit with the shirt's top button closed to hide as much as possible of a tattoo on his neck that looked like a barcode right across his throat.

Everybody knew the plan. And everybody knew the goal: the capture of a man nobody had seen. But Daz had not told MacSec the reason why. They knew not to ask.

At five o'clock the bikes, labelled one to four, tore out of the car park and took their positions, creating a box with the hotel in the centre. This was because nobody knew which route Daz would take once he left the hotel. Matt and Daz went into the lobby café and sat and drank tea and waited, with Daz's phone in the middle of the table.

15

———

Daz's phone beeped at exactly six. The message was a postcode. By the time they had reached their car, Matt's phone already had an RAC route planner showing him the location of that postcode.

'Fourteen miles,' Matt said.

They headed west. The location was Horton Road, just off Junction 14 of the M25. Nearby was the A3113, which took traffic to Heathrow Airport. But there was nothing here. As they took a left turn off the A3113 before the southbound exit onto the M25, Bike Two and Bike Three went past them. One and Four had already circled the junction, returning onto the A3113 to find a place to stop. The Mondeo curved left and they found themselves surrounded by trees and fields, although the noise from the busy junction nearby was a constant soundtrack that ruined the peaceful setting. The road turned right, but an offshoot pointed towards Stanwell Moor. Some way along the offshoot they could see low buildings. A business park.

'Now what?' Daz said. He spoke into his radio, explaining to his team that they had stopped.

As if on cue, his mobile beeped.

TIM'S TUCKER. GRAB CAR FIRST.

The message made no sense. They took the offshoot, driving slowly, until the business park revealed itself on the right from behind high bushes and small trees.

'Here,' Matt said. He drew the car up to the edge, where there was a partially hidden lay-by on the left with a car parked there. It was the red Suzuki Swift.

'Christ, it's on. And look.' Daz showed Matt a map on his phone. It was an overhead view showing their location, and the significance of a thick green line around the western half of Junction Fourteen was obvious to both of them: Greater London's western boundary. So the race across London was going to be exactly that: all the way across London.

Daz spoke into his radio while looking at the map. 'Guys, give up the chase for the minute. We think the race is going to be from here all the way east. It might end at the City, but if it goes all the way across Greater London, I think we're looking at the Boroughs of Bromley, Bexley or Havering. I want a bike in each and one in the City, but be aimed back here, west, just in case we find out we're not going the whole way.'

He got affirmation from his team then turned to Matt, who said, 'For real? Right across London? Nearly forty miles, all chased by the cops?'

Daz shared his concern. 'Even at eighty miles an hour, that's twenty-five minutes of hard driving and chasing. The cops could have a hundred roadblocks up in that time. And ten choppers. Maybe we're missing something. We can't avoid the cops for that long. We can't race round London without hitting a traffic jam.'

'We'll see,' Matt said as he opened his door.

The Swift was unlocked. As they got in, they caught movement from the trees off to their left. Some guy who'd been there and now wasn't. A watcher for sure. Maybe someone whose job it was to make sure nobody stole the car before the client got there. He vanished from their minds when Daz's phone beeped again.

UNDER SEAT.

Both reached under their seats. Daz lifted a box of six eggs. Matt found a plastic bag with the ignition key and a hands-free headset. They both looked at the eggs.

Matt put on the headset. Immediately he jerked as a voice spoke in his ear. It was loud enough for both men to hear. *'For the next hour or so, you do everything I say, do you understand, driver?'*

Matt's eyes widened. The voice was American. This had to be the other one, the second Watchdog. The Expert. The man who had probably arranged the entire operation to kill Karen. Who had stood at a high window half a mile away from her body and viewed the comings and goings of the police as they processed the crime scene. He had met Orbach, and now he was in voice contact with the second man he had to kill. He tried to picture a face, but knew he could be wildly wrong so shut it down.

'Who's paying who here?' Daz said.

'You're paying me to make sure that when you next get out of this car, it isn't into handcuffs. Listen, driver, you do everything I say and you do not use your initiative, and you do not doubt a single thing, okay? Failure on your part puts us in big trouble. Say you understand.'

Daz laughed. 'What's with the *us* part? I don't see you in the car.'

'I understand,' Matt said, and it hurt his head to kowtow to a man who had had a hand in his sister's death. Her murder. He looked at Daz, who was indicating his radio, pointing out a problem: they couldn't use it if the Expert could hear everything they said.

'I will direct you through London, but it is vital that you hit checkpoints at exactly the second I require. That means even if the police are hot on your tail and I say drive at nineteen miles an hour, that's what you do. Deviate and it all goes wrong, and the handcuffs come out. Understand?'

'I said I did.'

'So what now?' Daz said.

'Now you wait three minutes by that dashboard clock. Give them time to settle. And then you drive to the business park a hundred metres ahead.'

'And then what? Give who time to settle? And what are the eggs for? A mid-chase break?'

'Glad you asked,' said the Expert.

The business park had a caravan in the car park. It had a hatch with a guy in an apron peering out. A sign on the roof said TIM'S TUCKER. There were three plastic tables and chairs out front and at one sat two police officers. Their patrol car was in one of the parking spaces. Matt and Daz had watched it turn in four minutes ago.

Each cop was tucking into a jacket potato and chilli from a plastic container when the Swift turned into the car park and parked sideways on to the tables, thirty feet away. Neither officer looked up as Daz exited on the far side of the car.

The first egg was dead on. It hit one of the cops on his wrist as he was lifting his fork to his face. Gunk and shell sprayed both men. Both jerked and looked up as egg number two flew between their heads and hit the caravan. By the time they had gotten to their feet and pushed back their chairs, all six eggs had flown and they were splattered yellow. The Swift was screeching out of there before the cops had gotten halfway towards them, making them about turn abruptly. In his rear-view, Matt watched them racing back to their vehicle. And they were on their radios.

'What if they saw the registration?' he said.

The Expert said, '*Did you sign a logbook into your possession?*' and Matt took that as a promise not to worry about such a thing.

He was told to take the next left, along a dirt track that circled the trees, then a sharp right. At the end was the A3113. Traffic was one way, racing past right to left, westbound. But the Expert said, 'Faster. Eastbound, to the right. Keep at sixty-one and do not slow. Don't worry about the blue bike but watch the fun in green.'

'What?' Daz said as the Swift bolted out of the side lane like a bullet. Right into traffic. Matt braced for a hard impact from a truck coming from his right, but the way was clear because thirty metres away a blue bike, going slow, was weaving all over both lanes. And slowing the westbound traffic.

The central reservation was fenced, but there was a gap. As if men with an agenda had lifted a portion. Tape and traffic cones made it look official, but Matt doubted it was. Steering one-handed, he blew across two lanes and through the tape and yanked the wheel right, joining the eastbound traffic that welcomed his arrival with a blare of horns. As he straightened up, he stared out the side window and watched a green car, old, long and heavy, race past the bike and past the side lane.

Or not.

The police car exited at speed, perhaps because the driver fancied his driving skills or because God had promised him a collar this evening. The green car slammed it dead centre, driver's side. Matt put his eyes forward after that, but he heard the rending of metal and the screech of brakes. And the loud noise of a bike engine, no doubt the rider who'd slowed traffic getting the hell out of there.

'*The speed limit is fifty. Go seventy and do not slow until I say otherwise. Hope you're up to this.*'

'I could go a hundred,' Matt said as he stamped the accelerator and blew by a tipper truck in the left lane. The trees lining the left side of the road blurred past. Cars in the westbound lane were beginning to slow and queue because of the accident ahead of them.

'*Do that and it all goes wrong. Seventy. Do not deviate.*'

'Was that it?' Daz said. 'A hundred and fifty grand for that? Where's the other cops?'

'*They're coming,*' the Expert said. '*Lots of them. That was but a prologue. The real fun begins soon.*'

The way was calm. They went straight over two roundabouts and down a dual carriageway south of Heathrow Airport. Daz looked for planes on the ground, but the runway was empty. Then the view was obscured by vast, long warehouses and lines and lines of trucks. On their right they saw houses, some town or village.

'Any police stations in that town?' Daz said.

The Expert said, '*That's Stanwell and it's in Surrey. It's the Metropolitan Police after us.*'

'*Us*, he says,' Daz said with a laugh.

Past another roundabout, and then Daz saw a terminal building with planes attached on both sides, like kittens sucking at a mother's belly. Onward, east off a ring road and towards a flyover. Although thirty metres out from it, the Expert directed Matt to slow down to thirty, leave the road and push over grass and down a shrubbery-encrusted bank that someone had conveniently cut a car-wide path through. Then came the next tense part, because the road ahead was another dual carriageway and he made them turn right, which was the wrong way.

'Are you doing this just to make me wet my pants?' Daz yelled at the Expert as they dodged cars to a chorus of horns. But soon a gap in the central reservation appeared and they took it and emerged onto the opposite side, where the traffic went in their direction. The limit was fifty and he told them to stay there.

'Everyone's doing the same speed as me right now,' Daz moaned. 'Are they paying through the nose, too?'

But ahead the cars started to slow at traffic lights. *'Keep straight on, but you're on your own at this junction,'* the Expert said.

Matt clutched the wheel tighter as the red lights approached. Still only one hand on the wheel, which Daz warned him about. Both lanes were taken, but there was enough space down the middle to allow them through. But through the gap they could see cars whizzing across their path.

Luckily for them, two kids ran out into the road, throwing water balloons. Or was it luck? Maybe the Expert had simply tried to give them a scare. Cars stopped, horns went yet again, and the way was magically clear. One of the kids saluted the Swift as it crossed the junction. Not blind luck, then. Daz laughed, but Matt was wondering about kids and their involvement with the Watchdogs.

'You're a good man,' Daz said. 'I may tip you extra when I can put a face to the voice.'

'Save it,' the Expert said, *'because we'll never meet.'*

Matt and Daz looked at each other with a grin.

They got as far as Hounslow before the cops found them again. Until then, to keep up the tension, the Expert sent them at dangerous speeds along roads made thin by parked traffic, through more red lights at numerous junctions, and shouted last-second orders to swerve down side streets. But Daz complained again and again about the lack of cops.

The Expert said, *'We decided that you should be able to claim you drove right across London, one side to the other, ten boroughs, with the police hunting you. Not all of it would be possible with the police hot on your tail. But they are still after you. Already a description of your car is doing the rounds. The Metropolitan Police employs over forty thousand men and women, but even that's not enough to place an officer on every corner. However, you're about to get lucky. Take the next left onto Harper Street and run down the bus shelter just past the chemist's.'*

They approached Harper Street and Matt leaned into the corner as he made the left, and Daz saw his face and marvelled at it.

'Look at you,' he said. 'Aren't you just loving this.'

Matt had been, but he cut it now. Not because of Daz, though. Because this was serious business and he shouldn't be enjoying himself. But he checked himself in the rear-view and found the smile wasn't fully gone, and he had to admit that this was fun. The reason he was here was anything but enjoyment – closing the gap between his killer hands and the men who murdered his sister – but this was the kind of thing Matt enjoyed. He did not enjoy social situations, couldn't find pleasure in chatting at a barbeque, would feel uncomfortable at a dinner table... but stick him in a scenario where he needed his wits about him, where danger was always ready to pounce, and he thrived.

Harper Street was all commercial places and full of pedestrians, but the bus shelter, thirty metres down on their side, was empty, and maybe that was a Watchdog design and maybe it wasn't. It was all tempered glass around a plastic skeleton and the car tore through easily. The shelter dissipated into nothing like a burst bubble. Twisted arms of plastic soared for five seconds. Fragments of safety glass landed in people's hair thirty metres away. And plenty of people saw it happen, including several men in a forecourt nearby. A police station forecourt. Cops standing around screamed STOP, as if that sometimes worked, and then scrambled to their cars.

And the chase was on. Shockingly, the Expert told Matt to slow down to thirty. He did, and was forced to watch the road open in front of him, while behind two police cars entered the fray and closed the gap quickly.

Hounslow gave them to Richmond. The Expert shut down two more junctions to allow them to blast through, and a coach swerved into one cop car's path, although they saw passengers on the bus and wondered if this event might have been simple luck.

They passed the gold post box dedicated to Olympic Gold medallist Mo Farah. The Expert fell silent for long periods while Matt swerved and skidded and thrust his foot almost through the floor. The Swift was smaller and lighter and mechanically-steroided to hell and the pursuing Volvo V70s were no match.

Daz spent most of his time on his knees on the seat, staring back through the rear window at those chasing them, a hand gripping his seat-belt buckle, as if that was safe enough.

Across the Thames and into the other portion of Richmond, the only London Borough split by the river. The Expert spoke for the first time in two miles, in response to a question from Daz.

'Bridges are risky. Are we crossing the Thames again?'

'One more time, yes. But not for a while. Now tighten up, because Richmond has three police stations and each is now aware of the nippy red Suzuki tearing up the streets. Units are converging.'

'Certainly sounds like an army man,' Daz mouthed at Matt when he looked over. Then he got his radio and put it close to his mouth. Matt covered the headset's microphone with his fist.

'All bikes, move to Havering and await.' He saw Matt's look and said, 'Of the three boroughs on the eastern border, two are below the river. If we're crossing again just one more time, then we can only be headed for Havering.'

So they had narrowed it down. Thirty-three boroughs including the City of London, over 600 square miles, and now they knew their target was in a portion no bigger than forty-three square miles.

They were closing in.

~

'Right off the B353 in six, five, four...'

Just past yet another junction, they swung right, cutting between traffic stopped at the lights. This, according to the Expert, was a private estate called Courtlands. The road curved out of sight to the left and Matt gunned it to try to vanish around the bend before the cops joined the road, but the Expert warned him, *'Drop to twenty.'*

'You're joking!'

But he did it, and soon the flashing blue lights were in his rear-view again. Up close and personal.

He was directed to stamp the accelerator and then to flick hard right six seconds later, between two buildings and towards a fence behind them. The Expert said nothing, but Matt could see that a portion of the slat fence had been unhinged from its concrete pillars and rested upright. They hit it hard, fragmenting it, casting it aside with ease. Immediately the world opened up in front of them as the Suzuki bounced onto the worn grass of a sports field.

'HANDBRAKE!' the Expert yelled. Matt yanked the lever hard and the wheels locked, and the car skidded.

He was aware of a scraping noise from beneath the car and

looked down to see a large wooden board under the vehicle, dragged along the worn grass with them.

'*Boot it.*'

He jammed the car into second and stamped the pedal and the Swift leaped off the board and away. In the rear-view, he saw the first cop car aiming through the gap, but suddenly its front dipped and it stopped with an almighty bang, front wheels vanished as if sunken into the earth. And they were. The board had hidden a rent in the land, exposed when the Swift's wheels locked and dragged it.

'Lovely,' Daz yelled, still on his knees so he could watch the rear.

'*Flick left, aim between the dots.*'

Matt spun the wheel and pointed the front at a line of trees along the eastern end of the sports field. He didn't see any dots and was about to say so when they appeared. On two trees spaced ten feet apart. Big red blobs of paint on the trunks. Apart from a portion left at the front edge for camouflage, the under-growth between the two trees had been burned away in a clear path to a road beyond.

'*Go right, and then that'll take us southeast for two-and-a-half miles through Richmond Park.*'

'He just said *us* again,' Daz said.

'*Enjoy the sights. Then Wandsworth. Seven more boroughs, a bunch more cop chases. You game or want to back out now?*'

'I'm guessing we couldn't back out now if we wanted to,' Matt said.

'*I have only the one exit planned, so no, you can't. Unless you chance it yourself.*'

In Wandsworth they were picked up by the police pretty quickly.

They were directed around streets in a zigzag until emerging onto West Hill, and it was here that a police car came at them. Standard Volvo V70 traffic unit.

It was in the opposite lane, but the siren came on as soon as the car was close enough that the driver could recognise the vehicle he'd been warned about. He swung into Matt's lane and blocked it.

'*Left here.*'

'This part of the plan?' Daz said.

'*I have contingencies, of course. Never can predict where patrol cars will end up.*'

The car pursued them down a road missing chunks of tarmac, as if there had been an artillery war here.

Left, then two rights. One street was in the process of renovation and an entire side had every house in a state of disrepair and a small plastic fence blocking the pavement. Craftsmen were drawn from the houses by the siren. A few cheered the Swift onward to freedom, although one guy tossed his water bottle and it bounced off the windscreen.

'Maybe he lost his entire family to a joyrider racing across a zebra crossing,' Daz said.

Another cop car, no doubt pulled in by radio, entered from a side street and added its whine to the noise.

'*Chopper en route,*' the Expert said. '*We lose him in Southwark.*'

'There's that *we* thing again,' Daz moaned.

'We've still got Lambeth to go first?' Matt said. 'With a chopper on us? You sure you got this planned properly?'

'*Right in three, two, one, go—*'

Matt flipped round the corner.

'*—and yes. The chopper can only direct ground forces. No machine guns. Don't worry. Did you want a Sunday afternoon cruise?*'

'Jam ahead,' Matt said.

'Shit,' Daz said.

'*I know,*' the Expert said.

At the end of the street, three cars were waiting to pull out into a wall of traffic on the main road. A hundred metres out, Matt started to slow the Swift, and the Expert warned him not to. Hard left, he was told.

So Matt gave a slight tug on the wheel and slipped down the left side of the trio of patient drivers, nearside wheels riding the pavement. His foot hovered over the brake, despite the Expert's instructions, but at the last moment he saw it. The reason for the traffic jam. Just left of the corner, the lane had been coned off and a portable traffic light was making the twin lines of vehicles take turns to use the opposite lane. Traffic this side was stopped at red to wait its turn.

He took the left sharply and quickly and blasted through the cones, into the closed lane, which was clear. Nearly sent the portable traffic lights into orbit. The whacked cones sailed over the opposite lane and were volleyed by the bonnets and windscreens of oncoming vehicles.

Behind them, the cop cars played monkey see, monkey do.

There didn't seem to be any work in progress in the empty lane, and no workforce because it was half-past six, starting towards dusk. And no machinery, except for something Matt saw two hundred metres ahead.

'Tell me that thing's part of the plan?'

A backhoe was parked in such a way as to leave just enough road for a car to pass between it and the oncoming traffic. But its boom was extended over the clear chunk, bucket low. Very low. Maybe too low.

'Is that high enough to get under?' Daz said to Matt.

But the Expert answered. '*Looks to be about 59.7 inches off the ground to me. Hope the brochure isn't wrong about the Suzuki Swift's 59.4-inch height.*'

Matt clutched the wheel, aimed straight, and both men

ducked with a grunt as the Swift sailed under the big iron bucket. There was no crunch of metal. No shatter of glass. They didn't slam to a halt instantly. Then the backhoe was behind them and the way ahead was clear. The Swift cast aside a wall of cones at the other end of the roadworks and they were on a lane that was clear for a couple of hundred metres because of the delayed traffic.

And behind them, a crunch of metal, shatter of glass. In the rear-view, Matt watched the great metal bucket cut a crease in the Volvo's roof. The windscreen shattered. The friction slowed the vehicle considerably but it got past, although its chase was over. It swerved and skidded and stalled as the driver panicked. The cop driving the Volvo behind decided he didn't fancy the paperwork and stopped short of the boom.

'*Those darned 60.4-inch Volvos,*' the Expert said.

'Did you have to cut it so close?' Matt said.

'*If they'd had soft tyres or a fat cop or it had been one of their BMW 5-series, we'd be in trouble,*' the Expert replied. '*Next stop, Lambeth. We're halfway.*'

'Stop with the *we* part!' Daz snorted.

And then overhead, faint but getting louder, the unmistakable drone of a helicopter closing in.

A few miles later, Matt noticed something. 'These cars your doing?' he asked the Expert.

Daz looked forward and behind and laughed.

'*Keeps the chopper away,*' the Expert said.

It was up there, but far behind, and the reason was the other cars. Two cars ahead of Matt's was another small red vehicle, and another one two cars ahead of that. Behind, he saw two more in the same setup. Five small red cars in a line. All Suzuki

Swifts. The line stretched a couple of hundred metres, which made sure the chopper pilot had to stay far back from the centre vehicle to keep all five in sight.

'You sure you're making a profit from my money?' Daz asked. He meant that this whole thing couldn't be cheap.

They could hear a siren behind them, but for the last minute or so it had kept its volume at a constant low level, meaning it wasn't gaining.

'Police unit waiting ahead to pounce. Don't look.'

Of course they looked. They passed a side street and saw a police car lurking there, but it was in no pouncing state. Another car had its nose attached to the cop car's busted back end. Two officers were in the road, arguing with a man in a suit. Another delay for the cops, courtesy of the Watchdogs.

Daz got on the radio. Matt put on a coughing fit so he could talk. 'Updates. Who's in Havering yet?'

'Bike Four. No way,' came back a crackly voice. 'I ain't got your kind of help. I'm in Brent.'

The others were having similar problems. They couldn't push through traffic the way the Swift could, at least not without alerting the police, which had to be avoided. Bike Four was north, in Brent. Bike Three was south, in Merton. Bike One, carrying Lisa, was behind them. Bike Two was supposed to complete the box position by keeping ahead, further east, but the Swift had overtaken it a mile back. It was behind them also.

'Shit,' Daz said. 'Keep at it.'

Lambeth next. This borough was narrow and they passed across without much trouble. A tunnel and a few roads under bridges almost lost the chopper, but always it returned like an annoying wasp you try to swat away at a picnic. Under a bridge they were directed to stop behind two parked cars. Two red Suzuki Swifts, probably the pair that had been riding along ahead of them. A minute later the two that had trailed them arrived. They blew past and the two in front of Matt's pulled into the traffic and followed.

Four minutes later Matt was told to set off again, but now the chopper was gone, away in pursuit of the four decoy cars. The chopper had magnetised other pursuit vehicles to its location, but each new siren had promised an appearance that never happened. Five or six police cars had joined the chase, but all had been misdirected or stopped somehow.

Then the chopper came back and brought five guests to the party. Daz whooped with glee. Winding, maze-like roads eventually proved too much for one police car's steering and it went out with a bang. Two bad-on-purpose drivers at separate junctions put out another two. On a street cast in gloom by twin rows of trees, a forty-foot oak chose an opportune time to keel over and die and block the passage of police car number four. The shock of that one – 'How the hell did you guys do that?' – almost caused Matt to smash into a parked van. The last one blew a tyre, and the Expert claimed that one was blind luck.

The chopper, though, came on. It followed them like the moon. But not for long. A minute over the border and into Southwark, it got rerouted to some call about a guy zipping round on a moped and wielding a sword – a plastic one, the Expert assured them. Not long after that they used the Rother-hithe tunnel to get to Tower Hamlets. It involved another stop, this time to swap cars. It was another Swift, but this time green. Deep in the tunnel under the Thames, a guy waiting in the green car took their red one and got out of there to risk the cops. The traffic noise in the tunnel was thick enough that Daz got on his radio without fear of being heard. He told his people about the colour change to their vehicle.

'Sure your guys won't talk if they get caught?' Daz asked the Expert afterwards.

'They won't talk,' was the blunt reply.

They entered Newham without incident, but there the Expert got them to play another prank and so interest the police again.

Ninety miles an hour with three in tow, soon lost when a truck that ran a red light spilled its load and blocked their path. The Swift took a corner into a cul-de-sac and entered a car port attached to a house with enough garden gnomes to cast a black shadow on the owner's sanity. A guy sitting on his doorstep pulled a string and a bedsheet fell across the port's entrance, obscuring the car.

'Kill the engine.'

Matt did. He looked at Daz and Daz looked back, both unsure what to do now. Matt had both hands gripping the wheel and Daz said, '*Now* you hold the wheel properly?'

Matt looked at his hands and released the wheel and laughed.

'Will Gnome-Man be bringing us tea?' Daz said to the Expert.

The Expert told them no. Just wait. Matt got out of the car and the Expert told him to get back inside. He dawdled because Daz was on the radio. With the engine off, it would be impossible to talk to the men on the radio without being overheard. Both men relished the break, because it meant Bike Two could get ahead again, back into position. Bikes One, Three and Four stopped in order to keep the 'box' intact.

Ten minutes later, the Expert told them the way was clear again.

Later, they were in Barking and Dagenham and taking a dirt path to avoid a rolling roadblock. Bike Two, ahead once again, had got past before it was put in place. They could hear a cacophony of homeward-bound drivers honking their horns at the police as they blocked the road, travelling slowly with their lights flashing. The Swift cut a winding path through quiet zones. They ended up in Becontree, which Daz delighted in knowing the history of.

'Built between the two world wars.'

'Spectacular,' Matt said with badly-faked awe.

'Part of London since sixty-five.'

'Awesome!'

'Was once the largest public housing estate in the world.'

'Holy shit!'

'Shut up, you donkey.'

The rest of Barking and Dagenham was easy-going, which prompted Daz to accuse the Expert of shooting his load early. 'Is the action all done now? You need me to get you a cigarette?'

They took a series of side streets and paths through rural fragments of London to avoid zones where the police had cars waiting to pounce. Or so the Expert said. 'Sure this ain't pillow talk now you've shot your load prematurely?' Daz asked. But it was a joke: they'd heard the odd siren zipping past like buzzing flies they couldn't see.

And then they were in Havering. Daz and Matt looked at each other after the Expert said, *'Soon we'll be at Gallows Corner. Take the Southend Arterial Road, the A127, east. Your final chase will be here.'*

That meant they were close.

As they joined the A127, two police cars fell in behind them. Sirens and flashing lights were starting to get monotonous.

'Drop to twenty-five,' the Expert said.

'Comedian!' Daz barked.

It was a dual carriageway so cars were able to go by as Matt obliged. The cop cars caught up, then one veered to the right to overtake, obviously planning to cut in ahead and slow them.

Matt tugged on his wheel and put a stop to that. The other car tried to sneak by the left side, but he swerved again. And then roadworks cut the two lanes down to one. The cop cars got stuck behind. In a comical moment, one slowed to ten and a young cop got out the passenger side and started running. In shorts and track shoes he might have closed the distance, but he was laden with boots and a thick coat and more utilities on his belt than Batman and he had no chance. For a few seconds he kept pace, but then started to drop back and had to get back inside his car.

'*Fifteen,*' the Expert said. '*Central locking.*'

Matt locked the doors and slowed the car. The traffic built up behind them, and a gap opened ahead. Big. In his rear-view, Matt saw the older driver of one car gesturing at the young cop again. Out he got for another chase on foot. This time he closed the gap, slowly, and drew alongside. Daz covered his face with his hands, but peeked out between his fingers. The young cop, panting, using one hand to hold his belt of utilities, rapped on the window, as if expecting that his quarry might not have realised the cops had been trying to get them to stop for all this time.

'*We also souped-up this second car and now it's all gone to waste,*' the Expert said with faked despair. Matt got the point. He hit the accelerator. The young cop fell behind with a flick of the hand, as if saying their actions were unfair. The Swift ate the road. The road went down like a hungry man's hot meal. Bare ahead because all the traffic had pulled away. The roadworks ended. Road buffet. The cops had no chance. Matt got eight seconds at close to 130mph before cars started to fill his windscreen and forced him to slow. Behind, the flashing lights were still there, but far back. Matt smiled as he imagined the young cop still running. Ahead, they saw Bike Two.

Daz showed Matt his phone. The map showed Junction 29 of

the M25 some way ahead. Another roundabout with a green line around its far curve. Eastern border of Greater London this time. The M25 ran north and south along the border. Past the junction the A127 entered Essex. Essex would not be part of the route, surely. So the end had to be right ahead, surely.

Matt kept his speed but dropped a gear. The engine noise increased and Daz used it as cover as he spoke into his radio.

'Endgame, people. Be ready.'

South of their current position there was a housing estate. Daz sent Bike Three, already south, there just in case, although a populated place didn't seem a likely spot for the Expert to be lurking. East of the Swift's position, either side of the A127 on the Essex side of the junction, the map showed two large plots of land that were interesting. An industrial estate on the south, a quarry on the north, like a pair of butterfly wings off the main road. Bike Four, already north, was told to hang fire and join the M25 if the Swift took it north. Bike Two, ahead, was told to continue east along the A127, although this would take the bike deep into Essex, which they didn't think likely. Except those plots of land looked so interesting. So the rider was told to prepare to take the exit, so he could either circle the roundabout, ready to follow the Swift if it went south or north along the M25, or rejoin the A127 if they continued ahead and into Essex. And if for some reason they took the M25 south, Bike Three could abandon the estate and join them.

Behind them, and behind the cop cars racing up, was Bike One. The rider was ordered to continue following the Swift. In the rear-view mirror, Matt saw Lisa give a thumbs-up.

Bike Three came into the estate from the south. It was a place of houses and shops cramped close together with rung-like streets poking off a thick main road. Parked in a bus lay-by outside a minimart was a British Telecom van with a guy in the driver's seat, hunched over a laptop.

The rider passed the BT van and slid in behind it. Close enough that they were in the driver's blind spot.

'Guy in the van must be a Watchdog,' he said. 'The old fake phone repairman trick. Do your slut thing.'

His pillion was a girl in a short skirt and a shirt under her biker leathers. Her nickname was Siren, because in her past she had made a habit of picking blokes up in bars and then robbing them at knifepoint. She said, 'Get real, Alfo, we're supposed to wait.'

'He might hit the gas, girl. Go get. Hero time.'

Actually, hero time sounded good. They quickly worked out a plan and Siren slipped off the bike, slipped off her leathers, and slipped alongside the van. A rap on the window got the driver's attention. His eyes looked her up and down. Down came his window. She pointed behind his van.

'Bike,' she said. 'Stalled. You must know engines, being an electricity man and all.' The driver was happy to help a pretty girl. So back they went, and there was the bike, no rider aboard. He leaned close and had a peek. That was when Alfo rushed in from his hiding place on the other side of the van. Good street fighter in his day, Alfo. A one-two combination as the driver turned his head to look at the new arrival. The guy went down heavy and smacked his head on the tarmac. Both bikers had their hands in his clothing, ready to drag him into the back of his own van, when the radio squawked.

'Taking the Junction 29 exit, so it ain't the estate,' said Daz's voice. 'It looks like the M25, north or south. Bike Four, prepare to join it north. Bike Three, cancel the estate and prepare to join the M25 if we go south.'

'Ah shit,' Alfo and Siren said together. They dropped the innocent guy on his head again.

They blew up the exit. A coach leading the approaching traffic on the roundabout veered out of its lane and blocked everyone, allowing them to fly across the junction despite a red light. It stopped all but a bike that slipped between two braking cars, veered past the coach and got in front of them. Right in front of them. It was Bike Two, which had already completed one revolution of the roundabout. The pillion turned and looked at them and gave a thumbs-up.

The first exit was signposted Stanstead airport and would take them north onto the M25, but–

'*Ignore the exit*,' said the Expert.

Daz said, 'Bike Four, it ain't north, ignore northbound. Get south, get down here.'

Next they came to the slip road delivering traffic from the M25 southbound lane and here the light was green. In the rear-view mirrors, they saw Bike One enter the roundabout, ahead of the cops, who were nowhere to be seen. They could still hear the sirens, though, so the hunt was still on.

The second exit was a private road signposted Cobham Hall. On the map, this road ran parallel to the A127 and had branches that could deliver drivers to both of Daz's 'interesting' places, the quarry and the industrial estate, the latter via a flyover. There was an A-frame advertising van parked on a grassy wedge next to the road, its sign proclaiming that you'd be mad not to advertise your business on this van for just a few £s a day. Everyone was mad, apparently.

The exit rushed at them, but they were not told to slow, or turn. They were going past. No point in rejoining the A127, so it had to be the M25, south, had to be. Daz blurted, 'Looks like we're going south down the M25. Bike Three, join–'

'*Exit now!*' the Expert yelled, and Matt tugged the wheel left with almost no time to spare. Taking this exit narrowed the options again. Daz barked a new order into his radio.

'All bikes, we're off, we're off the junction, so it's the quarry or the industrial estate. Go, go.'

'Too late,' said Bike Two as his vehicle whizzed past the exit. 'Coming round again.'

Bike One, though, had time. The rider saw the Swift's sudden change of direction the instant it happened. But instead of following, the bike swerved off the road and into the trees before the exit. Seeing this in his mirror, Matt realised the plan. They were taking the quarry, a direct line northeast through the trees. A car would have to make a longer route, down the lane, left, and left again to circle a thick wood and the quarry and come in from the other side.

Matt angled the Swift down the thin lane. He hit the gas, but the moment he did, the Expert screamed at him to brake. As the Swift ground to a halt just metres beyond the open gateway, the advertising van backed up, blocked the road like a gate closing. The Swift was just a few feet ahead, and hidden. And just inches over the border, two wheels in Greater London and two in Essex. The sound of sirens was loud, but had the cops entered the roundabout in time to watch where their quarry went?

In his rear-view, Matt saw the growing darkness torn by flashing lights that sailed past. Cops, gone. Swift, unseen.

'*From here it gets easy,*' the Expert said. '*Well done, gentlemen. Hope you enjoyed the ride. We made it.*'

'Fuck off with the *we!*' Daz yelled.

16

Lisa squeezed Judd's chest harder as the bike entered the woods and rumbled over uneven ground, snapping dead branches, throwing up waves of dirt and dried leaves. He let out a groan.

'I kinda need to breathe to stay conscious, sweetie.'

'Do you know what the hell you're doing?' she shouted above the roar of the engine.

Judd leaned aside and pointed at the satnav clipped to the handlebars.

'Quarry,' he said.

In the dark woods, the bright screen was unavoidable. It showed a fat little arrow meant to depict their vehicle floating over a graphic of trees. Northeast of the arrow was a brown expanse with pixelated text saying *Lightwood Industries*.

'You can't know it's the quarry!' she moaned.

And right then their radio: 'All bikes, move, move. We're taking the left turn. It's the quarry. It's the goddamned quarry.'

They were through the woods in fifteen seconds, which was good because Lisa didn't have the lungs or strength for a longer journey. When they emerged into open land, she breathed and relaxed so suddenly she almost lost grip of Judd and hit the dirt.

Ahead was an expanse of scrubland, brown and dusty and dead, like a landscape from an old cowboy movie or a sci-fi flick about a blasted Earth following a nuclear east-west falling out. In the flick, mutated beasts would rule the lands and whatever humans survived might construct a sanctuary and bar it with such a fence as faced Lisa and Judd now. It was chain-link, twice a man's height, and wrapped in some kind of plastic sheeting that blurred the view beyond. The plastic was tinted a pale red, as if from rock dust. Quarry dust.

The bike slewed to a halt and they both leaped off. Judd clambered onto the fence and perched atop it like a cat, offering his hand to help Lisa up. She slapped it aside and scrambled over.

In the darkness, the blasted Earth scenario reversed itself. No longer for the security of human survivors, the fenced area now seemed designed to keep evil contained. The land fell away from them twenty metres ahead, as if a meteor had landed. They ran to the edge and stared down.

The ground sloped away from them steeply. Below were dark yellow shapes, not aliens but earth-moving machinery, and darker slices and curves where the machines had cut or packed earth to create makeshift tracks so they could go up and down. But there were no cars, and no lights, and no buildings. No sign of a man. No place a man could use to sit at a computer and direct a car chase.

Then they noticed it.

To their left the land rose slightly, so that by the time the rim of the crater had curved a quarter circle, it was fifteen feet above where they stood. There the land had flattened out and they could see the top of a square building set far back from the edge.

Lisa ran uphill, followed by Judd. Like something birthing

from the ground, a large shipping container exposed itself the higher they ran. Soon they were on flat ground and seeing everything. Seven or eight such containers raised on low stacks of bricks, a door and window cut into each with a set of metal doorsteps. They were dark and dead, except for a tiny red light winking from each. A burglar alarm. Offices and utility units for the quarry workforce.

Here, a good place to hide.

She turned as light entered the world. Twin elongated triangles cutting through the night way down below. A car entering the quarry. Matt's car. The interior light was on, too, which puzzled her, because why would Matt announce himself?

She ran for the containers.

Matt wouldn't have chosen to announce himself, not at all. If the choice had been his, he would have gone in with no headlights, either. But the Expert had said, '*Now turn on your main beams and the interior light, then make a left.*'

'You want us naked as well?' Daz had said.

The left was nought but a gash in the trees, like a wooden tunnel with a leafy roof. Down the land sloped. The ground was laid with packed mud to allow easy passage for wheeled heavy machinery. Through the tunnel they went, lighting up everything, feeling exposed.

'*What are you doing?*' the Expert said. '*What are you saying to him?*'

'Insider joke,' Daz said. Then to Matt, 'Left a bit.'

A couple of hundred metres along, the trees ended and the quarry lay before them. Daz described it for Matt. They were at the foot of a large hill and the quarry was like a great bite taken out of it. The headlights showed them a chain-link fence dead ahead that curved away to left and right and made its way up the rising land. The high shelf of land at the top of the hill contained nothing they could see, which Daz found puzzling. If the Watchdog was here, surely he would be watching them from a high point. But apart from the moon, the only high point was that shelf of land, like a cliff edge, and there was nothing up there.

Which meant he must be in one of the earthmovers scattered around like big sleeping dinosaurs.

'Gate's open,' the Expert said. *'Nudge it open. X marks the spot.'*

'Forward ten feet, slowly,' Daz said to Matt.

'Why are you talking like that?' the Expert said.

'I boss my employees around,' Daz answered.

Matt touched the gate with the Swift's nose and it moved. A harder push swung it open with a creak. In they went at a crawl, like a nosey cat. He turned left and right so his headlights would wash everything, and then Daz said he could see the X. In a flat bit of land away from machinery there were two planks laid in a cross-shape. Matt drove over them and stopped when Daz said so.

'No, don't get out,' the Expert said when Matt reached for the door handle. Matt froze, but not because he had been ordered to stop. He froze because he had not opened the door, which meant there had been no sound of a door opening, which in turn meant the Expert could not possibly have known Matt was about to exit the car. But he had.

Which meant he could see them somehow.

Lisa and Judd went to the door of the first container, found it locked.

'Don't try the handles,' she said. 'If he's in there, he'll know someone's here.'

So they went to the window and peeked in, even though that was riskier because if the guy was here, then surely the window was where he'd be, so he could watch the car. Only the car was at the bottom of the quarry and you couldn't see the quarry from here. She looked around. There were high trees some thirty metres behind the line of containers, but a man would have to be right at the top of one, perched in the branches, and that wasn't going to happen.

Judd tried the radio. Called Daz. Got only static. Lisa didn't like that.

The next container. Dark, empty, dead apart from that little flashing red light to deter thieves. They moved onto the next at a jog.

Between containers three and four, they saw it. In the trees, a road, and parked in there was a car. Dead and dark and empty like the rest of this place, though. But a vehicle, and that might just mean someone was here. Somewhere.

'So now what?' Daz said.

The Expert said, *'Did you get your money's worth, Mr McKinley?'*

Daz and Matt looked at each other.

'Sure,' Daz said. 'Very good. Worth every penny. I owe you the other half, of course. Are you here? Got a computer I can use?'

The interior light turned the windows into mirrors. Nothing could be seen beyond. Matt grew apprehensive. The guy could be standing right out there and they'd never know.

Daz spoke into his radio. Quietly. No engine noise to cover it this time, but the risk had to be taken. Matt covered the microphone with his fist.

'Who's close? Update?'

'*Not this time,*' the Expert said. '*I let you get away with that for a while. Now your signal is blocked.*'

Matt reached for the handle again, but again the Expert told him not to move. '*Wondering, of course, how I can see you? It's called a Nightforce BEAST. That's a tactical rifle scope, fellows. The first thing you ever did on this planet was climb out of somewhere. Want it to also be the last thing you ever do?*'

He knew. The Watchdogs knew. They knew everything. Insane Janes after all.

'*It was nothing personal, you know,*' the Expert said. '*I understand your commitment to your sister, and I applaud how far you got. We only worked it out today. You got close. Normally, I'd be a man who'd let you get your way. Get your revenge. I like seeing people get revenge. Hell, it's probably the main reason I do what I do. But of course, I'm one of the guys you need to kill, so that can't happen in this case.*'

The headset uttered a click that both men, experienced army guys who'd handled guns, recognised instantly. A weapon being cocked.

In a quick move, Daz snapped off the interior light. And Matt opened his eyes. He had kept them closed since a moment before the interior light went on. To save his night vision. Hence why Daz had had to direct him. Now, when they snapped open, his retinas quickly adjusted and he saw the world outside in cool clarity, like a cat. Big yellow machines, starkly displayed, and the rocky land rising high above beyond them. His eyes ran around the rising edge of the quarry, quick. It was a neat curve, nothing there. But then he saw it, along the flat top of the quarry: a little blip in the line, an arc downwards. And nestled in there, a slight illumination from the world above, where the bright moon hung. A reflection of the sky. Glass.

He had followed the rush of his eyes with his hand, tracking their movement with the thing he held in his fingers, pointing it where his vision lay, and now he clicked the little button on that item and it sent a beam of red through the dark window and through the dark world.

~

Lisa and Judd felt they were on a wild goose chase when it happened.

'There,' Judd said, and they rushed towards it.

On the black window of container five was a wavering dot, like a red firefly.

Lisa grabbed a rock as they closed in. Judd rushed to the door. She lobbed the rock at the window. It bust through with a massive crash as Judd raised a foot and kicked in the door.

Just before she passed the window, meaning to follow, bright light pricked her eyes. She turned, facing the quarry, and saw something that explained everything. Everything. A thin channel in the land, sloping down, like a furrow caused by a fragment of the meteorite that might have opened the Earth. Shallow at the top, just feet from her position, and fifteen feet deep when it reached the sheer edge. Rugged and rock debris-lined, though, as if a natural collapse of the land rather than something engineered.

And it allowed line of sight from the container to a small portion of the quarry below. Where, like a target in a reticule, the Swift sat facing slightly away from them. Even in the dark she could see the shapes of two men inside. And she could see the beam of Matt's laser pen, a straight line from car to target along that channel, as if the laser itself had burned through the land.

She rushed into the container to find Judd on the floor and a man standing over him. Felt a wave of guilt, for her pause outside had allowed the standing man to gain the advantage. He wore a suit, but over it wore a plastic outfit, like some bio scientist in a quarantine zone. It covered his hands and his feet and even his head, the hood pulled tight by a drawstring. Her eyes took everything in in half a second. A desk and file cabinets, and maps and papers stuck to the walls. On the desk, two computers, their screens throwing enough light to show her all this. And on the floor, lying near the rock and amid broken glass, was a rifle attached to a bracket. Something remote-controlled, she guessed. Arranged at the window, ready to fire down the channel in the land and kill.

After that half second, she was rushing forward. The suited man turned to her and she saw a handsome face with a trimmed blond beard framed within the exposed circle that the hood didn't cover. And she saw the shock on his face. He did not have time to react against her blow. The smaller rock she carried was launched. It missed, but taking him out with a wild throw had never been her plan. He twisted his head, turned away for a second as she threw the rock. It was enough to distract him, give her a chance to slip by the knife he wielded, the weapon that had put down Judd. She crashed into him and they both went down.

~

Matt heard the action through his headset. Knew it was Lisa, knew she might be in trouble. He got out of the car, but Daz remained.

'If the Watchdogs know everything, Orbach will be waiting

for a call,' Daz said. It was all he needed to say. Matt understood. No time to waste. As he rushed across the dark quarry floor, the Swift came to life and turned and threw up soil and rock dust as it roared out of there.

'Lisa?' he called into the headset as he pounded along. 'Lisa?'

His answer was more of the same. The noise of violent action as two or more people fought.

Daz whipped out of Cobham Hall Road and turned into oncoming traffic on the roundabout. And nearly ploughed down Bike Three. He stopped the Swift and leaped out and ran to where the bike had swerved and skidded and finished up on its side. Alfo and Siren were sitting on the grass verge, shaken up.

'The hell's happening?' Alfo shouted over the honks of horns and shouts of other drivers as they manoeuvred around the abandoned Swift.

'Get rid of the car,' Daz told them. Then he lifted the bike and got on and got the hell out of there. Once he was up through the gears, burning around the roundabout, he pulled his radio and shouted one word: *Orbach*.

'Orbach's still there,' came a voice in reply to his question. Not all of MacSec had joined the pursuit of the Swift. Of the ten who had taken the train to London to help their boss, three were watching the casino. Watching for Orbach, in case he left. So far, according to the voice, Orbach hadn't left. So Orbach's Expert hadn't yet sent a warning. Hopefully that meant he was dead already. But how long would Orbach wait for confirmation that the men in the Swift were dead before he got suspicious?

Daz programmed the satnav as he rode and was back at the casino in twenty-two minutes. He had people watching the front and back entrances, but he chose the fire exit that Lisa had told them about. Orbach's bike was still there, in amongst the old bangers on the car dealer's forecourt. Daz's man was across the road, sitting in a bus stop with a newspaper. His plan was to watch and wait and follow Orbach if he left.

Daz sent his man away, gave him some bullshit task that had nothing to do with any of this. Then he took the guy's place in the bus stop.

Plan: watch and follow.

But two minutes later he scuttled across the road and hid behind one of the cars in the lot. He owed it to Matt to make this easy for him. No more running around London.

New plan: grab Orbach as he left the building and present him to Matt like a Christmas present.

But after two minutes lurking amongst the cars, Daz thought he might have a problem holding a guy hostage out in the open, especially tied up. Plus, this wasn't a good place to kill someone. Too much chance of a witness telling the cops, of the cops themselves cruising by. Especially if Matt wanted to draw out Orbach's confession.

New new plan: take Orbach in the casino.

The fire exit had no latch, only a padlock and chain to secure it. Daz busted the hasp from the wall easily. Inside, he found wide open office space, empty, but there were stacks of builders' items that suggested a renovation was on the cards. He ran through room after room, making his way the length of the building. In every third room was a descending staircase, probably leading into a shop below or even to a street entrance. He went down one, just curious, but found a pair of locked double doors on a half-landing. Locked this side by a chain and a dusty padlock. Clearly there was no way up from below. He moved on.

He entered the room he guessed was above the casino and confirmed this with a glance out the grimy window – there was the car park, right across the road. Last office of the row, because the far wall had no doorway, no way to progress. It was blank unexposed brick.

But there was no exit in this room. The last one had been two rooms back, nowhere near the casino. And it made sense that there should be no way down into the casino – not good for security.

He spotted a file cabinet in the corner. A file cabinet normally doesn't stand out in an office, but this one did because it was alone. Brother desks and sister computers and auntie wall charts had all gone, so this solitary remaining piece of the floor's former life seemed wrong. So he yanked it aside. And found a hole.

Floor level, three feet high, and lined with rubber padding. It was the padding rather than the hole that made Daz think he had found Orbach's secret way in and out of the casino. He imagined Orbach coming through the hole and catching his nice suit on a dusty brick. Up went the padding.

On the other side he found a small room. There was a door in the far wall. He opened that and found himself in a bedroom. The little room had been a closet once, now turned into some escape route.

The bedroom was clean, tidy, spartan. A single bed, a single armchair. The left wall bore a sole shelf lined with books and a large TV below. On the right, in a glass case, was a pressed army uniform, full-size, with photographs surrounding it. Daz moved in for a closer look. The uniform was obviously Orbach's, because he was wearing it in some of the pictures. Most were outdoor scenes from overseas, places where he had served the US army, but others were indoor shots. In some he was alone, in others he had been captured as part of a group. In some he wore the uniform and posed, in others he had been snapped in motion adorned in civvies. Sweet and memorable scenes from the life of the man Daz was here to capture. Daz's eyes flicked quickly across them and rested on the top photo, the one above the collars of the uniform jacket, the centrepiece of the tableau, maybe even more so than the actual uniform. His eyes widened as a new truth hit him.

The wall ahead had another door. Beyond, a living room. Here, there was everything you'd expect from such a place except for a TV. Orbach clearly had better things to watch than soap operas. One wall was entirely taken up by a bank of small monitors set around a larger one. There had to be over two hundred screens, each one displaying the feed from a camera down in the casino. The audio was off. One of the feeds was displayed on the larger monitor, sharing the screen with a graphical interface for controlling the system. A sofa with a big remote control on the arm faced the monitors, suggesting that Orbach enjoyed sitting to watch his guests, and seek those with problems he could help with. It looked very hi-tech and confusing and on another day Daz would have loved to play with it. Maybe he'd return when he'd finished with Orbach.

Next came a bathroom. The apartment reminded Daz of a luxury hotel room. There was another door. Small, thin. Daz grabbed the handle and pulled it open, and froze when he saw Orbach right in front of him.

Orbach was seated behind his desk, just feet away. The hidden door was in the back wall of the office, behind Orbach, so he hadn't seen Daz, hadn't heard the door opening, and that gave Daz all the advantage he would ever need.

Two steps put Daz right there, right behind Orbach. Daz grabbed his hair and stuck the blade in his neck enough to hurt.

'Hello again,' he said.

Orbach didn't flinch, or struggle, or seem surprised that someone had emerged from the wall like a ghost, and he didn't sound scared when he said, 'Well done.'

'Thanks.'

'Not you,' Orbach said, and that was when some beefy arm grabbed Daz round the throat from behind.

~

When Matt got to the top of the quarry, he found a group.

Bikes Two and Four had already arrived. MacSec stood around the container, watching the door. Each person wielded some item like a weapon, things taken from the site like spades and bricks. Lisa was sitting nearby, clutching her arm, which was bleeding.

'I think he killed Judd,' she said. MacSec were angry, wanted to storm the building. Lisa had stopped them. 'He has a knife. I had to get out of there.'

He checked her arm, then went to the door. Burst right in, no weapon, carrying only an envelope, and stopped dead.

A man in a protective suit over a business suit, sitting on a chair, was slumped forward over the desk. Lisa must have gotten off a lethal blow, although he could see no blood. Judd was on the floor, neck gashed wide, an island in a sea of his own blood. Matt stepped around him.

He walked behind the suited man, wary that it could be a trick. Grabbed a handful of plastic at the shoulders and yanked, and stepped away. A moment later he knew it was no trick. The man was dead. White foam filled his mouth. MacSec stormed in, crowding their dead friend as Matt unzipped the Watchdog's plastic suit and searched his pockets. He found only a driver's licence in the name of Alan Bates. Was Damon Mason Alan Bates in the same way that Teddy Riley was Anderson Orbach?

He clutched the envelope in his hand tightly, angry. All this time, all this way, all these obstacles, and one of the guys he had hunted was only three feet away, and yet the bastard had escaped justice forever by crushing a cyanide capsule between his teeth. Matt swung a hard kick at the guy's head, toppling body and chair backwards. There was no sense of enjoyment or relief. The guy was dead, but he had taken his own life. He had made a choice to escape the only way he knew, and it had worked because Matt could now never get him back.

He rushed from the container. Lisa came over, but he ignored her. Rushed right past, towards one of the bikes. He was a moment from getting out of there when she put her hand on his arm, and he paused. It hurt to do so, but he knew he could not just run out without a word to her.

'I'll find you after all this,' she said, and right then he loved her. For that, he loved her. She knew he had to go, right now. Knew better than to try to talk him out of it, or even to delay him.

He gunned it. West. Back to the casino. There was one man still alive, hopefully. There was still satisfaction to be had.

~

The casino was freshly opened, and he showed his membership card and looked at the camera. No klaxon. The dead Watchdog had not had time to call Orbach, so Orbach might not yet know, although he would suspect soon. Or maybe it was all a trap.

He went past the slots, which were filling up. Down the slope and into the tables room. He headed for the special door in the corner. Forty feet away, he noticed that the guy who stood there, same guy as always, turned his eyes Matt's way, as if sensing that he was going to be approached by a customer who might need redirecting. Twenty feet out, the guy perked up, clearly knowing that words were going to be exchanged. Five feet and the ape knew some action would be needed.

He stepped forward, edge of the steps, and put out a hand like a traffic cop telling cars to stop. Matt didn't stop. He pulled his left hand out of his pocket and flicked it towards the guy. As the sand flung into his face forced the guy to slap at his eyes, Matt used the first step as a launch pad, bent knees straightening fast, and delivered a mammoth uppercut, a move that was almost comical, like Superman rising into the air. But nothing was funny about the way the guy's head snapped back and his legs gave out.

He had to drag the door against the weight of the unconscious ape. He slipped through when there was enough of a gap and found the lift and rode it up and stepped out and went to ZE BOSS's office. He opened the door nice and slow, ready for a trap. It was halfway open when he heard Orbach call out from inside.

'Don't come in, I'm getting changed.'

Matt came in, but Orbach wasn't getting changed. He was behind the desk and he was bleeding. Numerous cuts, some long, some to arms and chest, some to face and neck. His torn white suit was splattered in red. There was a dead man on the floor, and Daz. Daz was dead, too. Both dead men were also cut and bloodied. Blood was all over the place. Any more and you'd be forgiven for thinking someone had splashed white paint on red walls. Daz had put up a good fight, but of course no fight is good if you lose your life. By Daz's own admission, this meant he no longer owed Matt. But Matt now owed him.

Orbach looked dazed and weak. But he was alert enough to show shock when Matt walked in. Then the shock turned to understanding. He lifted a pistol. Had barely the strength to raise it. Propped it on the desk instead, barrel aimed straight at Matt's midsection. That was when Matt noticed a neat round hole in Daz's cheek, and knew that Daz had held his own against two men until the cheating started.

'Damon was a tough bastard, so congratulations to you,' said Orbach.

Matt took out his envelope, extracted a picture, unfolded it, showed it. Orbach didn't glance at it. Never took his eyes off Matt.

'I don't need that. I know why you're here,' he said. 'A lowly dead prostitute, strangled in an abandoned train station.' He must have seen the puzzlement crease Matt's face, because he smiled and added: 'I did state to my client that it would be wisest to have her body disposed of, but my client was given a choice, and he chose to have her body left out in the open for the world to see.'

Matt felt light-headed as realisation crashed through his mind. He visualised the underground train station, and Karen, and a man strangling her, somehow without alerting nearby girls but with enough force to break a sliver of plastic off a camera attached to his body. He saw black figures escort the killer and the body away through the sewer network. The killer was delivered home, safe and sound, while Karen's corpse was heaved through a manhole, into a waste ground, and dragged to a position from which her body could be viewed from a faraway window.

Without looking away from Matt, he jabbed a finger into a mobile phone laid on his desk. There was a neat round blood droplet right in the centre of the screen.

The phone dialled a number and another phone maybe a mile or a thousand away started ringing. The speaker was loud.

Matt stepped forward. Three feet from the desk. Six feet from Orbach. Orbach rapped the butt of the pistol on the desk. Had barely the strength to do so. 'Not another inch.'

The phone was answered, but no voice spoke. Just a grunt of sorts. Orbach said, 'It's done. Died right on his knees, begging for his life. Damon told him if he begged, he'd make it quick. Guy begged like a homeless man.'

He jabbed another button, again without looking away from Matt, and the call ended.

'I couldn't tell him you killed Damon. That would just upset him and it's his son's birthday and all. Can't ruin the kid's night at the circus. But that's the only part I was lying about.'

Orbach jerked his eyes downwards and Matt understood. Orbach's words to his mystery friend had gotten the message across to Matt. Matt dropped the envelope and dropped to his knees. But he took a step forward to do so, and that changed a six-foot distance to five feet. Now their eyeline was level, same as if they had been standing.

'I know the man who killed my sister was a judge. I'm going to kill him, and I'm going to expose whatever corruption she found out, and I'm going to sink the lot of you. This isn't going to be a case of *satisfaction guaranteed.*'

Orbach gave a smile, but tried to hide it. 'It was to be the trial of the century, with a powerful drugs baron going to prison for the rest of his life, or so the world thought. But the judge had been bought, and both men were destined to see out their days in the Bahamas, surrounded by girls, swimming in money.'

'But my sister found out, and threatened to expose them, and for that she was–'

Now Orbach's smile burst forth, followed by a laugh. Matt felt his stomach sink as his mind cast back: the man in the casino who'd gotten a dancer he'd been overheard coveting; Daz, who wanted to drive a fast car around London. The business of not just problem-solving, but making fantasies come true. *Satisfaction, guaranteed.*

He tuned back in to Orbach to find the man speaking: '... drunk as hell at the bar, quietly spouting off to one of the waitresses, giving her hassle about how she should stop flaunting herself because not all men found it attractive, that she should watch out because if she caught the wrong guy's eye, she'd regret it. Some men, he'd hissed at her, got turned on by making women suffer, by dominating them, by hurting them, and with men like that her short skirt and red lipstick would be wasted effort – all she'd need was blood that flowed and a voice that could scream.'

He awaited a response, but Matt couldn't find words. He had had this all wrong, all along.

'So there's your answer, Armstrong. I'd love for your little tale to be true, I really would. Your sister could go down in history as a martyr, praised by all, maybe with a statue erected in her honour. But the truth of why your sister is in heaven is a little cruder.'

At the word *heaven*, Matt flicked his eyes upwards, to a spot on the ceiling right above Orbach. But not slowly, as if seeking that place of eternal rest: sharp and quick, as if he'd seen something move, and Orbach instinctively copied. Back went his head, and back went Matt's memory again. But this time to a place he wanted it to go.

He had visualised it all in his head, over and over. Orbach standing five feet away, chin up, neck exposed; the belt ripped free in a backhand motion, uncurling like a slingshot. Power plus weight.

Just before he swung, he closed his eyes and watched it unfold in his mind, accompanied by a real-life soundtrack that was barely out of sync. The imagined Orbach, immaculate in a pale green suit, dropped into his chair and leaned back with his neck like a garden sprinkler, blood washing the ceiling. When Matt opened his eyes, it was like flicking two pages in a flip book: the real Orbach jerked forward in a fraction of a second and slumped over his desk. Flesh and muscle and gristle: no obstacle.

Matt got to his feet and grabbed Orbach's phone. Fresh blood from his ruined throat had already pooled on the desk and soaked the phone. Matt didn't even wipe it off. He pressed redial and waited and heard a voice say, 'Forget something?' and then he hung up. Broke the phone apart and left the room by the open door behind Orbach's desk. It killed him to leave Daz as he was, but Daz no longer had needs, and Matt did.

17

———

The deeper he got into the urban maze, the less conspicuous Matt felt. The paranoia dripped out of him and evaporated. By the time he had found the house he wanted, he was all out of worry and approached the front door like a man who had legitimate business there. Which he did. The house was dark, but he pretended to knock, just in case anyone in the houses across the street was watching. Then he went around the back. There was a high wooden fence, but the gate in it was swinging to and fro in the light breeze. He took that as a clear sign he was meant to succeed here.

Through and to the French windows at the back. They were locked, but they were old, and he yanked hard and the door made a cracking noise and slid open. Some broken-off piece of metal bounced on the carpet. A cat scarpered over, sniffed it, saw Matt, and dashed out between his legs. He shut the door and went through a kitchen, though a living room. Normal rooms. A lot of quaint knick-knacks that made him think it was a woman's home. The living room was scattered with toys, and these made him feel a little guilty about why he was here, but then he reminded himself that he wasn't here for no reason. If they had left him alone, if they hadn't blown apart his life, Matt wouldn't be here right now. But he hadn't been left alone, not by a long shot. And a man with a child should have known better.

He went upstairs. Three rooms. One for a child, a small one. No older than five or six, given the wallpaper and the toys. A bathroom that was overwhelmingly female. He started to worry. Just a jot. Then he looked in the master bedroom and found a few items of male clothing in the wardrobe, but the relief he felt was short. Apart from the clothing there was nothing that suggested a man lived here, and the clothing could belong to an ex-boyfriend or a new current boyfriend or a brother. His hopes started to fade again, until he stepped back onto the landing and saw a padlock on the trapdoor to the attic. Nice and thick, too much security against the inquisitiveness of a child.

He got a wooden chair to stand on and tested the lock by shaking it. Tough. But not as tough as the trapdoor. He slammed a solid palm into the wood, near the hinges. Six blows, as many as the pain would allow, and finally there was a crack. He used his other palm to smack the crack wider, until wood splintered from around one of the hinges. A minute later he was able to twist the door this way and that until it broke free from both hinges. He moved it aside and hauled himself up.

Right by him was a standing lamp and he flicked the switch. Cool green light illuminated the attic. It was spacious, carpeted, like a den. All male, this part of the house. His hopes returned. There was nothing here but a desk with a computer on top of it. The computer was on. A screensaver showing the time and date bounced around the screen like a cat trying to escape an oven. He went over and flicked the mouse and expected a screen demanding a password. But the text vanished and was replaced with a desktop of icons. The password, clearly, was the big metal lock on the trapdoor. He was in.

A rare smile from Matt as he stared at the computer's wallpaper. It was an image he had seen before, and seeing it again now, here in this house, was confirmation that he was in the right place. Undeniable.

The photograph had taken centre stage in a collection arranged around the shoulders and arms of the uniform framed upon a wall in Anderson Orbach's bedroom. It had been the uniform that drew Matt's eye as he moved through the apartment to make his escape from the casino.

It was located at the top of the pyramid, the first photo placed, the one that mattered, chosen from a stack before all others, making all the others just scenery, ornamental. All were shots of army guys, some alone, some in large groups, some in full uniform and some barely dressed. They sat on tanks, cleaned their weapons, played japes on each other, or just lounged in the desert sun. Guys who smiled like they were on holiday, a far cry from what they were in that desert to do: make war. The good times, captured for eternity on film.

The main photo was different. The location was not a barracks or a desert but a club of some kind, with a bar and a jukebox. Three men, arms around each other's shoulders. Names and ranks were handwritten on the photo, three different scripts, as if each man had signed it. Three soldiers of the 3rd Infantry Division, smiling for the camera. Orbach on the left, and the Expert, Damon Mason, on the right. There they both were, comrades and friends, who had gone missing in Iraq but so hadn't, really.

And in the middle was their sergeant major, between his lost comrades, arms around their shoulders, their arms hugging him right back. A man Orbach had called moments before his death, a man who had been waiting for that call, a former superior in the army who was still running things now that the three close friends had become a unit in an entirely new kind of army.

Sergeant Major Tony Senior, a man with two lives.

In one he was a wealthy businessman who garnered respect because of his long service to the US Army, including tours in Iraq. Sergeant Major Tony Senior had left the army soon after two of his men went missing during a peaceful phase in Fallujah's violent history, overwhelmed by grief at the loss of his friends. He had moved into real estate and made good money. His teenaged son was today an All-American wrestler, his wife a New York socialite. He owned a large home and a nightclub in New York and a limousine company in Los Angeles.

And a casino in London.

Orbach and Damon had faked their deaths, but Senior had not. He couldn't. The Watchdogs needed someone legitimate in the world because no business team could operate totally underground. Someone who could live in daylight, not resigned to the shadows. A public face for their faceless organisation. As team leader, as cheque-signer, taxpayer, this man was accorded the right to not have to live a hidden existence. But maybe to the Watchdogs subterfuge and lies were overwhelming addictions, because Tony Senior had a secret second life. And both were right at Matt's fingertips.

Matt scrutinised the icons on the screen, forcing the image of the three Watchdogs into the background. The taskbar showed open documents. He checked them all. One was an internet banking page that had expired through inactivity, and this one did demand a password. There was another website showing a range of speedboats. Another showed a booking confirmation page for a plane ticket. New York. Tomorrow morning at 6.15 from London City Airport. Returning home now he thought his enemies were dead and the job was done? Some online game was there, too.

Immediately Matt's eyes were drawn by a folder called RESEARCH. In it were sub-folders, seventeen of them, each given the name of a city somewhere in the world. Seven were in America, four in Britain, two in France, and one each for Germany, Thailand, and the Czech Republic.

And Haiti.

He held back the urge to click on Britain, because he wanted to be sure first. So he clicked on Haiti, and within seconds was sure.

There it all was. Word documents and pictures all about Haiti, and boats, and Manno Bellile and Etienne Frecker and the Haiti National Police. There were charts and spreadsheets and local maps highlighted here and there. Phone numbers, bank account numbers, scans of newspaper clippings. And more, lots more. The whole mission, all laid out, prepared and planned right here. Matt was sure that there was enough here for the police to convict. And in the other folders, too. Enough to blow the Watchdogs wide open, expose them and their operation to the world.

But that wasn't going to happen.

He started opening the folders, if only to delay the inevitable. Some listed building felled in Germany, the blame put on vandals, not the guy who could then build upon the land. A murder in Thailand. The strange disappearance of hundreds of sheep from a farmer's field in France.

He checked them all, a minute for each, marvelling at the depth of research. The Watchdogs had seemingly taken no chances, even documenting weather forecasts on specific days. He even saw the vast file on Daz's car chase. The route in detail, photos of every stage, documents, documents, documents. London 2, that folder was called. There was one subtitled Norfolk. He clicked and read and marvelled. But then he ran out of folders and was left with the one he hadn't wanted to open: London 1. Their first London job. Karen.

No more reason to delay. He opened it. Dozens of images, dozens of spreadsheets, dozens of Word documents. And images. Each image's icon was a tiny version of the picture, and he clicked on one that showed a vehicle. And there was the florist's van, the one they had hunted. He found a map of London's sewer system, and knew right then how they had done it. The Watchdogs had gotten the killer into the underground station through the sewers. They had gotten Karen's body above ground and into the waste ground using the sewers, which explained why there was a manhole near her body. He pictured men there, lifting her out, positioning her so that the Expert, half a mile away, could watch through his telescope.

There was a video. One video. Four minutes and fourteen seconds long. It was called KILL, as if he needed any more indication of what it might show.

He sat for long minutes, staring at the screen, fingers on the mouse, not daring to click open the video. He wanted to see, but also he didn't. And in the end, someone else decided things for him.

He heard a car pull up outside.

He leaned over and grabbed the computer and yanked hard, snapping screws, bending both sides of the casing open like wings. Pulled it off, tossed it aside. He tore at the innards of the machine like a psycho, until he was sure it would not work again. Wires were torn, chips snapped. The hard drive went into his pocket. Not because he wanted it as evidence, but because it might, *must*, contain more names. Everyone who had helped the Watchdogs with their LONDON 1 mission. He wanted every one of them, despite what he'd told Lisa. Same as the computer, he would rend and smash the murder machine until nothing worked.

He froze.

Moments later he heard a key in the lock downstairs, and then two voices, one male and one female. The male was laughing, and he recognised the voice instantly. Footsteps thudded up the stairs. The landing light came on when they reached the top. Through the trap, he saw a female whip past and into the bathroom. The door slammed. Even through the door, even over the sounds of the male entering the house and talking to who Matt assumed was his son, he heard the woman urinating. The front door closed with a sharp bang. A child's voice called out for a drink. Sounded about four years old. It didn't give Matt any second thoughts about what he had to do. But he knew he had to be careful.

The female finished urinating. The toilet flushed. Out she came, down she went.

Or not. Matt pulled back as she stopped under the trap and looked up. He saw her face fall. Then she was running downstairs, whispering something that he didn't catch. The child was still talking, then abruptly shut up as his father hissed at him to be quiet.

Then Matt heard the front door open and feet pounding, and then the door slammed shut. Nothing but silence downstairs now.

He feared they'd all gone, and panic started to rise. And then the landing light went off.

And then there was the slightest creak of a stair that informed him someone was coming up in the dark. Carefully.

18

Carol was in the car, phone in hand, finger poised over the CALL button, 999 already on the screen. After what had happened a few days ago, she was rightly terrified.

But the terror vanished a few moments later when Tony came out of the house with another man, a big guy with a soft face. Both men were smiling.

She got out of the car, carrying her son.

Tony said, 'Hey, babe, this is Matt, from work. We're just going to pop to the shops, catch up a bit. You go inside. It was a false alarm. Matt here thought it would be funny to scare us.'

Matt said, 'Sorry about that.'

Carol didn't know what to say. Her heart was still racing. Tony touched her shoulder and ruffled his boy's hair. Ten seconds later he and his strange friend were in the car. It pulled away, with the other guy driving. Tony waved.

Puzzled, Carol carried her son into the house. But she stood on the step, watching the car drive away. It rounded the corner and was gone. Carol shut the door.

∼

'So where are we going, dead man?'

Senior said it with confidence. Matt had noticed that Senior hadn't given his wife or son a proper goodbye, such as you would have expected from a man who feared that he would never see them again. He was too smart, too experienced, too goddamn big-headed to think he was in a jam. A minute from now, ten minutes, an hour – at some point Senior expected his enemy to leave an opening, let his guard down just for a moment. To give him that single fractional chance to turn things around.

Matt stopped the car just around the corner. He tossed a pair of handcuffs into Senior's lap. He put a roll of duct tape on his own lap.

'Get in the back seat, face down, and cuff your hands behind your back.'

Then he did something surprising. He placed Senior's gun on the dashboard, equidistant from each man. Almost as a challenge. There was a heavy pause, no movement from Senior. Clearly weighing things up. Maybe working out if he could grab the weapon and kill Matt and get to his wife and son before it was too late. Maybe trying to decide if his own safety mattered more than that of his family. He had been waiting for an opportunity, and they were away from the man's family, and so surely he realised he would get no better chance?

But Senior did not go for the gun. He got out of the car. There was a moment when he cast his head around, as if considering fleeing. Then he got into the back. Lay on his front, arms behind him, and snapped on the cuffs.

'You don't know the size of the mistake you're making, Armstrong,' Senior said. 'People will come after you. Lots of them. I have more connections than your brain. This can only end bad for you.'

Matt picked up the duct tape. 'It was a family thing. I had no choice but to protect them. It's my weakness, and it's yours, too. That's how I got to you. *Filius est pars patris.* A son is part of the father.'

~

Sergeant Major Tony Senior, a man with two lives.

In one, he had a jobless wife and a young son and a semi-detached house lost in an urban maze in London, England. He worked as a sales rep for a fitted kitchens company, so went his cover, which explained why he could visit New York for months at a time, and hop back into his other life. Doubtless he used overseas work as an excuse for his New York wife, too, when he visited London to see his youngest son, and to check on his casino and hang out with his old army buddies. And to participate in Watchdog jobs, when he fancied taking some cool role. Like taking the wheel to race a car through London.

Tony Jenkins, a man who had played the part of some low-level cog, just some guy hired to drive a car, but who in fact occupied the top rung. A man Matt had stood just inches from, oblivious.

When Senior/Jenkins had poked his head through the attic trapdoor, Matt had been sitting in the chair, facing him. Senior had carried a pistol, the barrel aimed his way, but Matt had simply raised his mobile, pointing the screen at Senior.

He did not see the screen straight away. He climbed up, careful of his bad arm, which he carried quite well for a guy with a recently broken elbow. Matt expected him to try to pretend that he was nothing more than a driver, but Senior said, 'Well done for getting this far, Armstrong. No one can fault you, even though it ends here. Did you kill my two boys?'

Still holding out the phone, Matt said, 'It doesn't end here. It ends a few miles away. We have to take a short drive. You and me, as best friends.'

Obviously puzzled and a little perturbed by Matt's nonchalance in the face of a loaded weapon, Senior stepped forward, trying to see what was displayed on the phone held towards him.

He saw a photo. Dark, because it was night. But it was clearly a picture showing the back of Senior's house. By the back door were two men and a woman in dark clothing, grinning and holding up knives for the camera, like holidaymakers with pina coladas posing for a group shot.

'What the fuck is this?' he hissed.

'That's a team of bad people, and unless I give them a code word to abort, their plan goes ahead. Their plan is, shall we say, to cut all your ties to this country.'

The mind was racing, Matt could see. Senior still pointed the gun, still glared at Matt, but his brain was elsewhere, thinking of the men outside, the ones with the plan to harm his wife and boy. And thinking of a way out of this mess. Evidently, he came up blank. 'What do you want, Armstrong? Some kind of revenge?'

He had dropped the English accent. The one he had invented to go along with the persona of Tony Jenkins, sales rep, urban rat. Matt was suddenly sorry for the man's wife, who didn't know her husband had lived a lie for years. She didn't know she was just scenery, a hobby, a prop in the bogus life of her husband. She didn't know about a wife and teenaged son in America, who were swimming in millions while she balanced on pennies. She didn't know he was probably only still in her life because she'd gotten pregnant. He was probably her whole world, but she was his dirty little secret.

'I want two friends to take a ride,' Matt said. 'So we'll go down and you'll tell your wife that, and we'll go quietly away, and I'll give the code word and your wife and son will be safe. So give me the gun, Tony. Hand it over or I'll come for it, and that means my plan will go to shit and whatever plan you're working on will go to shit and everything will go wrong for everyone. Newspaper front page type of wrong. Choose now. But first think about how much safer your family will be if I'm far away from here. You want to kill me, but you don't want to do it here, in front of them. That will just get people looking at you, and your sham life here will be opened up. Think about how much better it will be for you to have me miles away, somewhere remote, when you turn the tables and kill me.'

Either it was a good sales pitch, or Senior had already been thinking that very thing. Regardless, he tossed the gun on the carpet.

Now, Matt stopped the car and killed the engine and lights. He got out and opened the rear door and grabbed the Watchdog's feet and hauled him out.

They were outside the waste ground, where Karen had been found. The fence had a hole in it, cut earlier by another of MacSec. Matt dragged the Watchdog through and across the concrete. Positioned him carefully. Same place where Karen had lain. And all the while, the Watchdog was shouting, perhaps just venting, or perhaps hoping someone would hear and come to his rescue. But the area was empty. Just as it had been empty when Karen was brought here.

'I have such connections as you wouldn't believe, Armstrong. You think I don't have plans in place in case some weepy relative comes hunting? Anything happens to me, and the rest of your family pays the price. You want that? That worth your petty revenge lust?'

Just blatant bravado, as if he thought he really could threaten his way out of the mess he was in. But his eyes betrayed him. They said he knew he was in trouble.

'So what happens now, Armstrong? Strangle me like she got strangled?'

Matt knelt on the man's chest and grabbed his hair with one hand, tight. The Watchdog knew something unfortunate was coming and tried to wrestle free, but his arms were trapped under him, and Matt was the bigger man.

Matt raised a pair of pliers up to one of the Watchdog's eyes. The Watchdog screwed them shut, but it didn't help. Matt pinched the eyelid hard and tugged back, and away it came like a sticky label off a new shirt, nice and neat. The Watchdog stared at him wide-eyed, and probably not just because of the missing lid. He screamed, more in shock than pain, although the pain was there, too.

The second lid was more stubborn and half tore away, which meant Matt had to have a second go. He put the pliers aside, lifted a little bottle of superglue. Not a brilliant piece of surgery, but it stopped the blood flow. He wiped the blood away with his sleeve. The look in those wide eyes was no longer fear or shock. Just anger.

'You piece of shit. I'll kill your whole family for this. I was the one who chose her, you know, not that stupid judge?'

His voice was surprisingly calm.

'I cruised the street and just picked her. Thought, *There's one the world could do without. Total skank.* That's what you call them over here, isn't it? That was her. *Skank.*'

Maybe he suspected Matt had torture planned here and hoped to stir up enough rage that his kidnapper would explode and end him in a flash. Wasn't going to happen. Anger was long gone. All that remained was a sense of duty. He knew what he had to do, how to do it, and nothing was going to change that. It was akin to autopilot.

'Maybe we can work this out. I have money.'

A sudden change of tactic, from a man who knew tactics very well. Still no panic. Still that calm voice. A tactic thought out. A businessman making a business proposition. But he was pleading to deaf ears. Matt held up a photo, aimed down, so that the Watchdog could see it. Couldn't fail to. He tried to thrash again, but Matt's weight kept him there, and a fist tight in his hair kept his head in place. So up he stared.

The photo was of this place, the crime scene. A body lay where the Watchdog lay. Karen, dead. Some photo snapped off a phone before the cops got here to cover her body, probably by the guy who discovered her. The same photo that the whole country had seen in a newspaper, but the Watchdog stared at it as if he'd never come across it before. Maybe that was just the impression his wide, lidless eyes gave, but maybe not. Maybe the Watchdog had not viewed his own handiwork. It was one thing to see a 'skank' across a dark road and point and say *her*, and quite another to view the product of your plan. And that was why Matt brandished the photo. His way of saying:

This is who you murdered.

He tossed away the photo and used the glue to fill the Watchdog's nostrils. He clamped them tightly shut, held them. Ten seconds. Had had to peel his fingers away because they'd stuck to the guy's skin.

'What about the guy who killed her? What about him?' the Watchdog moaned. He reeled off a name and an address. 'He gets away with it, does he?'

Matt shook his head and held up another photograph. Karen in a summer dress, seated at a garden table with a piece of cake. Another party Matt had missed. He held the photo just inches from those wide eyes to make sure the Watchdog saw it clearly, every pixel. It was one thing to see a ragged corpse, and quite another to know that your victim could present as a smiling, sweet, vibrant young woman, a work of art.

This is who you murdered.

The breathing was hard, the throat constricted with fear.

'Killing me changes nothing. She's still dead. I'll go to prison. But don't do this. Please.'

Matt smiled at him. Just to show he was beyond reason. Just to increase the shock. He placed the photo carefully aside. Reached for the glue. Lips this time. He forced the lips tightly together when the Watchdog closed his jaws to gulp against the glue that had gone into his mouth and throat. Ten seconds again. Lips joined, teeth melded, throat closed up. He met the Watchdog's eyes and held them as the body tensed and the cheeks puffed as air was sought and air wouldn't come.

The final photograph was grainy, low quality. Not here a ragged corpse or even a vibrant woman. Not even close. It was one thing to see your victim as a handsome young lady, and quite another to know you'd orchestrated the brutal murder of *this*. Here was the beauty and innocence of a thousand summer flowers and a million sparkling blue oceans, clad in a pink dress, smeared around the smiling mouth with chocolate, her eyes showing the eternal fascination of a brain just nineteen months into the world.

This is who you murdered.

THE END

Two Years after Don Jones lost his home in a fire and moved to Sheffield, he was killed off by Ian Smith, who fled to Newcastle under the guise of a man who'd decided to relocate after his wife shacked up with his best friend. Three years after that, Ian Smith winked out of existence and Peter Jackson, rising from his ashes, resettled in Glasgow with a claim that he'd lost his job and had chosen a new home by sticking a pin in a map. A month after Jackson had vanished, the man who had lived as all three was back in London and hiding from no one the fact that he'd spent seven years floating around the island on fake names.

Today the man, whose real name was Matt Armstrong, woke early, but not alone. He sat up in bed and reached to his shoulder, as he had every morning for three weeks. But there was nothing stuck to his skin. Every day for three weeks, his sleepy, conditioned brain had to remind itself those days were over. Matt found his phone on the bedside table and slipped off the protective cover. The SIM card was stuck to the back of his device.

On the other side of the bed, Lisa turned towards him and grunted, but she was still asleep. Again, he felt a stab of self-hate that he was hiding such a secret from his girlfriend. To make amends again, same as he'd done for the ten days they'd shared this flat, he inserted the SIM card without her knowledge, but left the phone visible on the bedside cabinet.

He went into the bathroom to shower while the phone booted up. In five minutes he'd be back. He would check the phone, and hopefully there would be something. One man other than him had the number for that SIM card and in three weeks Matt had never received a call or a text on it. Every day for three weeks, he'd prayed he would. If that wasn't the case today, he'd return the secret SIM card to its hiding place and enjoy another day of life.

It was as he was from the shower that he heard his phone perform the unmistakable double-beep of a text message received. A voice from the bedroom announced this, too. A cold snake of apprehension slipped down his spine.

It had taken three weeks, but finally it had happened.

Matt pushed open the back door and slipped inside. The kitchen was dark, but his eyes were already adjusted to the lack of light from his time waiting out in the garden. He moved through the room, through a door in the far wall.

He found himself in a tiny hallway. There was a set of stairs, and two doors, both open. He saw a dining room beyond one, a living room beyond the other. The TV was on in the living room, but nobody was there. The dining room was empty, too.

He crept up the stairs, flexing his fists, warming the muscles up, ready for what he needed to do.

He could hear noises from the bathroom, but first made sure the other rooms were empty. The bathroom door was ajar, light spilling out. He kicked it open.

A cat had been on the edge of the bath, splashing a paw in the water. As the door flew open, the cat leapt down and scampered out past his feet.

A man was in the bath, but he wasn't relaxing.

Matt stumbled like a drunken man and had to steady himself by sitting on the toilet. He stared at the dead judge, at the still bathwater, where there floated a medicine bottle. Empty. Just to confirm, he reached over and touched the man's arm. It was pale and wrinkly and very cold.

Was this really him? Karen's killer? If so, he was dead and beyond the reach of justice. Beyond Matt's reach.

He stared at the face, running his eyes over every detail. He had expected to be overcome with anger and lost hope, but that hadn't happened. Instead, he felt a sense of... calm, because the hunt was over. Perhaps, when he'd heard about the suicide of the man the police had blamed for Karen's death, he hadn't felt like this because he hadn't fully believed the killer was found.

Perhaps, as Lisa had suggested, the fiery obsession had burned itself out.

That was when his eyes were caught by something lying on the closed toilet lid. A diary with an envelope on top, which was addressed to someone called Alain Barker at Hardman, Barker and Co. Matt tore it open and found two things inside.

The first item was a photograph of Karen.

And now it was real. He had finally found her killer.

In the photo she had red hair and a fluffy white coat and a glittery tank top that barely covered her breasts. She was standing as if facing the camera for the shot, but her head was slightly turned, eyes off somewhere other than the lens, and

Matt got the impression she had been snapped without knowing it. Behind her, part of a window in a brick wall. An outdoor shot. Combined with that outfit...

He wanted to tear the photo into pieces. He knew the photo had been taken not long before her death, out on the street while she hunted clients. Taken by someone to give to the judge, so he would know which girl had been selected for death.

But he couldn't. She looked so different to how he remembered her. It was how she had looked at the end, and that meant a lot to him, although he wasn't sure why. He turned the photograph over and saw something scribbled on the back, which almost stopped his heart.

In time, its beating resumed a normal rhythm, and he turned his attention to the other item in the envelope.

It was a folded sheet of A4 paper, bearing a suicide note, which he quickly skimmed through. It was actually two notes, separated by a line drawn in pen. The first, at the top, was typical of someone's goodbye. Apologies to his family, good wishes to all friends, and blame upon a frail body and an empty life without his wife for his decision not to continue. The last words of a sweet old man, nary a prostitute slaughter in sight. Matt wanted to spit and stamp on it. Then he reached the bottom note, and here he read slowly.

Alain, I have done a terrible thing. It is all in my diary. I am sure you will read it and hate me, but I need your help. Please inform the family named at the bottom of this note. I want them to know I am very sorry for what I did to that poor girl, their daughter, their sister. A moment of sick madness, which finally I could not restrain. Please insist that with my death, I have been dealt justice. I cannot be punished in this world, but my innocent family can. The family of the murdered girl will want to go to the police, but it will not help matters and they will only cause suffering to another family. Tell them, please think of my family. I want you to destroy this note and the diary and pass the top note onto my own family.

However, if my crime should be exposed, I would like the true facts to be known, and the true culprits apprehended. You must keep a copy of the diary for this reason. And you must find the answer to the clue on the back of the photograph.

It was a shaking hand that picked up the diary and Matt had to sit on the side of the bath, in splashes of cold water left by the cat, to prevent a collapse. If the diary contained the ramblings of a man slipping into insanity as the pages flipped and the days rushed by, he didn't want to be part of the journey. He would not walk alongside Karen's killer on his inexorable path towards violent murder. Instead, he flipped immediately to the date of her death. Somehow, immediate submersion into his sister's final moments was easier to accept.

They are almost dragging me, but I go willingly. Onward, ever onward, as if towards the centre of the earth. The journey seems destined to never end, and then it does.

I see a wall and my first thought is that something has gone wrong. Some bend or corner or crossroad misjudged, and we are lost. Eight years becomes an eternity in the dark depths of the planet.

A small light comes on. The light from someone's phone. In that mediocre illumination, I get my first real glimpse at the five men escorting me, and I am surprised. Normal faces. Typical clothing. Nothing memorable about any of them. They would not have stood out on a street. Just like the van they collected me in, from right outside my house. Only now do I realise the significance of the fireworks. A great but short blast of light exploding in the sky above my street, but not to celebrate a birthday or anniversary. To divert the eyes of my neighbours, so that none, if pressed, would remember a plain black van this night.

Then their hands are on me, taking off my clothing. I let them, knowing it is all part of the plan. Their continued silence unnerves me. I have paid for this, I am in charge, but I feel violated. I am helped into black trousers and a dark brown sweater and training shoes. A man fiddles with my collar, fixing something to it. A small black item, plain-looking, no bigger than a thimble. I am told not to touch it by a voice equally unmemorable.

My palms are sprayed with a thick liquid that smells like cumin and dries on my skin in moments. I am told to close my eyes and open my mouth and stop breathing. The same spray on my face and neck, in my mouth, my nostrils. All over my head. Again, it dries almost instantly. Nobody explains, but I suspect the liquid is something to prevent the shedding of skin cells and hair.

Another man approaches me with a photograph. It shows a pretty girl, red hair, slim, outrageous outfit. This is her, then. The one they have chosen for me.

Then it is time. One of the men steps up to the brick wall and lifts out a portion that has handles. My first thought is that the wall is wood painted to look like brick and has a pre-cut section. But it is real brick, given the scraping noise, the rain of dust, and how he struggles with the weight. This begins to seem dreamlike.

I am helped through the hole and find myself in a large room. It is dimly lit by a ragged row of candles by the wall on the right. Their flicking flames show me an arched ceiling some forty feet above, with stubs of metal protruding, as if lights had once hung, and fixtures that had carried cables. The flat floor is littered with trash. There is a stone protrusion on the left side of the tunnel, like a giant shelf. Poking out from the back wall of the shelf is a series of what looks like wooden fence panels, spaced ten feet apart as if to create a row of booths. In a few of the booths there is a lone woman, while in others a man and a woman get intimate.

I understand. The shelf is a platform. I am in an abandoned underground train station. The local red-light area girls are using it as a place of business. This is where it will happen.

A female calls to me from one of the booths. Although the light is dim, I see she is staring at me. And she is alone. Waiting for me, I know. Because this is part of the plan.

And she is the chosen one.

But in the booth beside hers a man and a woman are having sex. Just metres from where I am supposed to do it. But as I climb onto the platform and step into her booth, onto a blanket on the stone, I feel as if I have entered an enclosed room. I feel alone with her.

'They said you'd come,' she says as she takes my hand. I squeeze back, but there my input fails. She has to lead me. Within no time at all, I am knelt behind her, and she is bent forward on all fours to receive me. For the first time since leaving my home, I do not think of what is to come. I think of my wife, before the cancer took her away from me and she was strong and fit and we were able to do what I am doing now.

My hands from her hips, up. To her waist, then shoulders, then higher. I lean forward and lay my fingers lightly around her throat. This is the precipice, I realise. I feel myself go instantly limp inside her. She feels it, too, and tries to pull away.

I know that if she does, the moment will be over and I will lose my nerve. Knowing this, my brain sends shockwaves into my hands and wrists. My fingers close around the girl's throat, tight. I feel her airway shut off. I hear her grunt in shock, then try to suck in air, then try to scream. Then I feel myself start to grow hard again. And squeeze harder.

The moment it is done is something I don't understand. I am not aware of time passing. It seems that one second I am beginning to squeeze, and the next it is all over. I do not understand, but the others do. A man grabs my hands and pries them off the girl's neck. Other hands pull me away, away from the grimy blanket of white and blue and red on the ground; away from the girl, who almost appears to be sleeping. I feel my legs moving, and the ground beneath my feet, but I do not power myself.

And time seems to rewind. I exit through the hole in the wall. The little black box is plucked from my collar. I am returned into my original clothing. I am led away down the tunnel. Everything becomes a blur and the next thing I know I am being lifted up, out through a manhole, through the hole in the bottom of the van parked above it. It drives away.

Now that the worst is over, the men in black are talking amongst themselves, just like regular guys. I want to join in, because we did this together, but I cannot find my voice. Instead, I watch the man across from me scrutinising the little black box that had been clipped to my clothing, as if something is wrong with it. I see a little corner of the plastic missing.

When I hear fireworks again and the van stops, I know I am home. The man closest to me holds up a small tablet.

'The first night will be hell,' he says. 'Swallow this and you'll sleep like a baby. All night. That's part of the service, to make your day go perfectly. Any guilt or terror you feel tomorrow is your problem.'

I take the tablet without question.

'One final point,' the man says. 'You were already asked this, but I've been instructed to ask again now the act is over. Do you want the body to be found?'

Later, in bed, I return to this question. It has been with me for days. I did not do this for notoriety. I do not crave reading about my crime in the newspapers. I do not want to taunt the police or the victim's family. I had a sick desire to murder a prostitute, that is all.

So I do not understand why I said yes. Yes, I would like the body to be found. And before I could change my mind, I find myself on the street, looking up at the fireworks. When I turn to look at the van, it is driving away around a corner. In that moment, the fireworks illuminate the shiny residue of a sign that had once been on the side of the van.

My final act that night is to lie on my bed, in the dark, and await an influx of emotions. But there is no guilt, no shame, no fear. I will emotions to come, but again there is nothing. Is this the calm before the storm? Is the drug inhibiting my brain? Is the rush on its way? Will I wake tomorrow with a sense of achievement, as if I have passed an exam? Or will I dissolve under a wave of self-hatred?

Days later, as I write this and trawl my mind for something, anything to give the poor family of that girl, I cannot recall the make of the van, or any faces or accents. I paid cash so there is no bank account to trace. The man I dealt with always met me in places with no security cameras and no witnesses, late at night. I still cannot fathom how these people found me and knew my desires. I have nothing, no clue except the lasting image of the decal remnants on the side of the van. It is probably nothing. But it will have to do.

Again, Matt turned over the photograph of Karen and stared at the drawing the judge had made. He had seen it before, of course. Back then, the diagram had given him a million questions. Now, it answered everything.

A letter C on its back with a child's version of a cloud inside it: three bumps together.

The judge had not taken his own life to avoid judgement and punishment, but because he was wracked by guilt. Every waking moment spent with the photo in his hands, using the image of the girl he'd killed to fuel his examination of the only clue he had: a ghostly logo glimpsed on the side of a van used by the Watchdogs. Unable to trace the van, and knowing he had a date with death, he had somehow passed that clue onto someone who would have a greater determination to find the truth.

Matt had assumed he was being watched, tested, but that was not the case. The clue had landed in his hands simply because the judge had figured the family of a dead prostitute would be the only ones who would care enough to try to use it to find those responsible. Maybe the lack of an accompanying explanation was in case the family went to the police, because the diagram alone offered no clue to the sender and was no evidence of wrongdoing.

Afterwards, he sat and tried to work out his next move. Eventually, he left. He had come here intending to leave a dead body behind, and at least that had happened. Not by his hand, but dead, nonetheless. The judge had felt overwhelming remorse in the end, and had tried to make amends with the only fragment of information he had about the team that had helped him commit murder. And Matt couldn't ask for much more than that.

A little more, at least.

Outside, he saw a car with its lights on full beam. Someone knew he was here, but there was no panic. Here was a problem to deal with, that was all.

The car's radio turned on, loud, and the vehicle came his way and drew up alongside.

It was Lisa.

Angry, he jumped into the car and turned off the lights, and the radio. Now there was panic. 'What are you doing?'

He was so concerned that her actions had drawn attention that he'd overlooked the main aspect. Which now came to him.

'How did you know I was here?'

'Is he dead?'

'How did you know I was here?'

'I know about your secret SIM card.'

He thought of the message he'd received from Alfo of MacSec. *I found him.* The text had contained a postcode. Lisa had clearly understood that the found man was the one remaining enemy. The man who had physically murdered Matt's sister.

Matt had understood something, too. Transparency. Lisa had convinced him not to shield who he was any longer. No more false names, no more hiding. And no more secrets, especially from each other. Yet he had that secret SIM card.

'I didn't lie to you, Lisa. I never planned to come here.'

And he really hadn't, not at first. As former army, Matt understood that the real culprits were those who worked the mechanism of murder, not the cogs within that machinery. In the days that followed once the Watchdogs were dead, he and Lisa hadn't even talked about recent events. She hadn't asked a single question, so he hadn't offered a single answer – including what he'd learned in Orbach's office. And he had turned his focus away from the pair of hands that had actually closed around his sister's throat, onto future life. Somehow, that man had slowly ceased to matter.

Until that morning, when Daz's man, Alfo, had sent a text.

He explained, which elicited a nod of acceptance, but still she looked grim. He remembered her unanswered question.

'Yes, he's dead.' But instead of explaining further, he considered something. Trust. Yes, he had kept a secret, but so had Lisa. She had kept tabs on his SIM card, and she had followed him here, and that meant she hadn't believed his promise not to hunt the single remaining man involved in Karen's slaughter. So, instead of an explanation, he said, 'What if I killed him? He did deserve it, after all.'

'You didn't kill him. You promised you wouldn't. And if you did, then you lied to me and I won't miss you while you serve thirty years.'

Something warm sparked inside his gut. She trusted him after all, although that didn't explain why she had followed him here. 'He killed himself, Lisa. He's dead in there. Four days ago. There was a suicide note.'

She let this sink in. 'Then the police will have my car. So, no more lying. We go to the police now.'

And now that final puzzle was solved. He knew why she'd made herself obvious here this night. They couldn't just flee and forget. Until a coroner ruled suicide, the police would investigate and her car, remembered here tonight by residents, would be traced and questions asked.

Matt unfolded the piece of paper he'd taken from the judge's house.

'What's that?' Lisa asked. He held it out for her to read, which she did. Twice, given the length of time he waited, silent, just staring at the dashboard.

'It doesn't tell the story,' she said. 'It doesn't mention Karen's name, or why he felt he had to kill her.'

He had suspected the truth behind Karen's murder back in Orbach's office – *satisfaction guaranteed* – but with a chance he was wrong, that Orbach was lying, he had shut it out. He hadn't mentioned Orbach's claim to Lisa.

But now, after tonight, that horrible truth wouldn't be denied. 'He didn't have to kill her, Lisa. This wasn't about a grand conspiracy by a man scared of losing his power. He didn't murder my sister to save himself or powerful people or to protect a corrupt establishment. All along this was just…' He sought the correct words, but only two came to him: 'Evil punter.'

She was silent again as this sank in, but quickly became practical again. 'You shouldn't have taken this. The police will expect a suicide note if he killed himself. It might make them doubt your version of events when we tell them.'

'He did leave a suicide note. A more truthful one.'

She ran a finger across the torn bottom of the letter. In her face he saw realisation. She said, 'Why did you take this part?'

Matt looked at his phone, at the picture of Karen. The original photograph was still in the house, now in a dead man's hand along with the diary and the only suicide note that mattered. He wondered if Danny, when he learned about the judge, would be thankful there hadn't been a lofty conspiracy – his brother didn't and never would know the truth behind Karen's murder. And Matt hoped his mother, despite her claims to the contrary, would find peace in the knowledge that her daughter's killer had been brought to justice. But above all he hoped that tonight's events wouldn't upset a nice balance – tip the 10-4 – that his family had found over the last few weeks.

'Matt? Did you hear me? I know what he did to your sister

means he doesn't deserve anything from us. But, like he said, we should think of his family.'

'He should have thought of mine.'

THE END

ACKNOWLEDGEMENTS

Once again thanks go to all at Bloodhound team, with an extra dose for Heather, the new pup Ashley, Betsy, Fred, Clare, Tara, and Ian, in Scrabble-score order so there's no favouritism. Respect and a high-five to the Bloodhound authors, although if it wasn't for their awesome books stealing my time, this one would have been in your hands a lot earlier. Mind you, it wasn't only their great novels that burned my hours, so it's only fair to mention Tomb Raider games, YouTube fails videos, a new garden fence, and Scrabble research for the dull joke above.

A NOTE FROM THE PUBLISHER

Thank you for reading this book. If you enjoyed it please do consider leaving a review on Amazon to help others find it too.

We hate typos. All of our books have been rigorously edited and proofread, but sometimes mistakes do slip through. If you have spotted a typo, please do let us know and we can get it amended within hours.

info@bloodhoundbooks.com

LOVE CRIME, THRILLER AND MYSTERY BOOKS?

Join our mailing list to hear about our latest releases and receive exclusive offers.

Sign up today to be the first to hear about new releases and exclusive offers, including free and discounted ebooks!

Why not like us or follow us on social media to stay up to date with the latest news from your favourite authors?

www.ingramcontent.com/pod-product-compliance
Lightning Source LLC
Chambersburg PA
CBHW051643180726
48284CB00006B/1840